T0094538

TRANSPARENCY

TRANSPARENCY

MAREK BIEŃCZYK

Translated by Benjamin Paloff

DALKEY ARCHIVE PRESS
CHAMPAIGN / DUBLIN / LONDON

Library of Congress Cataloging-in-Publication Data

Bienczyk, Marek.
[Przezroczystosc. English]
Transparency / Marek Bienczyk ; translated by Benjamin Paloff. -- 1st ed.
p. cm.
"Originally published in Polish as Przezroczystosc by Wydawnictwo Znak."
ISBN 978-1-56478-711-8 (pbk. : alk. paper)
I. Paloff, Benjamin. II. Title.
PG7161.I319P7413 2012
891.8'537--dc23
2012002797

Partially funded by a grant from the Illinois Arts Council, a state agency

This publication has been subsidized by Instytut Książki—the © POLAND
Translation Programme

www.instytutksiazki.pl

www.dalkeyarchive.com

Cover: design and composition by Sarah French
Printed on permanent/durable acid-free paper and bound in the
United States of America

CONTENTS

September–March

13

Gabriel and Snow

15

Nighthawks in Twilight

22

Why Transparency?

27

Mlle Lambercier's Comb

30

Diaphanes

38

The Heart's Language

42

A Single Sentence

49

The Bandoneón and the Muleta

55

A Room by the Sea

63

Light and Reaction

66

Such a Lovely Word

73

Transparent Poland

87

The Vanity-Bag Co-op

95

A Bell-Jar of Blue Crystal

100

Cover Your Tracks

116

Glasarchitektur

125

A Digression in the Cathedral

130

The New Hygiene

133

Melancholia and the City

140

The Crystal Palace (1)

146

The Laboratories of Power

158

The Crystal Palace (2)

164

Three Houses

173

Rowe and Slutzky

186

Transparent Things

193

Icy Meditations

195

The Silent Way

202

A Spider, Poor Devil

208

Aerofanie

211

Hysteria

218

A Pure, Transparent Block

223

Olga

230

The Plural

234

Cake in Arcadia

236

Jean-Jacques: A Suite

246

June, Again

254

TRANSPARENCY

September–March

Over the last couple of months, whenever I've switched on the radio for my morning coffee, I've heard serious, generally hushed voices talking about the fundamental need for complete transparency if we are to enjoy a properly functioning economy and the rule of law. Or else about total transparency in government affairs. Or about the need for transparency in all administrative decisions. And in the financing of political parties. Or else about the campaign for a "Transparent Poland"—an actual public campaign. Or about unblemished, unclouded biographies. These words have resounded like the echo of a voice I've heard for a good long while now. I was having a hard time getting up, one coffee wasn't doing it, it was autumn again, a damp September, a damp November, the leaves turning tawny in the park nearby. Twenty-five years earlier I had walked through this same park, among these same trees, just then liberating themselves from winter, on my way to the other side of town. In my oversized backpack I was carrying two rolls, most likely with spreadable cheese, bags of Chinese tea, a blue mug and immersion boiler, a spare shirt, maybe some book: the strike survival kit.

It was March 1981. On the following day a general strike was to break out all over Poland to protest the so-called Bydgoszcz Provocation: the police beating of the local leaders of the Solidarity movement. All around, people were saying that the Soviets might not yield this time, that they were on the verge of intervening, that we had to expect the worst. I left the house much too early; I could have gotten a ride to the university that night or just walked the next day, first thing in the morning, but impatience drove me into the city, which is where I wanted to be. I sat down on a bench by the tennis courts; they had not yet recovered their color from winter, and without white lines they recalled a fallow field. I looked under my feet and made out the shapes of stones, their shoulders, heads, backs growing out of the clay, the sand, the gravel. They were like the remains of bodies pushed up to the surface, the preserved detritus of events. I pulled them out, took them into my hand, brushed off the soil, and chuckled to myself: you are the Hundred Years' War, you the French Revolution, you the Warsaw Uprising. I was a bit ceremonious, I had only myself for an audience, no witnesses. I crossed the bridge; some time earlier the river had already cast off its gags of ice and was driving forward with renewed vigor. For the first time in my life I felt no fear, and that alone was happiness. Never before, nor at any time since, have I known such freedom from dread, neither during the Solidarity demonstrations—when I would rush into a doorway, faster than many, at the first sight of the ZOMO riot police—nor going about my life, day in, day out, from one year to the next, when fear is like a shadow, sometimes nearer, sometimes barely visible, but always by our side. I was ready for anything, finally, just this once, ready for anything, free like never before or since. I walked across the city and saw the azure sky both above me and fading off to my side, toward the borough of Praga, in the still wintry, idyllic hues of twilight. You could see far and wide, nothing to obstruct your view, and everything became transparent, lucid. Myself, my country, its fate, everything coalesced into one clear blue glow over the Vistula. Transparent, lucid; it seemed like we were all transparent, that for myself and others transparency had burst its banks, that it connected us without words. Some of us later died, beaten or shot. Their faces, displayed in a yearbook, are great, silent books in themselves, while I was left with the luxury of weighing words, of choosing the wrong ones, so here, this impression—the strike having been called off in the night—is my most powerful recollection of that day.

Gabriel and Snow

It was already December, a Christmas party, a little snow on the ground, but a long way off, not here, because it's warm and vibrant at auntie's house, everyone's dancing, people are singing, the fireplace is keeping the many guests warm, the plates are full of goose (minus apple sauce), just a small slice of breast for Miss Furlong, that's Gabriel Conroy carving the roast, later he gives a speech, ceremoniously, with zeal, having memorized the speech in advance, including the quotations, and there's wine and beer arranged in three rows, so there's also laughter, jokes, conversation, light, familial, or else about the most recent production at the Theatre Royal, about the tenor Caruso and the wonderful air on Mount Melleray and the guesthouse run by the monks up there, and there's strife, albeit contained, Freddy Malins drunk as always, though basically a good guy, friendly, and Gabriel insufficiently of his nation, not Irish enough in the eyes of Miss Ivors, the bastard writes to English newspapers, and now the young lady is hissing something into his ear, and Aunt Julia is singing another aria, you have to sing her praises, and the pudding, too, is divine, though perhaps not as brown as it should be, and finally the party dies down, good-byes, a few more jokes in the foyer, on parting, reminiscences of grandfather Patrick Morkan and his beloved horse Johnny, with whom he loved to banter, and then the carriages pull up, Bartell d'Arcy is quietly singing some song upstairs, and Gretta, rapt, asks what it's called.

That's the first sign—Gretta leaning on the banister, her face in shadow—from the other side, like another hue within the warmth of evening, like a note from some other partita, though we'll forget it in a moment, we suspect nothing. They—she and Gabriel—get into their carriage and drive to the hotel along streets already thickly covered in snow; Gabriel, however, has now caught sight of something, has caught wind of his wife's sudden and beautiful pensiveness; he plays it back within himself to his own melody, in his own masculine way, to his mounting desire for her body, her sadness.

They enter their room, Gabriel duly informs her that Freddy Malins has finally paid back his pound, and suddenly, after the few hours of the Christmas party, after forty pages of storytelling, everything speeds up. Gretta, sparingly, in a few words and through tears, will tell Gabriel about a love long past, a love whose memory has been rekindled by song, though it wasn't even love, but the contact of two youthful beings. She and Michael Furey, the sickly boy who stood beneath her window, went for long walks together, and on that winter evening before her departure he'd caught his death beneath that same window. Of course, he was a lovely singer. Then there is Gabriel's jealousy, so real, so common, selfish, and vain, and the vain sense of his own smallness ("He saw himself as a ludicrous figure [. . .], a nervous, well-meaning sentimentalist, orating to vulgarians"), and his reflections on his marriage to Gretta, their many years together, and then, so oddly—so suddenly—something gives way, something bursts, and everything opens to the other side, to the snow outside the window.[1] The whole evening spills out—the scenes, the people, the sensations—tears free of the day's tether, escapes its frame, turns silently white beyond the window and hardens in that whiteness, which is covering the entire country and perhaps all time as well, what has been and what is now, in a single shapeless blur.

She was fast asleep.

Gabriel, leaning on his elbow, looked for a few moments unresentfully on her tangled hair and half-open mouth, listening to her deep-drawn breath. [. . .] His eyes moved to the chair over which she had thrown some of her clothes. A petticoat string dangled on the floor. One boot stood upright, its limp upper fallen down: the fellow of it lay upon its side. He wondered at his riot of emotions of an hour before. From what had it proceeded? From his aunt's supper, from his own foolish speech, from the wine and dancing, the merry-making when saying good-night in the hall, the pleasure of the walk along the river in the snow. Poor Aunt Julia! She, too, would soon be a shade with the shade of Patrick Morkan and his horse. He had caught that haggard look upon her face for a moment when she was singing "Arrayed for the Bridal." Soon, perhaps, he would be sitting in that same drawing-room, dressed in black, his silk hat on his knees. The blinds would be drawn down and Aunt Kate would be sitting beside him, crying and blowing her nose and telling him how Julia had died. He would cast about in his mind for some words that might console her, and would find only lame and useless ones. Yes, yes: that would happen very soon.

The air of the room chilled his shoulders. He stretched himself cautiously along under the sheets and lay down beside his wife. One by one, they were all becoming shades. [. . .] The tears gathered more thickly in his eyes and in the partial darkness he imagined he saw the form of a young man standing under a dripping tree. Other forms were near. His soul had approached that region where dwell the vast hosts of the dead. He was conscious of, but could not apprehend, their wayward and flickering existence. His own identity was fading out into a grey impalpable world: the solid world itself, which these dead had one time reared and lived in, was dissolving and dwindling.

A few light taps upon the pane made him turn to the window. It had begun to snow again. He watched sleepily the flakes, silver and dark, falling obliquely against the lamplight. The time had come for him to set out on his journey westward. Yes, the newspapers were right: snow was general all over Ireland. It was falling on every part of the dark central plain, on the treeless hills, falling softly upon the Bog of Allen and, farther westward, softly falling into the dark mutinous Shannon waves. It was falling, too, upon every part of the lonely churchyard on the hill where Michael Furey lay buried. It lay thickly drifted on the crooked crosses and headstones, on the spears of the little gate, on the barren thorns. His soul swooned slowly as he heard the snow falling faintly through the universe and faintly falling, like the descent of their last end, upon all the living and the dead.[2]

Every time after I've finished reading these last two pages of the story, and I can read it no other way than in a single breath, the velocity of my reading, my devouring of these words, makes me feel the acceleration the words themselves convey, and I am swept away with all these words, with the soul of Gabriel, toward the whiteness of the snow. Just as the story's slow, languid flow changes imperceptibly into the unbridled rush of the closing passages, the time it takes to read them becomes an avalanche that yanks us out of our safe, quiet moment. One more time, then: an hour has passed since the party, and now there is only this hotel room, the string of a petticoat hanging off the chair, the boots tossed carelessly to the floor—empty shoes are always innocent and awkward, like sad little kittens—Gretta's even breath, and Gabriel's lonely, increasingly lonely, and now increasingly bitter thoughts. Which hold initially to one side, wandering among the events of the last few hours, among faces seen just moments before, but which then carry all this into the whiteness and describe an ever-widening circle, catching a bird's-eye view of an increasing portion of space and time: not only the streets of Dublin, but also the cemetery on the hill, and the Irish plains, and the entire Earth; not just a moment, but eternity; and not only the fates of the living, but also the stories of the dead, who are connected to the living, with whom they form one community, whether of nothingness, whiteness, or sleep.

This strange Christmas night brings Gabriel to an experience of transparency, different, but not altogether different, from the one I described moments ago. Quite quickly, over the course of fifteen minutes or so, his entire existence loses its cohesiveness and dissipates; from behind the curtains of the immediate Gabriel starts to catch a glimpse of something he has never before perceived, the untouchable and eternal background that, white and indistinct, is now growing, so much so that it starts to absorb everything, to clear away the concreteness of events and to silence the voices, to join the living and the dead in a single, unattainable, and now visible glow, in which we can already hear an overtone of lament. Before Gabriel, staring at the window, the world penetrates the edge of time and loses its forms and colors in the snow, which falls not only on places, but also on all moments, those that have been and those that are now, for those are all that are left. Being is white and transparent, as the philosopher Michel Serres once said—where or when, I don't remember—and whatever that was supposed to mean, I feel that we could say the same of Gabriel's discovery. His final vision puts us on edge, where everything that has been up till now fades away, taking with it a whole array of colorful veils, leaving us with the pure, unadulterated figure of existence, which demands to be regarded in precisely this way: white and transparent.

There is no story, no text, to which I have returned more often than to James Joyce's "The Dead." The last two pages give me a chill at any time of year, and it always seems to me that Ireland lies in the Far North, and that people there get around on skis. I see Gabriel staring at the snow; despite the fact that it's nighttime, the whole picture is clear and vast. It reminds me of Tomáš, the hero of Milan Kundera's *The Unbearable Lightness of Being*, born of a similar gesture, that of looking out a window. Gabriel, however, is not a hero who will rise at that moment; his biography ("a ludicrous figure [. . .], a nervous, well-meaning sentimentalist, orating to vulgarians") is already known, and most of his life has already passed by. Thus I always return to him as I would to an acquaintance, as a brother of the gaze, a kindred witness of transparency, in a Dublin hotel room, on an unknown street, somewhere close to O'Connell Bridge, the bridge between this world and the other.

Nighthawks in Twilight

I have wanted to write a page or two about transparency and translucency for some time, for many years. Transparency, I told myself, is summoning me, digging into me like a probe: it is mine. In foreign cities, I chose to lunch in restaurants with panoramic views; evenings I would stop in front of illuminated shop windows, and my friends started to make fun, to buy me glass balls as gifts. I have a pretty good collection. Glass was my quirk: I went into pet stores to gawk at the aquariums, I went back to museums where they'd set up the exhibits behind bulletproof glass (in Bolzano, that bizarre Ötzi, the Iceman frozen down to the bone, our progenitor discovered in a glacier with a quiver full of arrows); about Lenin and Mao Tse-tung, in their glass tombs, I preferred to forget. Working on some text, I would unwittingly thin out the concreteness of meanings, the words would flee their sense, metaphors lost track of their ideas, everything inevitably tended toward abstraction: a whiteness shone out from behind the sentences. It's funny to say it now, but I loved clear broths, dishes with gelatin, fish or meat in aspic, head cheeses and other such deli foods. On the walls of my apartment I hung reproductions of Edward Hopper paintings, which gleamed behind their glass like garish dorm-room posters.

I loved Hopper the way others love their memories. Sometimes I experienced his paintings as if that's what they actually were. In fantasies and poems I became the hero of each successive work, that guy on the glassed-in veranda, looking out at the endless horizon, or the customer at the diner peering out the window at an empty street. Occasionally I embroiled Olga in these fantasies;

she quickly became irritated when I talked about it, so I shut my mouth. Of course—so I imagined—we were first of all the *Nighthawks*, birds of darkness, night owls, moths after twilight, when we would sit down in glassed-in bars, as deserted at midnight as nests after springtime. We would nurse drinks with American names—Bronx, Manhattan—and by our last whiskey it would already be just the two of us, immersed in the solemn silence that follows when life has flown away. It filled us like helium; we floated gently over the ground, over ourselves, winged guardians of the planet, its emissaries in a cosmic night. We felt homeless and free; our union, Olga's and mine, could stretch out somewhere over the city, not dying in its walls, but given to wander aimlessly along the sky's alleys, the fields by the Vistula, neighborhood parks, anywhere. *Nighthawks*, Edward Hopper's most famous painting, had been showing up more and more often on book covers, postcards, even on shopping bags, from which, against the backdrop of the customers' anonymous features, the faces of James Dean and Marlon Brando, and occasionally Marilyn Monroe, stared vacantly into their own solitude. This left me a little annoyed and unsettled: my imagination, my daydreams, my favorite snapshot of ourselves, copied and dispersed so banally on gleaming laminate, made—like the cover of *Abbey Road* or a photo of the Chrysler Building—into one of those German Gelini puzzles you can get at any supermarket, and now too cropping up in all the stories and poems growing out of the Hopper painting like mushrooms in underbrush. There were a lot of them, a bit too many: too often "my" painting appeared on the covers of books and calendars included free with the kinds of magazines one no longer wished to buy, and yet I also went along with this general fascination, because yes, there was a kind of unstated human longing concentrated there, because it spoke of our common matrix of dreams, it took on weight. Though rendered as a banal stereotype, it told of some desire that, like hunger, could touch everyone. Thus I existed, or so I imagined, in order to shoulder this burden myself, to elucidate it over glasses of wine in the name of us all, over glasses rattling with ice on July evenings, over glasses of grog (and what the hell is grog, anyway?) when frost traps steam against windows and summons it from the mouths of passersby, like *fumata bianca* for a new winter religion.

I knew what others had declaimed. So many trembling voices trying to hold Hopper's painting on slumping shoulders of verse, to roll its fragile ball across them. They drowned in the penumbras of that night and quickly petered out, leaving single words as traces of their gaze. The "cheap gardenia perfume" that Sue Standing smells on the neck of the woman in the red dress ("Hopper's Women"); the "patrons of life" whom Samuel Yellen discerns in the gathered trinity of customers ("Nighthawks"); news of the Allies' most recent victory that Ira Sadoff hears on a radio not shown in the picture ("Hopper's 'Nighthawks' (1942)"); scraps of counter conversation about the war, Hemingway, and Fitzgerald, which reached Susan Ludvigson's ear as she was writing her poem, with that enumeration of prosaic details characteristic of American poetry, the no-longer-hot coffee, the four salt shakers on the counter, the automobile most likely parked somewhere nearby—oh, and of course, there, sitting at the bar, those are her parents, now they're arguing about the "American Dream" ("Inventing My Parents") . . . All these poems—and many more, and whole novels (French, English) derived from *Nighthawks*, lifted on its wings—were touchingly irrelevant, like the Earth seen from the moon: from inside these poems someone was looking into the café with its ad for Phillies cigars, into its transparent mass, and trying to make the image his own, and after that he said something or muttered something, told the story of his insignificant little life, his moth's dance around the interior's yellow light. He looked; the light behind the windowpane, that gentle Medusa, riveted his gaze, robbed him of his eyes the way you can be robbed of your sanity; the pane separated words from selves, words that fell along this side and vanished in the darkness.

For years we have felt the weight of these eyes pressing in on us from all around, and Olga's were (I imagined) at times so intent and abyssal that I could not reach their shores. She did the looking for everyone, as if, from her post, she'd been sent to the crow's nest, to the highest point, while I was still being consumed by the temptation of yet another long story. She saw more from the get-go, perhaps the majestic silence of that ancient night, the immobility of the bodies planted on their stools like the statues on Easter Island, and that wraparound window like an amniotic sac in which a person had taken shape but decided not to live and so hardened immediately in the eternal, dull, superfluous willingness to clutch glasses of cheap bourbon, and all the while I'm still looking for ways to identify with their fates, with the loneliness of the one and the conversation of the others (about how you can't depend on Harold, how the Rangers would never win the Stanley Cup again), with the bartender's thinking about a tough day that, like others, was now over; that New York at night, early spring,

1942, when the anticipation of the events that would follow the attack on Pearl Harbor had cleared the streets and dug an even deeper furrow into the night, had so tensed the air in the glass diner with the Phillies ad that the gestures of its inhabitants were all limited to a radius of only a few centimeters, and the loneliness of the trinity of customers underscored the sadness of their bodies in the face of a higher power, the great onset of war.

So many windows, so many panes, so many glass doors had been erected by Edward Hopper that if one were to take them all together and arrange them end-to-end, the world would seem to have been sliced in half by a new Great Wall, dividing it in two, cutting through cities, rising up suddenly around motels and forgotten country houses, its invisible snaking glass bordered here and there by doorways, window frames, the sharp edges of half-drawn drapes and curtains. Whichever side we happen to be standing on, whether staring into the rooms, foyers, and halls held behind the glass or the other way around, staring out from their interiors at the streets, houses, or sky, a vague longing awaits us, either a longing for life, which is still going on at any given moment, so very near to time that it brushes up against it and tears at its seams, for here is a scrap of paper in a book, an open letter, a raised cup, a folder taken out of a drawer—or else a longing for stillness, unaffected by time, pilfered from the interiors of our rooms, calling out to the afternoon light, to neon signs in the evening, and covering the nervous bustle of the day in a transparent silence.

Why Transparency?

But why transparency? Why this word, which sounds as beautiful to me in English as it does in French, Spanish, or Polish? Transparency, *transparence, transparencia, przezroczystość*. No, the Polish really is the nicest, where we have our choice of the lovely *przejrzystość*—something along the lines of "lucidity"— and the even more beautiful *przezroczystość*—"transparency." Is it the sound of these words that I have always loved? Or those half-words, those other words, their collaborators? Clarity, "eyes"—the *oczy* in *przezro*czystość? Eyes, with their refined *y* in the middle and *s* at the end, because it's one thing to "look someone in the eye," when staring can only mean staring someone down, but quite another to look *into* someone's eyes. Transparent, apparent, appear, appearance in the eyes of another. And then there's that other thing denoted by the word "transparency," the image placed on an overhead projector in childhood, a word that held a little bit of magic, as well as the pleasure of anticipation. Such images were not quite so democratic in those days, you couldn't use them to oversalt your doses of the everyday; the image approached, announced itself, appeared mysteriously on white screens, on the very walls (we would pick out the lightest ones). Just as when, some thirty-odd years ago, in some Beskid mountain hamlet, someone, some city slicker, came along to show the old highlander women the desert and camels, African landscapes, dunes with bodylike curves. They sat in the village hall on chairs arranged a bit more orderly than usual, in ironed kerchiefs, as a sign that they appreciated the evening's sense of occasion. Apparently, transparently; I was curled up in the corner, freezing from traveling all day in the rain and snow, and I saw those motionless heads in their kerchiefs, fixated on the undulating bands of sand, the golden light that radiated off the wall and likewise drew you in. Yes, those were transparencies, *trans*-appearances; the images had the power to transport you, and the creases they made on the bright paint revealed an open, limitless space, a clear azure over the desert, over the cupolas of sand. Cinema had already been around for well over seventy years, but imagination was still three-dimensional, it saw far, *trans* wall, *trans* brick, *trans* the white of the screen, *trans*parently.

Why transparency, from my earliest years? Where did this desire come from, among my toys, my favorite games, child's play whose precise geometric principles, as in hacky sack or bottle-cap races, were delimited by my field of vision, by a strictly defined space? Was this simply a schoolboy's dream of travel to distant lands, an escape from school, a great adventure, setting sail across the infinite ocean? But wasn't it right there, on the other side of the window? Beyond the classroom, couldn't I make out an inaccessible world that I would someday finally enter? Or did transparency arise somewhere else, off to the side, not within but parallel to the buffalo hunt, nights spent in teepees, the endless wandering from port to port? Or did it instead admit shafts of light into a room where there had been a kind of darkness all along? Or did it rather brighten the wall where, as the poem we've learned by heart has told us, "the low, heavy sky weighs like the giant lid / Of a great pot upon the spirit crushed by care, / And from the whole horizon encircling us is shed / A day blacker than night, and thicker with despair"?[3] Lucidity, transparency, *transparencia*—I have made no essential distinction between what is simply lucid, truly transparent like muslin or a windowpane, and what strikes us right away as pure light, immediately visible. For I have also always felt that pure light is never directly given; the veil between it and our eyes, between light and ourselves, has become invisible, has kindly consented to purge itself of all shadows and smudges; light has turned out to be nothing more than a transparency we tolerate.

Why transparency, transpicuousness, *transparencia, przezroczystość*? Might this light have come to us from elsewhere? First of all, perhaps because of this: Couldn't I say that it, transparency, is the first thing I remember in life, like an icon or roadside cross? The first image: a bright, empty room in the morning, with an enormous patch of sunlight, a yellow square on the wall. The air thus became illuminated, with quivering bits of dust, so pure and full in that light that it seemed its interior had been revealed, so that transparency allowed the gaze to penetrate its bare surface to see an even deeper purity. Thus it lay dormant through long years, occasionally broadcasting a covert desire for solitude, quiet, absence; it was a visual projection of life, of life's unexcavated proto-Gospel, until at last it burst out in the fullness of its name, transparency, *transparencia, przezroczystość,* as a theme, as truth and illusion, as the hobby of existence, the graspable handrail against which we may lean our very being, something we might even try to pour into text.

Is this, then, where transparency comes from? Transparency is always approaching, just as the slideshow was always approaching. I don't remember it exactly; I recall only how it tasted. The flavor of the slides, for example, of the colorful squares projected across plaster.

Mlle Lambercier's Comb

Where might all of this have started? Jean-Jacques Rousseau was eight years old when one of Madame Lambercier's many combs was ruined. The combs were drying on a plate in the alcove of the room adjoining the kitchen; the heat emanating from the kitchen stove warmed the air, the first rays of spring sunlight illuminated the wall, and Jean-Jacques had the pleasure of reading in this very spot the Latin exercises that had been assigned him. Several of the combs were multi-sided; Madame, or rather Mademoiselle Lambercier, the strict Mlle Lambercier, must have had long, strong, thick hair. When the maid returned to the room, she saw that all of the teeth along one side of the largest comb had snapped off. She let out a shriek, and the echo of her cries resounds in the ears of some to this very day.

This called for an investigation. M. Lambercier and his family conducted interrogations, a capital inquisitory; the interrogator had no doubt that it was Jean-Jacques who had committed the offence—nay, the little murder: no one else had been in the room, no one else had been seen going in: guilty, guilty, guilty. Jean-Jacques objected, he protested, he swore; his Uncle Bernard was summoned from a great distance; the severity and authority of his relative did not compel Jean-Jacques to admit guilt: "They were unable to force from me the confession they required. Though the punishment was several times repeated and I was reduced to the most deplorable condition, I remained inflexible. I would have died rather than give in, and I was resolved to do so."[4] For the misdeed itself, but also for his resistance and impertinence, for his insolent denial, for his recalcitrance, for his stupid eight-year-old life, for his squinty blue eyes, for his proudly tousled bangs, for the flush on his face, for the serpent hidden within the garden, for man's original sin, for the failure to live up to the maturity demanded of him as well as of his cousin, who had also been up to no good—unintentionally, by his own assurances, but deliberately in the judgment of the court—a fitting sentence was carried out. Locked in their room, they lay in the same bed and, with a feeling of helplessness and injustice, embraced one another, lifted themselves up from under the covers, stood on the bed frame, and cried out furiously, in perfect Latin: *Carnifex! Carnifex!* Executioner! Executioner! You are all executioners!

When Jean-Jacques recalls this event in his *Confessions*, he is already an old man, but his hand trembles, waves of blood rise to his face, and he feels that "my pulse beat faster once more as I write."[5] Nearly half a century has passed, half a century, and nothing has changed, the plate is still steaming, it's as though it happened just yesterday. Yesterday the comb was broken, yesterday he was falsely accused, yesterday he was punished, yesterday doubt was cast on his innocence, the voice of his heart was left unheard. Half a century! "It is now nearly fifty years since this occurrence, and I have no fear of a fresh punishment for the offence. But I declare before heaven that I was not guilty. I had not broken, nor so much as touched, the comb. I had not gone near the stove, nor so much as thought of doing so. But do not ask me how the mischief occurred. I have no idea, and I cannot understand it. But I do most positively know that I was innocent."[6]

In his beautiful book *Jean-Jacques Rousseau: Transparency and Obstruction,* Jean Starobinski speaks of the whole affair with the comb as if of the expulsion from Paradise. The young Jean-Jacques had lived in the conviction that Paradise is the mutual transparency of hearts, complete and immediate understanding among people, that words and feelings pass from one to the other, from Jean to Sophie, from Sophie to Paul, like a ray of light from eye to eye. But then he learned that his own feelings, his own certainty—as to his innocence, for example—could not be transmitted, expressed, or told. An obstruction now stood on the path to the hearts of others; the conviction that flowed from the depths of his own heart could no longer reach them. The world had been so clear, so transparent. That morning, the sun had squeezed impatiently into the room, but then everything suddenly changed, the darkness of accusation and rejection fell upon that day. The world had become gloomy, clouded over, and had lost its luster, which before had cleared his eyes' course all the way up to the horizon. Now, somewhere in the depths of that darkness, the innocent heart of Jean-Jacques could only flicker like a burning, useless crystal. From that incident onward, he tells us, he could no longer enjoy unperturbed happiness. This marked the end of his childhood. Here had been the catastrophe that bisected his life, leaving the time of purity, innocence, and naïveté on the one side, and opening, on the other, which was infinitely longer, the laborious, daily game of appearances. "We began to be secretive, to rebel, to lie."[7] Later, just once, he will even say, "I became indeed what I appeared."[8] The destroyer of the comb, the cunning fox, the clever little liar, someone other than himself. Like that time in Turin when he stole Mlle Pontal's ribbon, the pink ribbon with the silver edge, though it was already a little worn, a bit frayed, and the guilt for this act was born by Marion, Madame de Vercellis's cook, pretty, modest, and sweet, "a good girl, sensible and absolutely trustworthy."[9] He regretted it for forty years; he hoped that he had done penance for this crime with forty years of integrity and honor, as well as with the avalanche of misfortunes that had crashed down on the waning years of his life and burdened his dying.

It seems that it was precisely Jean-Jacques Rousseau, the unfortunate guardian of the comb, who awakened the ancient concept of transparency and first introduced it as an intrinsic object (of ideas, feelings, phantasms) into the imagination and literature of Europe; it is in his writings that it comes to mark the ideal, the highest value, of which his, Jean-Jacques's, own existence was or might have been—if not for the closed hearts of others—the fullest embodiment. "My heart has been as transparent as crystal," he repeats several times in his letters and in the *Dialogues*.[10] When he starts to hold forth on honesty, he likes to speak of himself not only in the first person, but in the third, to assume a distance, to establish the objective measure of his statements: "His heart, transparent as crystal, can hide nothing of what happens within it. Every mood it feels is transmitted to his eyes and face."[11] A heart of crystal, a transparent heart: here is an ideal as much spiritual as it is physiological. "For, if I understand the hearts of Julia and Clara," he writes of the heroines of *The New Heloise*, "they were to each other perfectly transparent."[12] One can believe in such hearts, and even imagine them not as metaphors, but as a transparent material.

The dream of an originary transparency would remain the metaphor for the utopian state of happiness, and Jean-Jacques would surely never have reached the verge of his own great and extraordinary madness, which continues to arouse hatred and aversion (how many accusations from writers, philosophers, and critics to this day? how many reproaches—those abandoned children, those foibles, those strange relationships with women, that French Revolution?), were it not for his fascination with transparency as a state as much spiritual as physical and chemical. Transparency not only as a zone for interpersonal relationships and the social links derived from them, but also as a psycho-physical state. He was very interested in processes of vitrification, about which he wrote in his *Institutions chimiques;* he was intrigued by the work of the German physicist Joachim Becher, who believed that "man is from glass and to glass may return," and who was convinced that by the right process it was possible to transform a corpse into "lovely, transparent glass" (which the latest technology, used commercially in America, has mastered to perfection; for an appropriately high fee the dead body can be converted into a crystal signet ring—with a deep blue tint—to be worn on the finger).

Besides, at this time—the mid-eighteenth century—the conceit of imagining the body as though made of glass is gaining currency; it appears, among other places, in Fontenelle's then widely read *Conversations on the Plurality of Worlds,* as well as in a philosophical tract by La Mettrie. This image gained traction from technological advances in the production of glass and from its increasingly common use as a practical material over the course of the preceding century. The seventeenth-century image of glass was still negative, bound up with the Baroque discourse on the fragility and vanity of existence. In his *Anatomy of Melancholy*, Robert Burton discerns among the "fearful melancholics" those who "are all glass, and therefore they will suffer no man to come near them."[13] Descartes, in his *Meditations on First Philosophy*, also speaks of melancholics who, under the influence of vapors of black bile, imagine that they "are a totally hollowed-out shell or are made of glass."[14] The idea of glass's fragility (because of cups and goblets, because of transparent spheres, because of the instantaneous bursting of soap bubbles) likewise stretches through the entire seventeenth century in *vanitas* portraits and in still-lifes.

But the eighteenth-century sensualist discourse valorizes glass in another way, positively, by connecting it for the first time with such values as purity and openness. In Rousseau, the image of one's own body as glass is favorable, and not ominous, as it had been in those melancholic obsessions over fragility. In the aforementioned *Institutions chimiques*, Rousseau spends a long time pondering the physical properties of transparency, and he recognizes that fluidity is fundamental: "no bodies could be transparent were all their parts not fluid in equal measure." Transparency is for Rousseau hardened, arrested, or frozen fluidity, and this is why the crystal of the heart does not submit to time, but continues in its own, immutable, pure form, like an eternal river. If it were possible to erect a new monument to Jean-Jacques today (for example, in Warsaw's

Skaryszewski Park), I imagine that it might take the form of the "Man of Glass," *L'Homme de verre,* the statue that greeted visitors to the main hall of the Paris World's Fair in 1937. Illuminated by a shaft of light from above, it reaches into this brightness with a glass hand that flows with artificial blood; it tenses its glass torso, in which one can count all the ribs; while the glass legs, with their tangled muscles and glass arteries, hold the trunk in a straight posture, firmly planted, yet ready to raise it lightly, even to launch it into the air. Or else it might look like a figure from the tribute paid to Rousseau (*Hommage à Jean-Jacques Rousseau*) two hundred years after his death by Emmanuel Saulnier, a sculptor for whom transparency has become the chief subject; this glass Jean-Jacques was placed on the promenade in Annecy, in Rousseau's native alpine haunt, near the lakes upon whose surface he jotted down his dreams and strolls. And were it possible to memorialize Jean-Jacques on the pedestal in words befitting his imagination, I would select these, from a poem entitled "Transparency," by Jan Twardowski:

> I pray Lord to take no cover
> may that no matter what I am transparent
> that you see through me the duck with the flat bill
> the yellow primrose that blossoms in the evening
> always from the beginning of the world four poppy petals
> a heart that sketches emotion in a letter

Rousseauian transparency is all-encompassing, absolute, and, like every Rousseauian ideal, elemental as well as mythic, a given from the get-go. Its expression knows no shadow, nothing falls between the heart and the face, they exist in a commonness of purpose, like communicating vessels. Here there is nothing of degrees, nuances, evolutions, middle grounds, instances of unknowing, there is no dialectic of essence and appearance, no libertine *larvatus prodeo,* no living out one's life behind a mask. The only thing that might disrupt it is an obstruction imposed from the outside, one that cuts off the radiance of transparency, its immanent duration in time. This confrontation, encapsulated in the title of Jean Starobinski's book as, precisely, "transparency and obstruction," penetrates all of Jean-Jacques's work, creating two distinct categories and the basis of his social and political theory, which is dependent on the dichotomy of clarity and obscurity.[15] The obstruction to the transparency that Jean-Jacques had sensed within himself, the obstruction that will in time be elevated to the realm of negative social experience (people have gotten stuck in obscurity and no longer wish to live without it), is the impossibility—to use today's language—of communication; that is, of the complete disclosure and transmission of transparency, of its eternal duration. In other consciousnesses, there arises a false image of Jean-Jacques, destroyer of combs, and this denies his absolute transparency, which would otherwise be the ideal model for this kind of social communication.

Thus, the tragedy of Rousseauian transparency is the fact that it is left defenseless within its own innocence: it can't defend itself from being clouded over, from the darkening brought on by the unrestrained activity of mankind, from the false judgments of others. Simply looking at other people isn't enough to achieve this transparency, nor does looking seek to do so. Now and then

the world goes dark, and Jean-Jacques wants to account for it, illuminate it, write books about it, to make sure that, for the first
time in history, he is presenting man as he truly is, in all his transparency, and he, Jean-Jacques Rousseau, will be this man. He ac-
costs people everywhere, at salons, on the street, he pushes their
buttons, he awaits their smiles and understanding, for them to
entrust him with their faith, to admit him into their hearts, but
darkness continues to envelope the world, and he feels like kick-
ing and screaming, like letting his body seize and convulse and,
when his strength fails him, to just sit there and cry. All of the
most important characters in his work cry, and Jean-Jacques is
always crying himself, and in their faces the tears carve tracks by
which to return to times long past, to a childhood that smells of
thyme, when everything was as clear as the palm of your hand,
happily right there before your very eyes.

Diaphanes

When he spoke of transparency or clarity, Jean-Jacques availed
himself of the word *transparent,* which is derived from the nearly
identical-sounding Latin neologism *transparens,* coined in the
Middle Ages. In ancient Greece they used the lovely word *diaphanes.* You can repeat it for its pleasure alone, not knowing
what it means, but feeling how it fills the mouth with clear air and
opens it to the sun with its double *a.* It has survived in English
as *diaphanous* and is found in the Romance languages, as *diafan*

in Romanian, and in French *diaphane*. In Romanian it refers to something light and delicate, like a feather or a spring dress; the French usage puts greater emphasis on admitting light: not entirely, but noticeably. Porcelain can be *diaphane*, or an autumn leaf, or parchment, the old or aristocratic skin on one's hands. Broadening this meaning, one can also use *diaphane* to describe a silhouette ("it was beautiful, elegant, and *diaphane*") or even sunlight seen in a particular way ("The sun was clear and *diaphane*, like white wine."). (Despite their delicacy, both quotes are drawn from Sartre.)[16]

In her research, Anca Vasiliu has found that the word had many uses in Greek. In several ancient authors, it's used to suggest light at the moment of dawning, while in others, such as Pindar, it describes bright, shining phenomena, like the flames of a burning pyre; *diaphanes* was used for the moon when its disk passed across the disk of the sun. It was a common word for Plato, one he uses to describe the stream Illissos, on whose bank Socrates and Phaedrus discourse on love and the beauty of souls: "So beautiful is the water here, so clear and transparent," Phaedrus says in the Wright translation. In *Phaedo*, the land on the other side, that distant, other country, whose stones emanate such brightness that the most beautiful stones from this, our land, emeralds and rubies, are as worthless garbage beside them—that land is described as *diaphanes*. Finally, the word appears in the dialogue *Timaeus*, in the discussion of the mechanism of sight, of the conditions for discerning things. The concept *diaphanes* means utter transparency between the ray emitted by the eye and the ray emitted by the object; they meet halfway and penetrate each other in a state of complete consonance, without any mediation. This is a state of self-evidence, one in which there is no obstruction; in the Middle Ages, it was called "angelic." Between that which is seen and that which does the seeing there is nothing out of place, everything is obvious, clear, and unambiguous. Despite their distance from one another, the two rays, that of the eye and that of the thing, interpenetrate and become one. In that single moment, the world becomes crystal clear. But as Jean-Jacques would know best of all, the kingdom of *diaphanes* does not last forever.

The term *diaphanes* is taken up by Aristotle and his commentators. Among the ancients, it was indeed the native son of Stageira who paid it the most attention, for by using this word he explained more precisely than Plato how things become visible. In his treatise *On the Soul* (*De Anima*), Aristotle says that, yes, there is transparency. Perhaps most enticing is this one, naked assertion: "there is actually transparency." In any case, that's how it reads in French; in the Polish translation (where, significantly, *diaphanes* is translated as "transparent") the sentence reads, "assuredly there are things that are transparent"; in English, however, it is a little different: "We must then first say what light is. We can take for granted the existence of something transparent."[17] Aristotle's characterization is not entirely self-evident—his commentators wrestle over its meaning—but this affords us a bit of freedom in mulling it over, in repeating that "there is actually transparency," in questioning whether transparency exists as such. After all, we must recall that, formally, the philosopher is tasked above all else with describing how things reveal themselves.

For Aristotle, transparency is almost light. Almost, because they are not exactly identical to one another. For the given thing to become visible, its color must be perceptible. For its color to be perceptible, it has to appear in light. Light is generated through the medium of the transparency that obtains in all things. When this hidden transparency is activated, it becomes light. "The actuality of the transparent," Aristotle writes, "is light."[18] When the transparency in a given thing rests there passively, however, when it is inactivated, merely "potential," it remains invisible, dark; it is, as Vasiliu writes, "the other face of the visible."[19] Aristotle speaks of the "substance" of transparency that obtains in things; light activates it somehow, or, to put it another way, in its activity transparency becomes light. *Diaphanes* thus belongs to the nature of things, but at the same time it is also the field upon which the thing reveals itself. This notion allows Aristotle to counter Plato's awfully la-di-da definition of reality as *images* of reality (i.e., reality consists only of its representations). In saying that "we can take for granted the existence of something transparent," Aristotle was saying at the same time that "there is only transparency": there is only light, either revealed or waiting to be revealed—such is the nature of things. There is no tension between what is seen and what is, no uncertainty as to whether the visible corresponds perfectly to the invisible.

Later commentators to Aristotle, including the Church Fathers, were divided over the concept of *diaphanes*. It subsequently entered medieval Latin in its own form, *diaphanus,* as well as in the aforementioned Latin neologism *transparens*. It appears in tracts on very different subjects—philosophical, cosmological—from the pens of such thinkers as Bonaventure, Thomas Aquinas, Roger Bacon, and Meister Eckhart. It also begins to be used in artistic discourse; it is indispensable to the art of stained glass and, with it, aesthetic theories of light and its perception. According to Vasiliu, between the twelfth and fifteenth centuries both notions—*diaphanus* and *transparens*—were taken for technical concepts, though also—such were the times—for philosophical ones. Later, with the transition to the vernacular and following minor phonetic changes, the words lost their "scientific" character, all the more so because new concepts in optics and cosmology had rendered them obsolete. Yet Burton's melancholics would need them, since they offer an expression of the fragility of the glass body; and Jean-Jacques would need them, so as to speak of his innocence a half century later and dream of the mutual understanding of human hearts; and public figures would need them in order to assure us of the good intentions behind their actions and the obvious conditions under which they have made their decisions; and we, too, would need them, in the quiet of our apartments, since the heart of man changes more slowly than the world.

The Heart's Language

"My heart is as transparent as crystal." The works of Rousseau, foundational for the idea of transparency, contain concepts of transparency that are social as well as existential, political as well as psychological. His children's generation (not his own children, allegedly—no need to believe this out of hand—abandoned, but other, better progeny) were to reach for its social dimension, translated into revolutionary terms: enough of pretending, of living a lie, from now on the people shall have access to truth as such, no more of the fakery and secrecy of government affairs, to the scaffold with the aristocracy, and may their heads fall into the baskets like discarded masks.

But the phantasm of transparency that Rousseau passed on to Romantic literature, which followed one or two generations later, emerges most distinctly in the problematics of language. Rousseau had been the first to express so forcefully the idea of a crisis in language, in that instrument of communication which no longer served communication; Romanticism would extend this idea and take it to an extreme. The Romantic crisis of language—for that matter, the Romantic consciousness of language—rests on the fact that, as Alfred de Musset wrote, "we no longer wish for words, it is words that should wish for us; one must experience them like an irresistible thought that liquidates all play," that annihilates all appearances heretofore revealed. Rousseau had already been well aware that in order to satisfy his need to speak of his own indiscriminate transparency he would have to strive for a kind of language that did not yet exist, "to invent a language as new as my project."[20] Did this have to be a literary language? Not necessarily; he himself regarded writing as a burden, as an ultimately indirect communication, quite imperfect, too slow, and unreflective of the rhythm of one's own feelings. For those like himself, Rousseau writes in the *Dialogues*, "The cumbersome sequence of speech is unbearable to them. They chaff against its slow progression. From the speed of the impulses they feel, it seems to them that what they feel should become apparent and penetrate from one heart to another without the cold intermediary of words."[21] The heroes of *Julie, or The New Heloise* generally have no need of language: not only written, but spoken as well; the understanding between them is unspoken, for they do not have to conceal their feelings with words or resort to the economy of utterance: "nothing has remained in our hearts that we wish to hide from each other."[22]

"And having known the way of worldly shades, / And having known a heart that said: I'm pure"—so begins an unfinished poem by Juliusz Słowacki. At the time he wrote these words, "purity of heart" had already become a common formula, but an elaboration of what its language should be was no easy task. Rousseau and Romantic writers had first sought a matrix for this new language in music. The Romantics (with Adam Mickiewicz foremost among them in Poland) regarded as one of the highest expressions of music that which was later commonly referred to as *glass music*. One of its most beloved instruments was the glass harmonica, invented by Benjamin Franklin in 1761. Among the other instruments used to produce glass music was the glasschord, invented twenty years prior, a sort of small piano with glass strings, as well as the musical oddities called "seraphim," "euphonium," and "clavicylinder." The earliest attested concert on glass in modern times was played by an Irishman, Richard Pockrich, in 1741; his glass arrangement was called the "angelic organ." Perhaps the most spectacular contemporary angelic-organ concert is that performed belowdecks in Fellini's 1983 film *And the Ship Sails On*. Those passengers who happen to hear it in the depths of the boiler room fall into a rapture that is so pure, so innocent, it is difficult to call it anything but "angelic"; on their faces, carefully recorded on film, one sees delight and bliss. When I was a teenager, I was just as enraptured by Mike Oldfield's album *Tubular Bells*; an awful title, though allegedly it is indeed the technical name of the instrument Oldfield uses after the somewhat pompous climax: after fifteen minutes of laying the groundwork with secondary instruments, these bells appear, repeating the central theme and bringing it to a conclusion. Their attack sounds like a somewhat jacked-up, though angelic, parade of crystal tones.

It was in these same terms—angelic, seraphic—that the Romantics described the melody of their favorite instrument, the glass harmonica. This was a music both human and inhuman at the same time, for it reached, unobstructed, straight up to the heavenly spheres, joining the hearts of mankind to divine being. Rousseau, who had had a musical education, cast off the role of the performer-interpreter; he was an enemy of virtuosity, which obstructs music's immediate access to the heart. Alfred de Musset, who probed perhaps most deeply of all the Romantics, unpacking the connections between transparency and the expressible, called music simply "the language of the heart" ("Die Aussprache des Herzens"), availing himself of the expression of the German pre-Romantic Jean Paul Richter.

Musset, a true nostalgist of transparency, would quote a fragment of poetic prose by the Rousseauian Jean Paul, in which the Genius watching over humanity asks Jupiter to give him another, better language than the one he has at his disposal:

> "Father divine! bestow on thy poor human creatures a language more expressive than any they now possess, for they have words signifying only how they suffer, how

they enjoy, and how they love." "Have I not given them tears?" replied the deity,—"tears of pleasure, of pain, and the softer ones that flow from tender passions?" The genius answered,—"O god of men! tears do not sufficiently speak the overflowings of the heart; give, I thee supplicate, to man a language that can more powerfully paint the languishing and empassioned wishes of the susceptible soul,—the recollections, so delightful, of infancy,— the soft dreams of youth [. . .];—give them, father of all! a new language of the heart!" At this moment the celestial harmonies of the spheres announced to Jupiter the approach of the Muse of Song. To her the god immediately made a sign, and thus uttered his behests:— "Descend on earth, O Muse, and teach mankind thy language." And the Muse of Song descended to earth, taught us her accents, and from that time the heart of man was able to speak.[23]

This musical "language of the heart" would become the dream-horizon for Musset's heroes, who seek out an ideal correspondence between experience and its expression, which would foster understanding with neither loss nor psychological games. As with Rousseau, however, this is attainable only for the initiated. Zygmunt Krasiński, the Romantic poet who for many long years sent love letters to Delfina Potocka day in, day out, and occasionally every few hours, wanted to speak to her in precisely this way, with his heart alone, and in his breaks between letters he would lock himself in his room and concentrate, surrendering to meditation and autohypnosis, focusing his energy so as to reveal his unspoken words to Delfina immediately and telepathically. He often fell into doubt, but with new swells of faith he believed that there is an ongoing development of the human soul, and that at some point these souls—and in particular his own and Delfina's—would achieve an unobstructed and everlasting mutual understanding. It could happen at any moment, and yet the true time of such understanding could arrive only—here Zygmunt was again overcome with doubt—in something other than earthly time, only "after centuries will the curtain fall, and these masks we are today will fall, and we will know one another not in part, but in our entirety."

Jean-Jacques liked people who met simply to spend some time together, in solidarity and sincerity, finding union in their mutual presence on this Earth, and celebrating it. He regarded the wine harvest as the most beautiful of all such celebrations; there was no obstruction between hearts, and the rows of grape vines signified one common path for all. Gathering grapes, people walked together, side by side, making the same motions, singing songs in one voice. Rousseau loved music; as I've mentioned, he composed from an early age, and he pondered music a great deal as a theoretician and wrote about it in his letters as well. He complained about over-complicated partitas, about the "bulk of notes" from which they are made, the hundreds of little lines, dots, and flecks. He proposed a radically simplified system of musical notation. Above all else he preferred music that went straight to the heart, unembellished, without displays of virtuosity, without rhetorical or technical transitions or bridges. For this reason he saw an opposition between French music, written as much for the performer as for the audience, and Italian music, which was much less acrobatic.

He writes about this in his "Letter from a Symphonist in the Royal Academy of Music to His Comrades in the Orchestra," in which he describes French music as refined and artificial, and Italian music as aesthetically transparent, "referring solely to its own sounds." Thus he did not value harmony, but rather melody—that which is most easily transmitted in music. French music offers itself to the interpreter, to virtuosity, and in this way hinders immediate communication between one soul and another. Italian music, in going straight to the heart of things, is much more melodic than harmonic, which means that it is much stronger in communicating feelings, whereas harmony favors only brief sensual pleasure: it occupies but a single moment, makes an impression, yet does not reach toward depths of feeling.

Rousseau sought an equivalent for melody in the language of words. He wasn't interested in the immediate melodiousness of sentences, but in the possibility of a completely undisturbed—though also unornamented and refined—transmission of feelings. He did not yet know that the coming Romantic literature—as well as later literature of the nineteenth century, which sometimes dreamed of a language of hearts—would come up with something that was utterly opposed: style. This, of course, would be a means of expression that was narrowly individual, ironic, reaching for what Roland Barthes calls "the mythic depths of the author," which arise "on the border between his body and the world," but which enclose the author in solitude, "in the splendor of his own imprisonment." Though life taught him to doubt it, Rousseau believed that the heart of man could speak, that it could speak directly. It could speak in song, but sometimes, at particular moments, it could speak in yet another way, in true, simple, short words. And this is when, in a state of rapture, he saw how language could become a transparent medium for the will of speech, for everything that wishes to be expressed.

A Single Sentence

"Tormented by the cursed ambition always to put a whole book in a page, a whole page in a sentence, and this sentence in a word. Here I am."[24] Thus Joseph Joubert—a so-called minor Romantic who has entered literary history with barely a handful of poems and short, aphoristic thoughts as well as the legend of many bits of unrecorded, incisive advice given to such great Romantics as Chateaubriand—expressed his suffering some twenty years after the death of Rousseau. Joubert was among the first writers to find himself tormented by the dream of crystallization and condensation, of concentration into minimal space, in the pearl of a single sentence and maybe even a single word, some whole that would express the whole of existence. I am speaking of myself, but no longer as one whose whole and honest truth, whose whole transparent soul, must be represented in lengthy confessions, but on the contrary, in the briefest form possible, in a formulation that contains the densest essence. From Rousseau to Joubert—or, more broadly, from the Enlightenment to the pre-Romantics— the phantasm of transparency assumes aesthetic and metaphysical weight, it extends from the social and psychological domain to poetics, the new minimal poetics, of which Joubert's dream of "writing on air," as he himself described it, is today, I would say, the classic model. Joubert writes: "The transparent, the diaphanous, the thin crust, the magical; the imitation of the divine that made all things with little and, so to speak, with nothing: that is one of the essential qualities of poetry."[25] He is searching for absolute concentration, for the reduction of the poetic utterance to the smallest possible expression, a minimal phrase reduced, as he describes it, to a drop of the world. "Here I am." This drop of the world would be a single word, and in its closed transparency—so Maurice Blanchot would write about Joubert's wish—the utterance would for once retain the whole expanse of language.

At this time, the notions of condensation and crystallization, popularized by technology (thanks at the very least to the invention of the microscope or the birth of magnetism), function as literary metaphors not only in the sense of common poetic ornaments, but more interestingly as means for revealing the essence of phenomena, for example (the best example) the peculiar phenomenology of falling in love, as described by Stendhal in his celebrated *On Love*. Stendhal compares the amorous process, the process by which feelings are formed, to the processes of material crystallization that one can observe in nature, and specifically to the experience of the so-called "Salzburg bough." "At the salt mines of Hallein near Salzburg," Stendhal writes, "the miners throw a leafless wintry bough into one of the abandoned workings. Two or three months later, through the effect of the waters saturated with salt which soak the bough and then let it dry as they recede, the miners find it covered with a shining deposit of crystals. [. . .] The original little bough is no longer recognizable [. . .]"[26] The lover's imagination operates in an analogous manner, also crystallizing, that is, transforming the object of his affection from something completely common into a diamond. Inspired by feeling, the erotic imagination cleanses and alters the image; where an indifferent eye would regard the person in the ungraspable magnitude of her various states—better or worse, more or less smart or stupid, beautiful or ugly—the eye of the lover discerns a single, enchanting, difficult to express, diamantine whole.

In Joubert, the imperative to crystallize the word, to excise any excess, brushes up against the unutterable, against silence; his ultimately unrealized *ars poetica* heralds the aesthetic problematics of modern poetry, the poems of Mallarmé and many others in his mold, hidden just over the threshold of the immediate future. This is not the silence of refusal and resignation, but the silence, or half-silence, of inspiration searching for creative power and summoned precisely by the need to concentrate words, to liquidate inessential excess, meanings that are only half-full and perhaps too common, too full of common "clay." For Jean-Jacques, silence, contemplated in the course of his solitary strolls and daydreams at Lake Bienne, brings with it the sweetness of the truth about his own existence and the language of the heart's superiority over expressed—and thus spoken, but especially written—language. Joubert and others think of delimiting expression for artistic and metaphysical purposes, of crystallizing maximum content—hundreds, if not thousands of pages—in minimal space. Even in Zola, so exceptionally prolific an author of prose, moving from one book to the next like a train driving endlessly forward, there appears the dream of the crystal sentence, a sentence that will not actually halt the flow of words in order to grasp everything once and for all, but will instead be so hard and powerful that in each instance it will establish a complete and lucid whole. In his "Letter to the Youth," Zola writes: "I want ideas so true and bare, that they themselves appear to be transparent as well as solid, like diamonds in the crystal of the sentence."[27] Zola, as we shall soon see, adored glass decorations and would introduce them—as he spotted them in the new, transforming Paris—into the pages of his novels, and it seems to me that he could not have dreamed of a crystal sentence without them.

The crystal of a sentence, often of one, single sentence (or even of a word), would, from the Romantics up to our own day, tantalize many poets, much as novelists (and sometimes poets as well) were drawn to the historically older dream of the one Book that contains and expresses Everything. On the balance sheet of cultural history, crystallization may be a fairly young phantasm, but it has already fixed itself in our imaginations, where, like all good phantasms, it masks its own history so as to give the impression of freshness, the better to seduce us, as it once did me on the tennis courts of Skaryszewski Park.

I was doing worse than usual that day, unable to keep the ball in play, serving right into the net, knocking it into abandoned birds' nests, and then suddenly, in the middle of all the rushing and reaching and the backhands, whose failure made me feel as though I were lost in a desert of brick dust—it was spilling out over everything, enveloping everything in its hot breath—there appeared this strange feeling of hope, a sort of light, peaceful hint of hope, and it felt like certitude and revelation. That only this one thing remained, and that it could eventually work out, eventually or finally, this alone, this one thing could work itself out, namely, that my whole existence could be grasped in a single sentence, by which I could say, "Here I am." And with this thought came the sense that my life could indeed achieve this one, future sentence, that it could lead me there simply by following the path of its own destiny, completely unawares. No, the sentence need not be mystical or sententious, nor even the kind that expresses the fullest essence of what one has experienced; it wouldn't have to be a summation, a dictum, a witticism, an official closing remark, a ceremonial ending, nor would it need to be dazzling and poetic; rather, simply a sentence that was full and somehow clear, pure, and transparent. But one that clarified nothing, that might even be absurd, a silly rhyme for example, see you later alligator, mere alcohol doesn't thrill me at all, with no pretensions to divine, magic power (nothing of Joubert), but in its own way exact and crystalline. I had no idea how this was supposed to come about, maybe the sentence would fall from above me like a rubber stamp; all I knew was the hope that at some point this one sentence, this word, even if it appeared meaningless, would arrive.

So long as I was still hitting the ball, this thought felt like a real discovery, a different sort of droplet that had formed among the cold beads of my sweat, but later, once my body had cooled down, once the chill had gotten into my head, the thought seemed increasingly banal, pretentious, naïve, until I was out from under the anesthesia of imagination, through which the thought had snuck out, and in which it had flared up as something ostensibly original. I didn't know where it had come from, and I was irritated and somewhat surprised by the desire it contained for the unreal and absolute, for crystallization, for an ultimate, admittedly somewhat melancholic, but nevertheless full sigh that would elegantly encapsulate my entire life. But my surprise passed too, for I saw that I was merely the humble repository of a desire that had been rolling through the centuries, finding those who were more worthy, as well as people who just happened to be out on the tennis court.

Czesław Miłosz opens his *Visions from San Francisco Bay* with the following statement:

> I have written on various subjects, and not, for the most part, as I would have wished. Nor will I realize my long-standing intention this time. But I am always aware that what I want is impossible to achieve. I would need to communicate my full amazement at "being here" in one unattainable sentence which would simultaneously transmit the smell and texture of my skin, everything stored in my memory, and all I now assent to, dissent from.[28]

Rhetorically, Miłosz wanted everything, and in his one sentence he also wanted to house his own great and unexhausted memory; modestly placed beside his, my own desire (there on the tennis court) for a single sentence instead harbored what I would understand only later, the opposite intention, a contrary calling: no trace at all.

The Bandonéon and the Muleta

What is *diaphanes*, which is transparent when it manifests itself at all, and do we, even in reading Aristotle, know how to answer the question of whether it is real? Is this notion, asks Anca Vasiliu, an Aristotelian philosophical fiction that allows us to describe the phenomena of sense perception right to their very limits—that is, attaining the unobtainable, pure light, and thus transparency in action? Does it exist as an invisible specter winding around space? Is it merely a feature, an attribute of things (of those flames over the pyre, of those butterflies on the wind); or is it the aura they might manifest; or else, as Aristotle suggests, their substance (there is transparency in all things); or is it also perhaps an independent form of luminosity, a tinge of air? If it isn't a fiction of the intellect, then is it a fiction of the imagination, a space in motion that one can enter or leave? Is it at all possible to imagine transparency itself, unseen, as something beyond our vision? Is it perhaps something that just happens, that arrives, that is generated somewhere among bushes, houses, and streams, as ice forms from water? From time to time it might pop up from nowhere, you could feel it welling up, swelling drop by drop or suddenly shining right here next to you, or among the sentences you were just reading, among the sounds you just heard; or else it was suffused with layers, like a distant background with bands of color, like a lower plane with another on top and another on top of that, drifting to and fro like a hidden stream that knows all the secret passages through the weightiness of things. There were times when that's just how it was, I knew the exact moment it peeled suddenly away from the buildings, when just a moment earlier it had been completely invisible, nonexistent, I knew the moment when the light became its color, when it flashed between the walls, among objects, when its scattered particles flocked into a V-formation and flew into my eyes.

It wasn't always there. It hid inside its haunts so as to burst out unexpectedly, appearing as a space in motion, like sand, to lure me in. Here it had its mediums, mysterious means, hidden emissaries who summoned it without warning, who released it, conjured it from piles of things, prepared its place. As, for instance, on that day when we were coming back from the cemetery in Portbou and heard the bandoneón.

The bandoneón, without which the tango wouldn't have taken so long (and perhaps circuitous) a route from the velour of cat-houses, the *prostíbulos,* to hardcore metaphysics, differs from its close cousin, the friendly accordion, in more than just range and timbre. The most important difference is the time each sound requires to be brought to its peak. The bandoneón's inimitable, odd, brash groan immediately reaches an extreme, the glass edge of emotion. The bandoneón affords the musician no chance to turn back or effect an essential change. To a great extent, an accordionist can shape a sound after pressing a key, extending it with the motion of the bellows: he has a moment to decide what to do with it, which direction to take it in, maybe to change his mind, or even to replace one pitch with another, to cut it off, not to allow it to rise to the surface completely.

The bellows of the accordion echo the beating of the heart; they expand and contract, and in both motions the sound rolls out like blood, it flows and fades, but in both motions it resonates. When an accordionist sits down to play—a good, fiery accordionist like Jesus Aured, who seeks out a tone, feels around for a silence, and then wants to tell us about it—his whole body works in concert with the bellows and seems to be listening to the rhythm of his heart; his body pulses, it explodes and cowers, tightens, expands and contracts as though momentarily dead. Jesus's inconspicuous figure, bald on top, hardly equal to his name, takes on a serpentine plasticity from the very first note he plays. His tensed body pops off the hinges of its everyday form in order to reach the full potential of scream and silence, the full force of suffering, creation, and dying. When the bandoneón player presses a key, however, he summons sound more quickly, instantly, and irreversibly. Though its construction is very similar to the accordion's, though it's operated by a similarly violent two-stroke inhale and exhale, expansion and contraction, growing and shrinking as in the labor of the heart, the instrument only allows you to modulate the sound upward or cut it off sharply, without its dying out the way an accordion's would. Thus, it doesn't allow you to go back, to shift the sound into a different register. The entire two-step phase is divided in the bandoneón: the bellows, actually singular, moves the sound ahead, but when it pulls back and shrinks it becomes mute, it actually casts off the sound, collapses and closes so hard that the two ends of the instrument smack against each other and, if the musician so wishes, with a dry crack, with a kind of scraping that recalls the dry rustle of stockings as a tango dancer presents her legs to begin a new figure, signal a new beginning, the start of the next dance.

If we are to trust Jesus—and if not him, whom?—the ban-doneón poses the tougher challenge for the performer, tougher not only technically, but psychologically. It's as much a matter of the speed of decision-making as the diminished opportunity for improvisation, which, more easily accessible on the accordion, maintains the regular flow of time and allows the accordion-ist the possibility of slowing down, dalliance, exploration, and even discovery. Playing the bandoneón is therefore all about the brashness of the sounds that follow and that, in their inability to be turned around or extended, are brutally pure and lucid and, when they are violently interrupted, carry us to the very edge, where the voice falls into the abyss of a silence expressive like never before and nowhere else. They seem like sounds written with capital letters; they go right to the heart of the matter, to the very essence, sounds that in that one moment become al-legories, sticking a sharp knife into life. Not so much "asleep," "loving," "anxiety," "despair (*despertar*)," and "fear" (the titles of Astor Piazzolla's *Five Tango Sensations*), but rather "Asleep," "Loving," "Anxiety," "Despair," and "Fear": feelings and states— the language of the heart—in their pithiest, tensest, unrelenting, unremitting form.

The accordion produces music that is deeper, richer, and that has a wider harmonic range; the bandoneón's is simpler, reduced, somewhat unadorned, but farther-reaching, going to a place where things seem mercilessly clear, irrevocable (the way love, anxiety, and despair are irrevocable), thrust into the void like a mountain peak into an abyssal sky. The sound of the bandoneón (especially when Astor Piazzolla is playing, though Aured can get there, too) contains in its very texture a kind of glass foundation, the undertone of the glass harmonica. Thus, the instrument's characterization as a medium of transparency is based in large part on its having the same aural substance as glass, and in this characterization, or else in this feeling of transparency—mine and perhaps also Aured's—there lies an image of glaring clarity, of a brightness in the light of which it is no longer possible to hide parentheses or other creases, a striking self-evidence, all of it—the clarity, the self-evidence, the brightness—speaking at once: yes, now. There it is, now. That's it.

This is why, when Aured plays the bandoneón, the moment in which the sound suddenly breaks off, cast violently into silence, is so essential. One immediately feels like furnishing it with choreography, with the steps of the tango, particularly to watch how the bodies suddenly stand still, how they execute a given gesture, how they take a figure, once initiated, all the way to its edge and suspend it in the air, how they slaughter it for show, cutting and slicing with an invisible cleaver, with a violent twist of the body, so that after this pause, marked so emphatically, they might start a new figure, sketching its lines on a field left blank from the one before, and which, after a few bars, will reach its own end, reminding us again: yes, there, that's it, no other way to do it, that's all there is, nothing but another end. Here we are quite far from the soft melodiousness and dancing of other melodies and dances, in which there are no scars between the figures and bars, no obvious bridges, and in which one moves smoothly from one note or pose to the next. When Aured or Piazzolla plays the bandoneón, we dance (or so I imagine) in space, where there's nothing behind us, and what unfolds before us all at once is transparency, a clear void, into which we cast our bodies with resolve. Just let it be graceful, added Claude, Aured's friend, who then told us about Dominguín and his uncommonly precise handling of a muleta.

Luis Miguel Dominguín, one of the most famous matadors, spoke little of the *corrida*, but he did pronounce one important phrase, perhaps the most important. He knew many artists who had gone around the *corrida* waving the capes of their own obsessions and imaginations or intellectual illusions. Picasso was most intrigued by the movement and violence, the scenes in which the *torero* faces off against the bull; he confessed to Dominguín that he would rather have been a *picador* than a painter. Salvador Dalí sought the mythological image of the Minotaur in this spectacle. Luis Buñuel found in it a pleasure that was as mystical as it was erotic. Hemingway—with whom Dominguín had argued, as Hemingway didn't value his expertise, preferring Ortega y Gasset's disputable knowledge of the *corrida*—sought manly heroism and the beauty of an extreme situation. Cocteau was interested in the poetic form. Of course, Dominguín says, "The ideas of the artists I met were completely different from my own. Their interpretations seemed wrong to me, but they were interesting." Cocteau believed, for example, that tauromachy is first of all a ballet. Dominguín told him that yes, sure, the matador is a dancer, but the kind who stands still, a motionless dancer; the beauty of his art consists not in the steps he performs, in their charm, virtuosity, or precision, but in their calm, in how they die out in a body that is itself suddenly lifeless, and in how within that body the next steps are being prepared.

Unsurprisingly, Dominguín's most significant statement concerns an inseparable couple: the corrida and death. Many others have spoken of death in the afternoon, both before and after him, but it is Dominguín who hits the mark: "I am convinced that death is a square meter that moves around the arena. The matador knows that he mustn't enter it when the bull is charging. But he does not know where this square meter is."

One square meter. Death in the arena, Dominguín suggests, is a transparent space with sharply defined, yet invisible sides; never before has geometry achieved such terrible precision. It may have taken thousands of bodies gored and hundreds of thousands of bulls killed for such a statement to arrive, for this definition—or, rather, this intuition—of death to crystallize over generations (of people and animals). Death hovers like an aura, its four surfaces brushing a meter's breadth along the matador's body, his hands, his head, his feet sliding along these hidden walls, around this hole bounded by air. There is no visible difference between its space and the space of life; each turns around the other like twisted, colorless ribbons whose paths will cross who-knows-where. Thus the dancer must stop, stand still. Reach the edge of his movement and stop there. When the bull charges, he must avoid Dominguín's square, even brush up against it (otherwise he'd be a lousy *torero*, they'd whistle him away, and he wouldn't get his token of honor, the *orejas*, the bull's ear), but then—not another step. Here, somewhere just beyond his skin, he feels that transparent air which is not oxygen. And it may be for this that he enters the arena; this may be what crowds gather to see: a communion with this pure, absolute transparency, no longer of this life.

The bullfighting critic and announcer Gregorio Corrochano drew an opposition between Dominguín's logical tauromachy and the magical tauromachy of Antonio Ordóñez, another famous *torero*, saying that in Dominguín the art of bullfighting often came out too dry. This characterization—logical and dry—refers to the manner in which Dominguín moved about the arena, *ad more geometrico*, as well as to the economy of his gestures, which were more conservative and didn't conceal his raw technique under an excess of style or exaggerated theatrics, just to hold the eye more powerfully and stir up the audience, bringing easier applause. This logic of Dominguín's seems to me to belong to the aesthetics of transparency. The matador, executing his sparing, reserved dance, cuts the figure of this aesthetic, which I am taking out of the arena, from the arena in Linares (where Manolete, the king of the matadors, stepped deep into the square), in Madrid, in Puerto de Santa María, in Malaga, in little Antequera (where Dominguín gave his greatest show), in Valencia (where he brushed up against the square too hard and a horn opened his stomach), and I will cast my heart some pages forward, now divorced from the *corrida*, for which one needs a greater feel than I have (though to have a greater feel one needs to be more feeling, and maybe that's why—as we are unlikely to have occasion to mention later—Jean-Jacques loved opera), an understanding that has now been transformed into imagination, replaced by safe speculation, yet in the afternoon sun, which casts no shadow on the arena, and in full view of Dominguín's red cape, I say that maybe it's not all that safe, that I would like to add my own heart, hushed and stilled, however momentarily, to the *torero*'s frozen silhouette, to his hands and feet leaning against the invisible square.

A Room by the Sea

A room by the sea, a light on the wall, a lustrous polygon. Among Edward Hopper's commentaries to his own art, the best known is this: "What I wanted to do was to paint sunlight on the side of a house."[29] That's all: the light, the wall. Something that happens, the light arriving, but free from the power to shock, from violent movement. It arrives, it is. It doesn't even enter, it doesn't creep in, but simply reveals itself, evidence of nothing but itself, increasing for the eye, but—for the air—no more than a modulation of the day. "The photosynthesis of being," the poet Yves Bonnefoy calls it, and this may be the most apt—at any rate it's the loveliest—of all the short, aphoristic statements about Hopper.[30] Gorging oneself on light in order to transform it into life, absorbing it in order to nourish our gaze and give us strength. To swallow light and get out of bed at the crack of dawn, to go outside, lean against a wall, and watch, and watch.

Light on a wall, passed down from one Hopper painting to the next, keeping it from going out along the way. And the photographs saturated with it, of special, favorite places in Hopper's life and that of his wife. The photograph of the apartment by the sea where the Hoppers went for the summer immediately recalls the famous *Rooms by the Sea*—paintings hardly less familiar than

Nighthawks from their thousands of mercenary reproductions—
but one is also struck by the differences. In this photo, the door
opens out toward the seashore, so that it becomes a kind of continuation of the wall. It must be latched to something, because on
top you can see the hydraulic door-closer, or maybe the clumps
of grass and pebbles on the narrow little strip of beach dividing the threshold from the water are holding it open; you can
still imagine the movement of the hand that pulled it back and
struggled momentarily with the latch or propped it open with a
stone. In the painting, the door, which opens inward, as though
once and for all, sort of disappears from the field of vision and
frames the sea from the side. There is no interruption between
the threshold and the sea, not even a bit of earth, the gentle waves
seem to come right up to the room, and the sunny block of light
(three right angles, one sharp, one obtuse), which in the photo
amounts to barely a ribbon beyond the threshold, has landed flat
in the interior, yellowing most of the space between the walls.
The painting has extracted that which is most important from
the photograph, like sucking marrow out of bone, like flicking
sand from nougat, and has placed it right in front of us, unbound,
purified, blown up to full scale. Thus the soul might rouse itself
from the mass of tissue it's wearing and reveal not just a patch,
but the whole.

In the painting there is yet another room off to the side, hidden
away, and that's where the rhombus of light has slipped, smallish, one geometric form among others, among furniture and art
reproductions on the wall. But here, in the empty, unfurnished,
unadorned room in the foreground, purified, prepared for that

peaceful event, there is nothing, nothing but the light on the wall. "Maybe I am not very human," Hopper warns in the aforementioned self-commentary. Maybe the light on the wall is only a sliver of cosmic caprice, of accident, happenstance. Maybe the wall arose here specifically to receive this moment's yellow glare. And this room is the ultimate, outermost outpost, our last base, where the inhuman is already breaking through unopposed, but has not yet taken full possession of everything. Elsewhere, in other paintings, the light still gets tangled up in our human affairs, it presses through among the objects on the table, it sets the water glasses ablaze, it creates evening moods beneath the streetlamps, it helps somebody read a book. Whereas in this room by the sea it falls, at first glance, like an indifferent, golden stain, caught up in nothing, or rather it has no foreign influence, no invasive imposition; though dispatched here and left untouched, it has more right to be here than we do. On this edge of water and floor, plaster and air, the delimited and the unencompassed, one would like to stand still—and should—in order to feel both sides at the same time, not knowing the difference between inhale and exhale, shadow and light, self and sun, and only then to experience this other, higher test—as gold itself is tested—of transparency, of something that is no longer the eye being stabbed through an aquarium, or looking through crystals, or seeking out spots of light behind the windows of cities, but the immediate penetration of light, what it's like to feel haunted.

Light, the light on the wall, a transparent square, a band of light on my eyes, a trembling warmth among shadows, the first crystal painting on plaster, a transparent doorframe, light: the light, a transparent gate left open for whomever now arrives from the water.

Light and Reaction

The transparency of the soul conceived by Rousseau is contained implicitly in notions of enlightenment, *Lumières* in French, *Aufklarung* in German, all of which say, one way or another, "Now we'll see." The idea of light and of perceptiveness, of consciousness that can see clearly and emerge in all its sincerity, had been growing throughout the eighteenth century; in the body of experience offered by Jean-Jacques, experience as much autobiographical as authorial, existential, and philosophical, it attains an exceptional expression, not quite reduced to concept, since it is authenticated by his obsessions, daily habits, and manias, which made themselves known to him more in his interactions with other people than through any given text. The "vengeful heart," "agitated by the continual recollection of offenses suffered"—how many times is this thought repeated, expressed with exceptional variety, as Rousseau relates his meetings with others in the *Confessions*?[31] Everyone takes advantage of his naïveté and openheartedness; everyone makes fun of him, everyone titters at him behind his back. Everyone insults him in turn: Diderot, Saint-Lambert, Madame d'Épinay, not to mention that intolerable Baron d'Holbach, that farcical villain: "But it is true that behind the baron's playful teasing a glint of malicious pleasure could be detected in his eyes, which would perhaps have troubled me if I had noticed it at the time as clearly as I later remembered it."[32]

Rousseau's idea of transparency is often interpreted as standing in opposition to the aristocratic theater of everyday life, cynical and libertine; purity of heart (which would be a feature of the bourgeoisie's entrée into the historical arena) would oppose the irony of the salon, the masquerade, keeping up appearances, those barons, counts, and princesses with their goddamned pranks; it would oppose language that is undoubtedly perfect, but that buries its contents in the folds of refined expression, seeking out detours and a perspicacity that cancels out direct transmission. "Everything was accounted for, it came from the brain, even a spasm." So E. M. Cioran writes of the theater of manners of the aristocratic salon, of "a class worn out by its own constant recourse to irony."[33] This theater of language and manners, in which the sometimes biting recognition of what motivates the actions of others was accompanied by one's clever entanglement in a game of essences and appearances, became so apparent (and increasingly glaring), had disintegrated so far into the frenzy of its own perfection, that Rousseau's gesture of revelation took on more and more social significance.

The jaded, disillusioned aristocracy, decadent in its superego, pessimistic in its view of the human being, who was contaminated by original sin and ultimately incurable, imprisoned in his own ethical and existential disability, was confronted not only by a new social class, but also by a new way of viewing the human condition—seen now, after Rousseau, as more primal, more natural, and therefore purer and innocent. Before it would give rise to political revolution, it was to have accomplished an existential revolution, one that would reveal man's other potential. Rousseau provided not only the idea for this revolution, but also its vocabulary. Purity of heart and transparency of soul became concepts resonant not only for psychology, but for social science and politics as well. This is why the French Revolution was the first lyrical revolution, to borrow Milan Kundera's formulation, an uprising of the innocent and transparent: "Here innocence danced! Innocence with its bloody smile."[34] The innocent and transparent: to go with his theory of sacrifice Rousseau had created a common alibi, a social alibi for all the downtrodden. What he had first said to himself, he now said to them, that it's the other guys who are guilty, that they're the ones making mistakes, whereas our intentions are always pure and perfectly self-evident, fully disclosed and coherent. The *Confessions* were composed on what Peter Sloterdijk calls "the white page of this feeling of innocence"; it was on such pages that the first generation of Rousseauians were to write their own, now universal, history.[35]

The libertine, pessimistic truths about the darkness of human nature and Rousseau's light, which likewise belongs to human nature, clear and immediate, came into conflict, which expressed itself so brightly, so to speak, as to determine how we would think about human nature further down the line. Is human nature absolutely dark, or absolutely transparent? Play and appearance, or an open heart and a bare soul? The Rousseauian odyssey of transparency was a radical interpretation, though also the last on so grand a scale, and at any rate the most powerful such explication to posit the complete legibility of the "I" and to remove all impediments to its reading. It was followed by an anti-Rousseauian revolution in European philosophy and the nascent psychology, a counterrevolution that Peter Sloterdijk calls "the critique of transparency."[36] It arose directly out of the discovery of the subconscious in human nature. Historically, this discovery has been variously dated: when we speak of the pre-Freudian sources of psychoanalysis, we reach most frequently for the German Romantics, who gave literature the themes of gloom, abyss: hidden sources and unfathomable depths. Another interpretation locates those first intimations of a deep-rooted *psyche* in magnetism and mesmerism, which at about the same time had begun to erect new obstacles just where Rousseau had removed the old ones.

In this respect, according to Sloterdijk, one of the most interesting of these obstacles is the peculiar experience of hypnosis, as discovered by a pupil of Mesmer, Armand Marie Jacques de Chastenet, the Marquis de Puységur. In 1784, six years after Rousseau's death, during one of the therapeutic séances to which he subjected one of his farmhands—having bound him, as was his scientific practice, to a magnetized tree—de Chastenet induced a state that he called "artificial somnambulism." Interested less, in contrast to Mesmer, in individual psychology than in the ability to condense and convey energy through the body, the Marquis de Puységur focused on the patient's own potential for self-therapy and self-understanding. Bringing the patient into a state of deep absence, of sleepy descent, by way of hypnosis, he also knew how to draw statements from that patient about himself, about his own character traits or, should he wish, pathologies; these were supposed to achieve exceptional accuracy and perceptiveness of a kind absolutely unobtainable by the patient once awakened and having immediately forgotten the entire ordeal.

From the vantage point of later developments in psychoanalysis, most important in Puységur's experience was the intuition that the patient should undertake the therapeutic activity on his own, that he should perform his own introspection, and that the one applying the magnetism could direct this imperative toward the one receiving it. For the reader of Rousseau, even today, even at this very moment, the most important conclusion arising from these experiments was a negation of the Rousseauian concept of ideal self-consciousness—that is, what Jean-Jacques himself called, using a term that would gain its own notoriety, *sentiment de soi*. Against the Rousseauian sense of having an immediate view into one's own soul, of transparent self-discovery with unambiguous intent, mesmerism (or, as it was developed later, puységurism, and eventually psychoanalysis) presented the "I" as hidden behind a protective barrier, its immediate feeling obscured, graspable only in extraordinary circumstances, demanding extreme techniques bordering on conscious dreaming. Jean-Jacques, however—even back then, on the shores of Swiss lakes, under a sun that burned away the morning mist; he could lose himself so deeply in dream that the Marquis de Puységur would have mistaken his motionlessness and half-sleep for a hypnotic state—knew perfectly well who he was, knew himself perfectly in that pure moment of simultaneous sleep and wakefulness, knew himself to be as pure as that moment and full of feeling, transmitting to himself another, equally full, equally powerful and self-evident sense of being, in which there were no secrets and no depths to be fathomed or understood.

The critique of transparency in the last decades of the eighteenth century started to destroy the Rousseauian phantasm—and thus also the idea—of transparency. The discoveries made through mesmerism brought on still another sort of night beside that already discerned by libertinism, which had left no illusions as to the purity of human motives. Experiments with hypnosis revealed that, beyond our conscious knowledge, there remain entire zones of shadow hidden right there beside the zones of light. No longer would anything from those zones be immediately and obviously attainable; self-knowledge would move along a path of straight talk, of painstaking and unpleasant affirmation of one's own contradictions, eventually reaching an awareness that it's still a long way to the self, that a vast distance stretches between "I" and "I," that one is quite the opposite of the person one believed oneself to be. What would later be called psychic reality would move into the zone of obscurity and be suppressed within injuries and traumas, though also in the very experience of their recognition, that is, in the endless process of unmasking successive illusions, of negating successive findings, which are themselves constantly undergoing their own transformation, given the structural nature of the unconscious. This was to happen many years later, after the waters of Lake Bienne had forgotten Rousseau's shadow: the consciousness of non-transparency was slowly to take shape, until it became the dogma of our soul.

But this would take some time. Peter Sloterdijk, whose argument I have been referencing throughout, believes that the error of the spirit of enlightenment is that it ignored mesmerism, regarding it as an anti-philosophical reaction, an aristocratic and religious reaction to the bright, illuminating understanding of *Aufklarung*, which drove the entire phenomenon into a "spiritual underground" and brought it down to the level of popular art, a mysterious store-bought occultism. In other words, the error was in depriving mesmerism of its rational character and, through rationalism's aversion to it, plunging it into the haze of a rather dull mysticism or Gothic ghostliness. The bourgeois-positivist background of *Aufklarung* could hardly bear the new categories' tendency to overturn the old, how they undermined the place of reason and of a consciousness that has faith in the kind of knowledge it has about itself, and which draws its strength from this certainty: the discovery of the subconscious, marking the end of traditional philosophies of consciousness, struck, essentially, as Sloterdijk writes, at the cultural narcissism of every class, not just the aristocrats.

Despite the triumph of psychoanalysis and the model of thought it has imposed, despite the relegation of the transparency of the heart to the status of open-air museum, non-transparency's battle with transparency continues to this day, and the two parties in this mêlée together create one of the fundamental oppositions, the conflicting pair through which we can present the spiritual history of the last two hundred years.

The non-transparency of existence is today a philosophical and psychological dogma. The more one resists it, the more conventional, bourgeois, conservative (and even right wing), naïve, blind, and hypocritical his way of thinking and living seems. But transparency was never completely suppressed, banished to the bright sky, its azure ideal. As a category of social and political discourse and an ethical postulate within the workings of institutions both political and economic, it appeared a quarter century ago and still seems to be spreading, becoming today one of the basic imperatives of social life. Or, rather, it didn't so much appear as recover after a period of dormancy lasting from the Second World War to the early 1980s. Because, once it had been expressed, it would never stop tempting and tormenting the imagination. Alongside the "critique of transparency" that I mentioned a moment ago, a counter-process ran throughout the nineteenth century and the first forty years of the twentieth, a process that we could call the "critique of non-transparency." On the shoulders of visionary architecture, literature (and not just the utopian kind), art (especially in the interwar period), and the philosophy of ideas (and not just of Futurists), transparency, lucidity, *transparence*, and *transparencia* are always crossing into new eras and nurturing the next aesthetic movements, the next political programs, manifestos, and languages, the next forms of existence, the next great projects, and the modest imaginations of small, quiet people.

Such a Lovely Word

"They took your word," Olga would sometimes say, laughing over her yellow coffee mug and still pointing a mocking finger in my direction. "They just took it. They stole it. You were there first!"

I would be pouring purified water into the espresso machine, nodding my head, or once again having a hard time finding the milk in the refrigerator. For two years now the words "unvarnished," "lucid," and "transparent" had been poking their way into our breakfast like gadflies, swarming out of the morning papers, the radio, interviews, articles, talk shows, testimonies, and debates, starting at the crack of dawn. They were becoming increasingly persistent, in everyone's mouth like a new and lovely tooth. We were assured of this or that person's transparency, things were made transparent, especially biographies, as well as the curricula vitae of public officials, and they announced the government's complete and public transparency, and that of the courts, the police, the banking system, the media, and they guaranteed the transparency of the work they had undertaken, all the while complaining of its absence from the work of others. Days would pass, and the cheese in the refrigerator would go bad—yes, with my appetite for the future I was always buying too much—and my word invariably kept cropping up in various forms and turns of phrase from morning on, and something clicked. No longer was there any doubt that the word had inscribed itself in the spirit of our times, entirely dependent on its obligatory jargon, which itself serves—as Milan Kundera wrote of the word "kitsch" in *The Unbearable Lightness of Being*—every side in the political arena, liberal or not, communist or not, one for all or one for self.

The concept of "transparency" as a normative principle for the function of government and other institutions came to Poland straight out of Western discourse. In its public application, it has garnered exceptional power in the West over the course of the last decade or so; today in France, which happens to lead the world when it comes to using this word, it belongs to the store of concepts exploited by the rhetoric of correctness. The word *transparence* ("transparency") and the phrase *en toute transparence* ("quite transparently," "in all transparency") are used so often that they lend themselves to quantitative analysis; an investigation into their daily use in the world press would require, as I have had occasion to confirm, the processing power of a computer. A couple of years ago I started to note down examples, to assemble a catalogue of public transparency. Today alone—it's September 10, 2005—I've counted six such uses in exactly one hour of looking through a few French newspapers and, at the same time, watching a French TV news magazine. First there's the television talking about the possibility of reopening the investigation into the Elf Aquitaine oil scandal, in which Roland Dumas, the former Minister of Foreign Affairs, has been implicated; the Minister of Justice is declaring that the investigation will be conducted *en toute transparence*. The weekly *Le Point* is reporting on the introduction of new, experimental technologies for food production; all trials and procedures are to be conducted under strict guidelines and in complete transparency, *en toute transparence*. Nicolas Sarkozy appears on the screen and announces a new initiative in the government ministry he was then running; all reforms will be applied *en toute transparence*. An article in *Le Figaro* about Israeli arms shipments to Africa is entitled "Israel Bets on Transparency in Arms Trade"; *Sud-Ouest* cites a complaint of the Organization for Security and Cooperation in Europe to the effect that the public mandate that was supposed to have been provided by a recent referendum in Belarus lacked "transparency." An article in *Le Nouvel Observateur* is reporting on new divorce procedures that allow couples to divorce *en toute transparence*. Back when I was recording these examples, I was still thrilled by the hunt: new butterflies of French, American, and Spanish transparency were falling into my net. I didn't expect that the following year, thanks to the Polish media, the collection would become impossibly overfull, rendering it a journal of the banal.

When, in the early eighties, Kundera composed a dictionary of his own keywords for *The Art of the Novel*, "Transparency," one of the sixty-five terms he considers, was still used quite differently from the way it is now, as a metaphor for social behaviors.[37] Kundera writes:

> A very common term in political and journalistic discourse in Europe. It means: the exposure of individual lives to public view. Which sends us back to André Breton and his wish to live in a *glass house* in full view. The glass house: an old utopian idea and at the same time one of the most horrifying aspects of modern life. Axiom: The more opaque the affairs of state, the more transparent an individual's affairs must be; though it represents a *public thing*, bureaucracy is anonymous, secret, coded, inscrutable, whereas *private man* is obliged to reveal his health, his finances, his family situation, and if the mass media so decree, he will never have a single moment of privacy either in love or in sickness or in death. The urge to violate another's privacy is an age-old form of aggression that in our day is institutionalized (bureaucracy with its documents, the press with its reporters), justified morally (the right to

know having become first among the rights of man), and poeticized (by the lovely French word *transparence*).[38]

Kundera, raised on the novels of Kafka and mindful of the Czech experience of life in a totalitarian police state, identifies "transparency" unambiguously with the violence perpetrated by government institutions against the defenseless individual, who cannot shield his own existence from a nosiness that has been sanctioned both here, by the police, and there, by journalists. For him, there is essentially no ethical difference between, say, the illegal wiretapping of a man under police surveillance and a newspaper publishing pictures of the singer Jacques Brel in tears while leaving the hospital where he was being treated for cancer. If ever transparency, conceived as something limitless, a universally uncensored "right to information," was a gift of 1968, or formed a direct part of its legacy, then, like several other "rights of man"—which Kundera analyzed in his later novels—it backfired against the individual. Kundera speaks of the continuous dictatorship of transparency that transcends political systems, extending from the totalitarian regime to the democratic administration. The communist, police form of transparency—that is, access to all aspects of private life, without exception—violated individual rights directly, whereas the odd perfidy of democratic transparency is that it actually pretends to be a democratic value (nothing to hide, the right to full knowledge) at the same time as it turns out to be, essentially, voyeurism, systematic surveillance, without respect for anyone or for intimacy of any kind. Transparency for Kundera is therefore not a public virtue, however poetically enchanting it may be—a beautiful and merciless lady, *une belle dame sans merci*—but arises from the sting of totalitarianism and is ultimately the result of democracy's fatal infatuation with its own dogma.

Since then, the notion of "transparency," which in Kundera's reflections had been directed against the defenseless, helpless citizen, a victim of the microphone and lens in the hands of the police or the journalist, has changed, or in any event its field of operations has expanded. It has been carried—or, as it were, pushed—in another, rather institutional-bureaucratic direction. Today it must also be realized in the domain of great, collective subjects: of government as such, or of its particular manifestations, of concrete institutions, or finally in the corporate body of enormous financial conglomerates. The word *transparence* appears in two of the declarations establishing the European Union (the seventeenth declaration of the Maastricht Treaty and the twenty-third of the Treaty of Nice), where we read that "transparency of the decision-making process strengthens the democratic nature of the institutions and the public's confidence in the administration" (Maastricht) and of the need for general "transparency of the Union and its institutions, in order to bring them closer to the citizens of Member States" (Nice).

In this new usage, shedding light on individual existence, whether through the media or government institutions, loses a bit of its negative connotation, its sense of bureaucratic oppression, of state-sanctioned intrusiveness. Of course, it remains a problem, but one that the individual increasingly accepts and forgets, whether because he's gotten used to it (as we have long since internalized and assimilated Kafkaesque bureaucracy); or because the paparazzi have ultimately triumphed in the media; or because society has assented to opening human privacy to the public, a form of complete access that the reality-show phenomenon has popularized, imposed, and rendered easier to swallow; or finally because of a growing sense that we are under threat (from criminals, from terrorists), which requires citizens to assent to more extensive surveillance of everything that moves on the earth, in the air, or in the ether. The vectors have been turned around, or at least they have been crossed: today, "transparency," shining continuously on the individual and his secrets, has been drawn into that snoopy bureaucratic "opacity" that, in Kundera's lexicon, had been its owner, not its object. It may seem that, considering the number of institutional scandals that have been made public, societies have discovered the virtue of transparency, a revolutionary virtue: we will investigate, we will be vigilant, we will expose everything, from this day forward nothing will escape our attention, no government will be able to exercise its power in secret.

The word *transparence* reportedly first appeared in its public sense in 1361, in a text by Nicole Oresme, a theoretician of finance; it was then used primarily in the language of mercantile law. Later, it mostly drifted in the depths of poetry. Over the last quarter century, however, it has come back to us in the titles of books, among them those of Gianni Vattimo (*The Transparent Society*) and Jean Baudrillard (*The Transparency of Evil*), finding use in meditations upon how society functions in its new media-virtual spaces.

But as an ethical principle for the workings of governments and other institutions, transparency has only recently acquired an explicit right to exist. We can acknowledge that Gorbachev's glasnost played a certain role in its resurgence and advanced a new way of reading transparency in the West, particularly in France; it wasn't long before the French press was even using the Russian word (printed in italics) in the context of strictly French affairs before at last reaching back for the native term *transparence*. Currently— reinforced by world events (and, at the same time, "affairs") like Chernobyl, tainted blood transfused in hospitals (a massive scandal in France in the early nineties), mad cow disease, the collapse of Enron ("Transparency is what was really lacking in the Enron affair," Laurent Fabius, France's former prime minister, wrote in *Le Monde* in February 2002), and a great many other scandals—the imperative for public transparency is clearly extending its range. It has an increasingly strong grip not only on the institutions of state, but on private enterprise as well. In the statements of spokespeople of every sort, transparency has become the lighthouse that guides discourse and guarantees the indisputability of every assertion. French sociological criticism uses a telling expression for this phenomenon; they call it "the removal of secrecy": the veil was once a sign of shame, of elegant prudery, but today it can be the opposite, a mark of shamelessness and chutzpah. When, in autumn 2006, a book appeared on the French market called *In Praise of Secrecy*, *Le Nouvel Observateur* entitled its review "The Tyranny of Transparency."[39] The reviewer wrote that the book's author, Pierre Lévy-Soussan, a psychiatrist and psychoanalyst, stands up to the "mythic god Transparency," which commands us to reveal not only the secrets of institutions, but also those of the private spirit, of our desires and anguish.

And also those of our lovely bodies. My friend François has sent me, along with yet another glass ball (this time with a caribou inside, on a snowy field: "I hope you'll like it, I found it on an Iroquois reservation."), the latest clippings from the Montreal press. They're reporting a scandal in a fitness club that's been operating for a couple of years in François's neighborhood. It's a high-class place established particularly with somewhat older ladies in mind, headquartered in a modern glass building. Great big panoramic windows, which are popular replacements for walls in Western fitness clubs, present passersby with the dramatic spectacle of scantily-clad people pedaling the air or racing to nowhere on the treadmill. This sight, however, has drawn the attention of more than just passersby. Students of a Hasidic private school that recently opened on the other side of the street, instead of leaning over books of ancient wisdom, have been taking a gander at the pendulous breasts of the fitness set. The school's director, concerned for the educational progress of his pupils, therefore suggested to the club's management that they replace the panoramic windows with Venetian ones, which would allow the ladies on their chrome steeds to go on enjoying the natural light while also raising an impenetrable obstruction to block the young men's stares. The club made the change, setting the stage for the scandal, for when the members discovered that their efforts on the treadmills and stationary bikes would be invisible to the world, they screamed bloody murder and informed the press. Their rights had been violated, they complained, their right "to exercise in their chosen outfits," to be seen in whatever costume they chose, a "hard-fought right, which they won't relinquish one inch," since doing so would be tantamount to "renouncing their identity." The leader of the club revolt issued a communiqué in which she maintained that she was "fighting against all forms of integrism and misogyny and against our feeble tendency to yield on the battlefield." Her arguments were picked up by one of the largest dailies in Montreal; one could read in the letters to the editor that in this affair the club members' opponents—particularly the integrist Jewish community (though it might have been any other), was "attacking the very essence of Western societies: the equality of men and women, which establishes the latter's right to have their bodies seen in public spaces without obstruction. In this matter, no other point of view can be tolerated." François, wishing to delight or else to tease me, wrote that the club-goers' battles for the transparency of the club's walls had determined the direction of history, and that "the future will see us all in the crystal palace." And I repeat his remark to affirm once more, on the basis of this quite typical Montreal incident, that transparency is redrawing the horizon of our dreams and aspirations; that exposing what had been private to public view and revealing, for the sake of our very identities, the mysteries of our bedchambers and our muscles—such is the latest imperative of the modern soul, of being "absolutely modern," as Rimbaud put it. In Witold Gombrowicz's novel *Ferdydurke*, the mark of modernity is the bold, provocative step by which Mrs. Youngblood moves toward "what had thus far been a covert activity—her now overt visits to the toilet."[40] The hypermodern man to come, *modernus modernus*, will be prepared to leave that door ajar, or even open; if the "god of Transparency" is to be of any consequence, he can accept no veil.

Was it not with faith in this god that on May 26, 2005, then-candidate for the presidency of the Republic, the aforementioned Nicolas Sarkozy, went to the studios of France 3 TV? "He had decided to take the bull by the horns and to bet on transparency in a live broadcast," Serge Raffy describes the scene in his book *The War of Three.*[41] Several days after news reports that his wife had left him for another man, before the eyes of millions of viewers, like the hero of a soap opera or reality show, Sarkozy spoke about his recent ordeals and troubles. "The truth is simple," he said with genuine tears on the ends of his eyelashes, "like millions of families, mine has had its difficulties. We're trying to overcome them." It's likely that Sarkozy was crying to benefit his image, but we also can't rule out the possibility that the politician had at the same time internalized the imperative for transparency, letting millions in through the windows of his own private existence: that he believed his confession was a natural, or in any case a valid, justified, logical extension and consequence of the need for political and institutional transparency that he himself had called for, and which he had answered with transparency of the heart. For today we have also come to the reversal of the historical situation: social and political transparency obliges us to have a transparent heart; for Jean-Jacques Rousseau, it was the other way around.

Transparency is demanded by the market, public opinion, the media, and even individual consumers, who want to know how the products they purchase were manufactured, and who write to various companies, to Nestlé and Dannon, to L'Oréal and Nivea, to dozens of others, with polite inquiries as to whether the next, new product, that delicious yogurt with flatulence-reducing bacteria, that lotion for our rough hands, will meet all hygienic standards, whether it's been tested on animals, whether the production process can be traced from raw material to finished product (the French call this *traçabilité,* "traceability"), whether labor laws have been violated, confirming that no Bangladeshi children or Congolese preschools were used. They demand proof of the "complete transparency" of the entire production process and express hope—like my childhood friend, the author of dozens of such letters to international corporations (in Communist Poland he would write letters to the State Railroad, demanding more frequent washing of the windows on the trains, as well as to high-circulation newspapers, demanding more frequent washing of the shelters at bus stops; back then I thought he was naïve, but now I see him as the vanguard of a movement, a warrior in its first battalion)—that the *pleine transparence* that the company has guaranteed will foster greater trust between business and customer, proof of which they would receive in the form of increased sales of their very fine products. As another tracker of industrial transparency has observed,

> [T]ransparency influences the architecture of enterprises and their products. Liquids are becoming crystal clear, their containers colorless, their packaging invisible. The product has to give the impression of absolute purity; it has to be as clear as possible, without additives or colorings. Soft drinks are becoming transparent, buckets of paint are sealed with plastic film on top so that you can be sure that they are properly labeled. Even cosmetics are

becoming colorless, so better to emphasize "our skin's natural glow."

Also, "investors don't want any unpleasant surprises and wish for enterprises to be increasingly transparent." This last sentence comes from André Boyer's 2002 book *The Impossible Ethics of Enterprise.*[42] "Enterprise," Thierry Libaert adds in his 2003 book *Transparency in Trompe L'Oeil,* "no longer has room to maneuver. Transparency is no longer negotiable."[43] "Transparency," Florence Aubenas and Miguel Benasayag remark in their book *The Fabrication of Information,* "affirms itself as the sole ideology that cannot be betrayed."[44] The media, consumers, and citizens form a common front in the fight for transparency. The word itself exerts such force that many companies have recently employed it in their sales and ad campaigns as a way to seduce their clients or customers. Now Cogema, rechristened Areva NC, a company suspected of breaking the law in its nuclear-waste disposal business, is letting us know, "We're transparent, we have nothing to hide." Now a Geneva bank rumored to be on the verge of bankruptcy is spearheading a campaign called "Transparency Live": thanks to a special telephone line, each client will have instant access to any information he wants. Now the Salvation Army is issuing a bulletin to its members in which it lists all its expenditures, "a guarantee of transparency." Here's the French division of McDonald's holding open houses in the name of transparency, during which the public may visit franchises, the warehouses where products are stored, and even the corporate headquarters.

In corporate operations the imperative for "internal transparency" is stronger and stronger, requiring a business's employees to know everything about its activities, financial situation, future outlook, etc. "If an enterprise wants to make real partners of its employees," wrote one financial analyst, "it has to invoke cooperation and transparency." His idea spurred the director of a corporation as large as France Telecom into action, sending an e-mail in October 2002 to all employees in which he expressed his commitment to a "policy of transparency as regards the facts, which is today a greater obligation than ever before." Business French has brought this notion into everyday use in the phrase *jouer la transparence*, literally, "to play transparency," though a better translation would be "to bet on transparency," that is, to make decisions, as all of these businesses and institutions have done, befitting someone who has nothing to hide, and who wishes for everything, but everything, to be revealed.

Transparency is an essential principle of public life, subject to complete regulation, and is increasingly being enacted through the letter of the law. General, public access to administrative documents, to draft bills, and to regulatory systems has in recent years been legally sanctioned in European legislation. Many laws from the seventies (like one in France concerning access to administrative documents in order to prevent corruption in political finance) have been reformulated with an eye toward increasing transparency, and the word itself appears triumphantly in the legal record. Now and then in France, also the global leader in transparent jurisprudence, we get these *hautes commissions de la transparence*—High Commissions of Transparency (really, though, that's actually what they're called)—which investigate everything from finances to nuclear security systems in the hope of preventing the next big scandal. These are not merely civic institutions, but government agencies as well, their existence demanded by non-governmental organizations and the media alike. Additionally, there has been a proliferation of social, public, and independent organizations along the same lines, sometimes connected more or less closely with the anti-corruption organization Transparency International.

Transparent Poland

Transparency broke out in Poland with the so-called Rywin Affair, a political and financial scandal in late 2002 involving prominent politicians and Poland's largest newspaper. It was said that Western democracies had provided the concept, and even a word— "transparent-*ność*"—while our own crisis of government had provided the impetus. Today the word is a linguistic magic spell, understood by all and generally taken as a motto, a prerequisite, and also one of the basic concepts of our new "political correctness," recognized or played out by all participants in public life, regardless of their ideological pedigree.

The word "openness," which had appeared earlier and was used more often, and which has largely disappeared, had lost its strength, its sheen of redemptive transgression (one of the benefits of the prefix "trans-") and by now had ossified within the stiff, routine demand for "openness in public life." Still less apt was the now quite partisan call for "clarity," a term that belonged then mostly to the last dogmatists of Polish Communist-era discourse. "Transparent-

ność" was gaining strength; the Polish synonym *przejrzystość* didn't yet sound decisive or "objective" enough and, though it was used, it didn't always quite fit all the necessary linguistic contexts, it didn't yet have currency, certain formulations couldn't seem to accommodate it: its poetic charge had yet to be tamed.

The term "transparent-*ność*" spread throughout the press during the formation and early work of the so-called Second Investigative Commission for Orlen-gate, Poland's biggest recent scandal; it was in this form that the concept started to appear as a keyword and basic demand in the reports of journalists, publicists, and politicians. It received a peculiar consecration in early December 2004, when the editors-in-chief of several of the most important weeklies and dailies used it in their appeal for full disclosure, "for the public good, by persons facing indictment or court proceedings." The editors wrote: "As a matter of principle, a gag order should not be binding against those in public service, politicians and businessmen whose interests depend on government decisions. All of their activities should be transparent [*transparentne*] to public opinion." The calque from French or English, the polonization of a foreign word rarely used before, lent the notion a sort of official flavor, elevated it to the level of a normative ethical principle, an objective principle that one could in no way oppose while remaining within the sanction of the law.

Over the course of the next couple of months, both words—the Anglo-French *transparentny* and the Polish *przejrzysty*—began to function side by side. One might have assumed that the native word was bound to win, that its metaphoric quality, undetectable in the foreign word, would sooner or later be assimilated. And that's just what happened. Yes, every so often "transparent-*ność*" makes an encore appearance, but more and more it's assuming a bureaucratic twang; our less-stiff politicians, bureaucrats, and journalists aren't really reaching for it anymore. Toward the end of 2004, the press started publishing reports—along with a pretty blue-and-white logo—about the creation of a non-governmental organization called *Przejrzysta Polska*—Transparent Poland. The poetic tradition of titles with "Poland" as their collective subject (even *Wingèd Poland*, an aviation magazine started in the thirties) has no trouble incorporating our own word, and by doing so it also lends the idea (of a transparent Poland) a ludic dimension, natural, non-juridical, not saddled with the cold that suffuses the international "transparent-*ność*"—all the more so because the transparent windowpane in which the movement's organizers posed in photographs lent the native word a concrete form, no less accessible for all its metaphoric content. The press reports accompanying the organization's appearance surely helped fix the word in public discourse; its old poetic overtones were soon undetectable, as was also true of another Polish word, *przezroczystość*, which eventually became interchangeable with *przejrzystość*.

No other new term could achieve the same range of meaning; the metaphor has been exhausted. Which means that the concept has already achieved its full potential, the apogee of its dynamic drive. In this self-delimiting form, having plateaued, it might still endure for a while longer, to become a verbal touchstone or slogan in the declarations and campaigns to come. Later, perhaps, after its ethical and revolutionary baggage is naturally depleted and flattened under an influx of short-term campaigns, of concrete, momentary political needs and maneuvers, it might become a strictly political term, that is, the kind emptied of its original meaning, and thus will take up all the necessary content while also concealing it from those who use the term, whoever they may be.

The paradox that comes with today's next cup of coffee is that, like speech before them, the psychology and philosophy of our day continue to be dominated by the Freudian concept of a fundamentally nontransparent subject who resists all attempts to grasp him, who is embroiled in an endless game of veils and masks, in a semiotic tangle; whereas according to the media's vision of the ideal operation of the state, generally recognized as an imperative, as a model of appropriate behavior, the state as a subject is potentially transparent: it is only its perversion that stands in the way of its complete transparency. The images of transparency utilized by representatives of the party in power or coming to power (as was the case in Poland in 2005)— always announcing that certain great changes are about to be made in the workings of government—are themselves already betrayals of their party's revolutionary *ésprit* on the level of language: the fever of a new beginning, of a dawn that is to dispel the surrounding darkness. The rapid proliferation of these images in recent years itself heralds a proliferation of radical sentiment. The Polish *casus* of transparency or clarity, whatever place it may find in common precepts, however it may draw on European experiences and fashions, has been fed for the last three years by precisely this spirit of transformation and renewal, anticipating the coming storm of purification.

This new Polish transparency brings together the aims of elites and non-elites alike, the "top-down" and state-institutional program, as well as (to a much lesser extent than in, say, France) the social and civic, that which fights for "grass-roots" access to government power. This transparency wants to penetrate and sometimes even force its way into history, into all measures of time, to make its demands not only upon the future—on which it places the greatest emphasis—but also to illuminate the past. Everything is supposed to come out into the open, biographical details are to be exposed, qualifications scrutinized, and all the folds of ink, print, and oblivion are to be ironed out like curtains cast open, revealing a flawless diamond of truth.

Does the notion of Rousseauism, of the new Rousseauism, apply to all of these activities? Jean-Jacques is often seen as someone who pushed the boundaries, as someone who broke down the wall between the private sphere and the public, between the domestic "I" (accused so ruthlessly of having broken the comb) and the public "I," devoted to social and political activities outside of the home. When he entered the agora, he said, "Yes, this blister pains me"—everyone knew about his shameful disease—"no, I did not abandon my children"—as they accused him, when convenient—"I stand before you transparent and pure"—as did no one before him in all of human history—"and when all of you, following my example, pile your snowballs on mine, you will be doing the same thing as when you admit to your weaknesses, expose your hearts, the fog will part on the agora, the avalanche will fall, and our lives together, the time we share, will be like a transparent, unambiguous heart, like a single drop of water added to itself." Some find Rousseau's attitude reminiscent of early Christianity, but in actual fact, as the Sermon on the Mount suggests, Christ assumed a separation between the public and private spheres. Political activity, according to this view, was supposed to be circumscribed by shadow, since the flash of light that illuminates everything also transforms the sanctity of the individual into pseudo-sanctity and hypocrisy. When, in early 2005, the Institute of National Remembrance issued a list—first it appeared on the Internet, then on the lips of everyone in Poland—what is now called the Wildstein List, publicizing the names of the tens of thousands of people registered as having collaborated with the Soviet-era secret police (some of whom would later be called "victims"), the question of the coexistence of the public and private spheres took on a sudden, renewed vigor, and the idea of transparency, which had already succeeded in fixing itself within social discourse, received an additional and robust boost. Among those commentators more favorably disposed toward Bronisław Wildstein's decision to make the list public, the voice of Jadwiga Staniszkis stood out, seemingly resonant with Rousseau's thought, echoing his belief—this, too, was Staniszkis's credo—in "man's natural instinct for good." Shortly after the list's publication, when the fever of talk it provoked had reached its peak, she wrote that it was necessary for everyone who had lived through those times to examine his or her past, to admit one's misdeeds to oneself and others, to stand in the presence of oneself and others in "the moral subjectivity they have achieved"—that is, to use Rousseauian language, with one's heart now gloriously transparent. "Today," Jadwiga Staniszkis wrote, "we can move beyond our crisis of unconsciousness, beyond the thick white-out within us, beyond the effacement of our moral subjectivity."[45] And then, thanks to millions of individual gestures of revelation and confession, our existence—from the national, administrative, and social spheres down to the private—would develop along a new track, based on new values and vigor. We, the individual subjects, would be transformed, and with this transformation would arise a new, better, collective subject. The moral heights we would attain would allow us to rejuvenate the state, as well as to return—each of us, individually—to the "blessed memory" that had been the Solidarity Movement. There would be a return to the "language of values as a language for describing the world," which had been lost with our faith that "good would triumph, and that it's on our side," and at the same time we'd regain the "lost memories" of our innocence, of the carnival of Solidarity, as it was once called. In her subsequent analyses, Jadwiga Staniszkis no longer expressed so open a hope for these mutually dependent transformations. In our own parlance we might say that Rousseau's existential transparency, his gaze into his own heart, was merely a moral appeal, whereas the only thing that could really be made manifest in this case—there was no general admission of guilt—was institutional transparency.

The transparency of public life, the transparency of institutions, the transparency of the past: all of this was to have been—and turned out to be, I thought later—the new Polish transparency, a quarter century after the carnival of Solidarity: a second Polish transparency, this time institutionalized, with a government guarantee, which the state put on display as much for society at large as for itself. Not as it had been back then—a paradisiacal transparency, idyllic, wondrously and childishly simple, unreflective, instinctive, romantic, unconscious, wordlessly bringing people together, bringing about an immediate understanding between hearts, with a feeling of great togetherness and with a common purpose, under the banner of that single word, "Solidarity," at the very sound of it, at its immediacy and spirit, like a lungful of air—but a transparency of the body politic, mediated, post-lapsum, a law and a word: that is, a system of arbitrary signs. To put it symbolically, this was a transparency no longer in the manner of Rousseau, but in the manner of the Jacobins, standing guard for the reason of state, not that of individual existence. Over the course of a quarter century, these two transparencies had more or less been lumped together; or, rather, one had transformed into the other. The path from a transparency of the heart to an institutional declaration of transparency certainly obeys a historical imperative, albeit one that's carried out but rarely; and yet, it has fallen to us to witness such a transformation within a single swift turn of events.

Nine months after the publication of the Institute's list, and a couple of months following the start of the "Transparent Poland" campaign—thus six months before the campaign for "Transparent Elections" and three years after the term had first penetrated our vocabulary—Polish transparency underwent its first general staging (in the sense that it was broadcast to millions of viewers), its first symbolic test. In front of the cameras, as they say, representatives of the two parties that were then in charge—both of Parliament and of the rhetoric of transparency—met in order to discuss the creation of a coalition government, there before the eyes of the nation (a new topos, or else a cliché: the blue screen, a material sky become transparent glass), with nothing to hide, everything out in the open from start to finish, from the first word to the last. More than a hundred and thirty days later, before the very same eyes of the very same Poles, the government, which had actually been formed elsewhere, held a full session on live television; you could see and hear everything, even the whispers of ministers halfheartedly following the remarks of their colleagues or looking impatiently at their watches. This may well have been the first actual public, political transparency ever seen in the history of the world, shown live *in extenso*, where the only thing missing was instant replay. This mandated broadcast was the crowning achievement of the entire phenomenon, its most spectacular triumph: in just a couple of years, Poland had forced its way from the rear of the pack to the head of those countries driven by a wave of words—"transparency," "clarity," "openness"—toward the immaculate light, the ultimate goal, the ideal of civic life.

The Vanity-Bag Co-op

Transparency—so I would digress at our subsequent breakfasts, having dreamily discerned "my word" since daybreak in the newspapers, on the radio, the television—for all the successes our society has enjoyed because of it, for all the scandals and malfeasance that it has revealed, transparency is the new opium being distributed to the people, the great civilized substitute for the feeling of having even a modicum of power. In some countries—I've already mentioned France—citizens' access to the associations and institutions that oversee transparency is broad and legitimized by the individual involvement of those same citizens, so much so that this gentle but firm social pressure—a new expression of their Jacobin genes, now transformed into a bloodless and velvety inflexibility—gives the impression of a permanent revolt within an absolute republic: here, in the immutable, inviolable state, a daily revolution is taking place that only solidifies that state's solidity. The citizens enjoy a sense of satisfaction, since they feel like rebels setting torches to authority, almost bringing it down but never quite overturning it, and the authorities (governmental, institutional, or corporate, all the way down to small businesses) are happy to keep it up for a relatively modest price, and they give the rebels bonuses in the form of assurances of the transparency demanded of them, statements to the effect that they are in fact itching for the citizenry to keep them in check. Big business and the structures of government have reached an accord that allows them to maintain their position and advantage; transparency is a concession and, at the same time, a ransom demanded for maintaining the status quo; it is a civic triumph, truly difficult to overestimate, that defers other triumphs *ad kalendas Graecas*.

In countries that, like Poland, have been deprived till now of a strong civic tradition, a similar imperative to keep the state or private enterprise in check is borne by more exclusive circles, imposed or guarded first of all by the press, without much will or determination on the part of the society at large, which remains distrustful with respect to political machinations and institutions, as well as toward efforts to keep these under control, because everything, secret and public maneuvers alike, strikes it as equally suspect. But this imperative ultimately remains for the most part at the disposal of these very same structures of power, which only use it to mark out their differences from the preceding government and to declare a new beginning, yet again, from zero.

So, had they really stolen my word? After all, it belongs to everyone, more and more it's common property, and it comes in handy at every turn. And it still hasn't reached its zenith. It flows through the centuries, rising and surging across many years, and despite so many revolutions, beginning with the French, it never loses its attraction, its novelty, its enticing qualities. Its stunning career over the course of the last decade, not only in political language but also in artistic endeavors, to say nothing of design or, especially, for over a century now, architecture—all this proves that it is far more deeply rooted in the imagination than we might otherwise have supposed. My word, their archetype. Our archetype, everyone's archetype. Why is it that we see more and more glass in buildings? Why do we hear assurances of transparency more and more often in political speeches? Doesn't this indicate some persistent, secret aspiration that, while hardly new, is increasingly assertive in seeking its fulfillment? We haven't even come close in the three centuries since Jean-Jacques, but listening to the politicians, journalists, and businesspeople proclaiming the need for complete transparency, or for total clarity, we can't reject the notion that at least sometimes, somewhere deep within, even when we're behaving contrary to these stated desires—let's say, deep within the imagination, or deep in our hearts—there is always a primal, child's voice to be heard, the voice of innocence and of our pure longing for light, for a new, true beginning, for erecting glass houses of state in which everything will be different.

If, however, nothing and no one, not even Jean-Jacques, has justified my naïveté, it is difficult for me not to succumb to the thought that transparency, in the contemporary, "politically correct" understanding of the word, has become, following the global collapse of ruling ideologies, their covert replacement: a new ideology that need not make use of concrete ideas, but that has instead supplanted them with images and plastic concepts. Instead of visions of an ideal society, now sorely faded—whether created by totalitarian systems or democratic ones—we have a dynamic vision of the ideal state, that is, the completely transparent state, illuminated on all sides like a brightly lit garden covered (like the new seat of the Bundestag) by a glass cupola. Governmental institutions, as well as the social and civic institutions that keep them in check, have set themselves a goal that assumes an air of finality, and this goal is the complete legibility and visibility of the activities and functions of those organs that manage political and economic power. If we can't have the ideal society, in which justice and plenty reign, and if money itself can't rule, then perhaps at least reason and honesty will be fairly distributed throughout the world, perhaps at least we can have a government that is flawless in its exercise of power, regardless of its political (conservative, liberal, social-democratic) character. Nothing will happen in secret, and in the best countries, the leading countries, a new, provisional paradise will arise, basking in the light of metaphor, in which everyone, the electorate and the elected, the givers and the takers, will see to it that every official gesture occurs in full view.

At least we'll have that; inequalities won't go away, nor will poverty or unemployment, social welfare systems will remain imperfect, the financial system far from ideal, excise taxes way too high, gas too expensive, but all decisions (even the worst of them) will be made "in complete transparency," *en toute transparence.*

But, on the other hand, in real social interactions, transparency is almost always relative, divorced from its metaphysics, which remains, of course, in the private gesture, awakening now in a Dublin winter, or by a lake in Switzerland, or in our wandering around a city. In the social sphere there is no transparency as such; no one will say that it exists in itself, absolutely, and certainly not within the framework of some social relation. Or at least no one bothers to hope for such a possibility: here, we can only speak of transparency in terms of the perception of discrete objects, objects to be probed and illuminated by someone's gaze; because here, even the most transparent heart must enter into the dialectic of revelation and concealment. Here, transparency exists solely as a function of the gaze, directed at something or other, and generally not toward a future that is supposed to come, but toward the past, which obstructs it. It is not a cosmic data point that's existed for a long time before us and is out there calling on us to discover it; it is, above all, a concept, a task to be completed, one that is sometimes even posed authentically, definitively, and rationally, though it's more often illusive or merely fleeting, dependent on the discourse that dominates at a given moment, on current needs. And this transparency by and large only sets the usual political game in motion, propped up by the manipulation of words. In political and social life, the catchword "transparency" is invariably accompanied by the concurrent production of new obscurities, of new shadow-zones. And if this is really how it's supposed to be, this way and no other, then maybe that time spent in front of those aquariums and Hopper's fences was all a waste. And "my" word too, a waste—to hell with it all. For, after all, as we read in Leopold Tyrmand's novel *The Man with the White Eyes*, "*the visibility and transparency of Philip Merynos's affairs clouded over once again.* At a time when private enterprise was still able to function, he converted his firm into a workers' co-operative called the 'Vanity-Bag.'"[46]

A Bell-Jar of Blue Crystal

True, I cannot separate—but then perhaps we're not supposed to—"Transparent Poland" from glass architecture, nor from the hypnotic interiors of aquariums, nor from the heart of Jean-Jacques. Imagination always walks its own path and juxtaposes, connects, or unites distant places and different stories. Transparency allows us to connect them effortlessly, without the exaggerated strain of metaphor: the dream is singular, it is deep, and it flows from a single source—and sometimes it strikes me as megalomaniacal to say (though I have witnesses to back me up) that there's no better phantasm, no imaginative object more expressive of so many dimensions of modernity at once. It works best in French, where the word *verre* (glass) is an imperfect anagram of *rêve* (dream), thus converting the imagination directly into a glassy material. Dreamed up by Jean-Jacques—though it is unquestionably archetypal—the passage from interior to exterior, the smooth interpenetration of the two sides, the revelation of the whole before one's gaze, such that the eye might encompass everything unhindered, the entire reality (physical, social) that has hidden its state till now, but also the unveiling of one's own soul, casting aside all protective veils and masks, the dissolution of secrets—all of these gestures are translated, transformed, or echoed in glass forms, in the architecture of glass, in *Glasarchitektur*.

So it was that the first real aquarium appeared in England around 1850, and the idea of glass construction picked up steam throughout the nineteenth century—and all of this started with innocent glass lampshades.

"Under the blue bell-jar / of my listless moods . . ."[47] Thus Richard Howard translates the opening lines of Maurice Maeterlinck's poem "Heart's Foliage." In the original, it goes like this: "Sous la cloche de cristal bleu / De mes lasses melancholies . . ." In Polish too we used to use the word for "bell" for this crystal—or glass— "bell jar," though today we use *klosz*, a calque of the French *cloche*. Paradoxically, it came into our language later, primarily in the jargon of home furnishing; it was our glass lampshades, *cloches*— and certainly not "bell-jars"—that were shattered by balls or other projectiles when we were roughhousing as kids. Had Sylvia Plath lived in the nineteenth century, the title of her book would have been translated into Polish using a completely different word, more reminiscent of "bell" than "jar." Zygmunt Krasiński, in one of his thousands of letters to Delfina, employs the image of the bell in the following peculiar question:

> Have you heard of those cats or birds that professors of physics place under a pneumatic glass bell, in order, by

the convulsions they produce, to demonstrate to their pupils how they are removing the air from under the bell? All around is light and air, yet beneath this glass—emptiness, nothingness, death. We are like these cats. The past, the future, the air of history all around us is life-giving, blue, bright! Only we, our fifty years of life, have been sealed beneath such a transparent bell, for beneath it we must die for lack of life![48]

Those experiments on those unfortunate animals (long after we knew how to demonstrate the existence of a vacuum) have become the stage upon which we witness the drama of nineteenth-century humanity, or at least of nineteenth-century Poles, since we're not just talking about Zygmunt and Delfina, but of people paralyzed in their actions, made to suffer for lack of access to a genuine space in which to live, whatever that might be—private or collective happiness, national independence and freedom—though above all else for the lack of a conscious potential that one perceives all around, that one can see clearly through the glass but cannot reach. For Krasiński, the notion of the glass dome is still negative, bound up with the feeling of being imprisoned, suffocated, paralyzed, all the while presenting us with an aesthetic illusion of beauty that calls out from the other side, yet remains inaccessible.

All manners of bell-jars, the *cloches* that appear here and there in the excellent plays of the aforementioned Alfred de Musset, more or less a contemporary of Krasiński, often appear, in keeping with the nineteenth-century convention, as "bell." Fantasio, the hero of the comedy that bears his name, directs the following question to his friend, Spark: "Doesn't Jean Paul say that a man obsessed by a great idea is like a deep-sea diver under a glass bell? Spark—I have no glass bell—no bell at all, and I dance like Jesus on the waves!"[49] And then Lorenzaccio, in the play that likewise bears his name, confesses that, sure, he too has taken these deep journeys underwater, unlike Filippo, a humanist who lives on abstractions, to whom he addresses these words: "Like a shining beacon you have remained motionless beside the ocean of men, and you have beheld in the waters the reflection of your own light. [. . .] But I, during all this time, have dived; I have plunged into this rough sea of life; I have traversed all the depths of it, covered with my diving-bell; while you were admiring the surface, I saw the debris of shipwrecks, the bones and the leviathans."[50] In his metaphor for authentic versus illusory life, Lorenzaccio outlines—to look at it with a technical eye—the project of the *Nautilus*, the submarine that would sail half a century later, Captain Nemo at the helm, twenty thousand leagues under the sea. Equipped with enormous panoramic windows, it would afford a comprehensive view of the ocean and reveal heretofore inaccessible mysteries. From the Romantic de Musset to the Positivist Verne, the idea of underwater travel changes, but both hold to a similar technical principle. As we know, the imagination of the writer and of the painter is conditioned by the development of technology, which submits its successive inventions to the game of desire and absence, providing us with a space to be filled with phantasms. Jean Paul Richter, and after him de Musset, makes imaginative, "humanistic" use of those early forays into the bathyscaphe. In turn, Jules Verne draws upon the reigning fashion for glass structures, which exploded in the mid-eighteenth century.

But, preceding him, Maurice Maeterlinck draws on it, too; in his poems, the related images of the bell jar and the greenhouse are both frequent and important. Greenhouses appear in the titles of his poems and in the title of what is perhaps his best poetry collection, *Serres chaudes* (1886). The surprising English term "conservatory" pleases, but Richard Howard's translation, *Hothouses,* is closer to the mark. And this is how Maeterlinck himself, a resident of Ghent, glossed his title: "The title came upon me naturally, since Ghent is a city of gardeners, of flower-growers especially, and is full of hothouses and conservatories. I've always been attracted to exotic plants and flowers. Summer days, when I was still a toddler, it seemed to me there was nothing more pleasant, more mysterious, than these glass houses, where the sun was king." Later on we'll take a look inside these greenhouses, and his lucid reminiscence will rather darken the lines of Maeterlinck's poems, but for now I'll dredge up a couple more dates and facts and a handful of glassy, hothouse quotations.

So, in 1886 there were already many greenhouses in Ghent, used mostly in agriculture of the botanical variety. Forty years had passed since what I have found to be the first appearance of the greenhouse in serious literature. In Baudelaire's *La Fanfarlo* (1847), the eponymous heroine's admirer is tempted by these quarters: "La Fanfarlo's room was thus very small, very low-ceilinged, stuffed with soft things that were perfumed and dangerous to touch; the air was charged with those bizarre scents that make one want to die there slowly, as if inside a hothouse. The lamplight [. . .] lit some paintings marked with a Spanish melodrama."[51] For Krasiński too, at this time, the glass enclosure still carries a sense of suffocation: sweet, exotic. The image of the greenhouse is connected to thanatic phantasms, though also to erotic ones.

Baudelaire had very quickly assimilated this new type of construction, which had been imported into architecture by the only recently developed technology for manufacturing and mounting large glass exteriors. In the history of glass, which, like all history, reaches deep into antiquity, one of the most important dates is 1676, when the British chemist George Ravenscroft replaced alkaline salts, which had been used in the production of glass up to that point, with lead oxide. The transparency and hardness of glass manufactured in this way were increased immeasurably over the types of glass made since early Christianity (and earlier technology differed still more), but because of the high cost—and likely because of technical limitations—this new kind of glass was not used in windows; window glass still had to be broken down into small rectangles reinforced by metal and wooden frames, which also obstructed one's view of the outside; more intimate meetings between interior and street (between the beloved behind the glass and her suitor at the bottom of the drainpipe) would have to be negotiated through the dialectic of the open window and the closed. But by the second half of the eighteenth century (by which time Jean-Jacques had already taken his leave) large glass windows, without internal divisions or reinforcements, were adapted to all manner of unoccupied wall space. The earliest caprices of this new glass architecture were the arcades that—beginning in the first years of the nineteenth century, but especially common in the 1820s and 1830s—demonstrate the heights of daring that glass construction had by then already achieved, if primarily used for roofs. The walls themselves were still being made from traditional materials. The next step, which builders now quickly achieved, was the house made entirely of glass, first to accommodate winter gardens, very popular at the time, as well as for metropolitan arcades.

The peculiar link between these two constructions, the greenhouse and the arcade, soon inspired the biggest building of its time, and the one that has fostered the broadest interpretation, by everyone from shoemakers to writers to philosophers: the Crystal Palace, the handiwork of an Englishman named Paxton. His rival, the architect Hector Horeau, who ultimately lost the competition to determine who would design the building that would house the Great Exhibition (thanks to which he would become one of the protagonists of Alessandro Baricco's 1991 novel, *Lands of Glass*), also harbored the fantastic idea of a glass cupola enveloping the whole of Paris; a certain Saccard, a dealer in real estate, would also express this idea a little later in the second volume of Emile Zola's *Les Rougon-Macquart*. Covering the city beneath a dome was supposed to change it into one huge hothouse; within its interior, glass galleries would branch out in every direction, allowing one to move about Paris without an umbrella (not to mention galoshes), regardless of the weather or even of severe fallout. In the twentieth century, these twin ideas would likewise occur to the architect Buckminster Fuller, who dreamed of enclosing the island of Manhattan beneath a glass dome. His vision was realized, modestly and practically, by François Dallegret (born 1937), whose domes covered individual buildings, as well as their surrounding grounds, gardens, driveways, three dogs frolicking among the bushes, and a bed of tea roses. And quite recently

Jaume Plensa, a Catalan artist, unveiled an installation on one of the squares of Washington, D.C., consisting of a delicate-looking steel truss; suspended high in the air, the mass of steel threads, which were separated by empty squares and which linked together houses that were otherwise distant from one another, looked like a transparent ceiling, and the whole of the urban space, roofed in this manner, soon became a kind of gigantic, warm interior space, one that I would happily inhabit.

But for the aforementioned Saccard, the "hero" of Zola's novel, the greenhouse becomes an inextricable part of his idea of the residence appropriate to the new man, the *Homo novus*—which he feels himself to be. It adjoins his own home, forming a whole, and becomes part of his living room.

> On summer evenings, when the rays of the setting sun lit up the gilt of the railings against its white façade, the strollers in the gardens would stop to look at the crimson silk curtains behind the ground-floor windows; and through the sheets of plate-glass so wide and clear that they seemed like the window-fronts of a big modern department store, arranged so as to display to the world outside the wealth within, the petty bourgeoisie could catch glimpses of the corners of tables and chairs, of portions of hangings, of patches of ornate ceilings, the sight of which would root them to the spot, in the middle of the pathways, with envy and admiration.[52]

We're starting to breathe easier: the revision of the image of the glass dome, when compared to the descriptions provided earlier by Baudelaire and Krasiński, is striking. Things have expanded, taken on life; the feeling of suffocation has disappeared, and a sense of happiness is building; the interior encased in glass transforms into an exhibit that steals up toward the eye, which now approaches from outside: it is an accumulation of things, a collection that creates an entire world. A small world, though full and alluring in its way, calling on us to possess it, if only with our eyes. Things ostensibly haphazard, dispersed, trapped under a glass cover become powerfully present, and this presence has a positive purpose—perhaps just being, being here.

Looking into windows thus gave rise to a new kind of pastime—it became fashionable and pleasant and, as is frequently the case with fashions, in certain of its applications quickly fell into self-caricature, comedy, and pretension. Already in a novel by Champfleury (a second-rate writer), published in 1856, we find a hilarious scene in which awful bourgeois, fond of touristic herborizing throughout the countryside, go out to the provinces to look at the fields and trees through the multicolored windows of the village residents, installed specially for this purpose, at the same time as the servants look at the landscape directly, with the naked eye. According to Philippe Hamon, author of a book on the connections between literature and architecture, from which I have borrowed several quotations and ideas, Flaubert had had a similar notion as he was working on *Madame Bovary*, but in the end he rejected it. Which makes me think that one could surely write a more detailed history of the gaze than we've had till now—a look at looking, at where our eyes have alighted, where they couldn't get enough, where they turned away. Just as I know people are writing a history—a fragmentary one, for the time being—of hearing (the French historian Alain Corbin has written an excellent book about sounds, particularly those of church bells, in the countryside of nineteenth-century France), so too should we look deeper into our love for aquariums, which has been growing since the mid-1800s.

Kordian, the eponymous hero of Słowacki's drama, felt that he had been enclosed in a "crystal ball," and the Doctor at the insane asylum where he's incarcerated says that Kordian is "a goldfish in a crystal bowl"; he speaks of "the small crystal of air in which he washes his gills," about being imprisoned in a glass jar.[53] At the time Słowacki wrote his play, there weren't any glass prisons for fish—due to technological limitations—large enough to give Kordian the idea, or rather the feeling, that the entire universe was such a jar, a crystal bowl, the prototype of the aquarium. The first aquarium in the modern sense of the word is said to have arrived around 1850, twenty years after the publication of *Kordian,* and a little before the construction of the Crystal Palace. The images it inspired were generally happy ones, happier in any case than Kordian's, imprisoned in his crystal cosmos or glass jar.

This was an image that Stéphane Mallarmé especially loved to ponder. Mallarmé, whom we should also mention as one of the most outstanding practitioners of hermetic *poésie pure,* was also the founder of a general-interest magazine called *La Dernière Mode* (The Latest Fashion). He wrote in its inaugural issue about jewelry and crystal; transparent objects had always fascinated him—it's no wonder he was a Pisces. In the next issue, he imagined how he, left to his own devices, would decorate a restaurant's interior. It would have a lot of Indian silk, Japanese rice paper, and then some kind of undersea landscape. But how to convey the magic of the bottom of the sea? Mallarmé asks himself:

> [S]o what wall coverings can give us the aquatic world, which—monstrous, frail, rich, obscure and diaphanous with weeds and algae—is so decorative? Any picture, whether painted or embroidered, casts a sort of veil, an immobility, over the mysterious life of these riverine or oceanic landscapes. How shall we possess these watery depths in their reality?[54]

A picture, Mallarmé says, would itself cast a veil, and this veil would have to be torn apart. So then he imagines replacing the picture with glass, a kind of aquarium whose effect would be "magical, living, moving and extraordinary."[55] It would be illuminated by daylight during the day, by gaslight at night, and the inside would be alive with swimming, floating—real or imagined—"goldfish, scorpion-fish, polypuses, starfish, Japanese telescopefish."[56]

But there is no more happily imagined aquarium than the aforementioned *Nautilus,* the ship dispatched to the depths of the sea from the port of imagination called Jules Verne. A good many of us, maybe most of us, sailed on that tub as children, once or perhaps even a couple of times, if we found it to be an especially good read, so I'll note just a couple of details: the *Nautilus* is a museum-ship, though not entirely of this world, moving like a shadow through the ocean's deepest abysses. It has everything: twelve thousand volumes, collections of paintings and musical scores, specimens of natural oddities. Much like the Crystal Palace, it is a saturated world, full, closed, and self-sufficient, in which the crew can even, as Captain Nemo assures us, "manufacture all the air [they] need."[57] The *Nautilus* is equipped with two enormous crystal windows; the extraordinarily powerful lighting affords the viewer half a mile of undersea visibility. "And what a sight!" the delighted Professor Aronnax exclaims. "What pen could ever describe it? Who could ever depict the effects of the light on those transparent mantles, the gradualness of its progressive fading away into the upper and lower regions of the ocean!"[58] Thanks to these panoramic panes aboard the *Nautilus*, the entire undersea world seems to change into one huge aquarium, which passengers can examine at will, with a sense of delight, curiosity, and security.

Captain Nemo's eyes seem to have adapted to this expansive view, to this breadth of vision spread out before the ship's windows. He can see more deeply than others; his gaze can illuminate things and render them transparent:

> One particular detail: his eyes, set rather apart, could embrace nearly a quarter of the horizon. This faculty—as I later confirmed—was accompanied by an eyesight superior even to Land's. When this curious personage was looking intently at something, his eyebrows frowned and his broad eyelids contracted to circumscribe his pupils and thus restrict his visual field—and he *did* look. What a gaze! How he made distant objects larger, and how he penetrated your very soul! How he could pierce the liquid

depths, so opaque to our eyes, and how he could read to the bottom of the seas![59]

If the evolution of the species were even more contingent on our desires—more than it already is, I mean—the future race of Nemos would have eyes three times larger than their ears, their pupils would grow to cover half their faces, as in cinematic representations of extraterrestrials, and their auricles would atrophy from the silence, cutting us off once and for all from our ancient brethren, the bats.

But in the literature of the second half of the nineteenth century and the beginning of the twentieth, it is not the ocean that is subject to observation, but the city. Hamon talks about the new urban phenomenon that he calls "the proliferation of scenery."[60] The city doesn't simply build outward—it develops like a spectacle. The new optical technologies employed in architecture—large glass panes, display windows in stores, marquees—together with new technologies for gas illumination that utterly transform the city's urban landscape ("We are violently enamored of gas and glass," Edgar Allan Poe notes in "The Philosophy of Furniture"), expose interiors to the outside, celebrate the gaze, deepen its capacity for peeping. Peeping becomes a privileged mode of looking, and urban space produces more and more exhibits, it theatricalizes itself, arranges itself into a series of performances, just as for Proust's narrator the glassed-in courtyard of the Hotel de Guermantes forms "an exhibition of a hundred Dutch paintings hung in rows."[61] Urban life seems to unfurl on an illuminated stage, on—as Rimbaud would say in his *Illuminations*—"crystal boulevards."

The idea of the exhibit, the exhibition, the collection, of revealing a structure's interior, is common during the period we are discussing, and it gives the eyes free rein—to take it in, to peep, to look into, to bring into full view, to leave nothing unseen: these are the new existential imperatives and the aesthetically determined modes of inspection and description. In his brief text on the *Nautilus*, Roland Barthes characterizes Verne as having "an obsession for plenitude":

> [H]e never stopped putting a last touch to the world and furnishing it, making it full with an egg-like fullness. His tendency is exactly that of an eighteenth-century encyclopaedist or of a Dutch painter: the world is finite, the world is full of numerable and contiguous objects. The artist can have no other task than to make catalogues, inventories [. . .].[62]

The encyclopedic temperament, however, is not peculiar to this one imagination. The "obsession for plenitude" affects many, becomes a sign of the times, and grips a whole host of writers. Already in 1861, in his *La Mer*—to keep us deep underwater— Jules Michelet, the most famous of the Romantic historians and in his time a friend of Adam Mickiewicz, proposed the creation of museums in which one would find a "complete exhibit" of all the monsters of the deep. And in England and France there had been since the 1840s a wave of quasi-encyclopedic publications, catalogues, guides, directories, physiologies (of marriage or whatever), portraits (geographic, for example—*Scenic France*—or mental-geographic—*England and the English*—or "comparative-specialist"—*Paris Prisons*), in a word, of all that Walter Benjamin calls *livres-exhibitions,* "book-exhibits."

The first World's Fair in London in 1851, which was quickly followed by many others, seemed to focus this inclination and summon its new forms. Zola's famous maxim, "To see everything, to say everything," summarizes this need for utter universality, for the euphoric exercise of the gaze, and to translate it into an authorial task. For Zola, looking at something becomes a pleasure in itself; rarely does one find in literature protagonists who are as happy as the lovers Renée and Maxime in *The Kill:*

> The tall houses, with their great carved doors and heavy balconies, with inscriptions, signs, and company names in great gold letters, delighted them. As the brougham rolled on, they gazed fondly at the wide pavements, with their benches, their variegated columns, and their slim trees. This bright gap, which stretched as far as the horizon, grew narrower and opened upon a pale-blue square of space; this uninterrupted double-row of big shops, where the shopmen smiled at their fair customers, these currents of stamping, swarming crowds, filled them with absolute contentment, with a feeling of perfection in the life of the streets.[63]

In closing this brief litany of images, might I present just one more instance of the pleasure of looking and the delight in exhibition? I have a painting, just a print, that dates from not much later on, and which soothes the eye with its pastels and bronzes much the same way as balm soothes a wound. *The Vegetable Garden with Donkey* (1918) is a canvas from Joan Miró's initial, more figurative and narrative period. Since we're speaking here of the pleasure of looking itself, of happiness that flows in through the eyes, this vegetable garden draws us in more than Hopper's paintings, which are full of the fascination of looking, but which are also less delighted, colder, given more to the light itself than to the assembled objects portrayed, perhaps more concerned with contours (of windows and plate glass) than with the interiors themselves, which are more exposed to eternity than concentrated in the moment. *The Vegetable Garden with Donkey* is not enclosed in a greenhouse, yet it reminds me of, or rather it makes me conscious of, what visionary glass architecture could have accomplished, those gigantic domes encompassing whole swaths of land, entire spaces of habitation. It's only an impression—after all, Miró didn't paint glass walls or roofs—but the geometric outline of the garden's edges, of the hills and the clouds above them, seems to be the support for a roof made out of sky, for a glass shelter beneath the heavens. And in the midst of so much, of so much goodness, of so much accumulated life, of bushes, trees, crops in neat rows or on evenly planted trusses, branches offering their leaves like a peacock its tail, a single donkey, just one, quietly grazing, yet shown in such a way as to embody the majority of donkeys or even the entire donkeyness of this world, the sand-colored hacienda (the people are likely having a delicious nap; it's siesta-time) and everything else have been gathered together, arranged, concentrated in such a way that for the viewer, here, in the foreground, in front of what could be a glass wall, everything is for the taking, available for purchase, ready for you to set your heart on it, for you to give in to your whims. Much like in its kindred painting *Farm*, from 1921. This time it's night under a full moon, but the hacienda and its adjoining property are gleaming as if in sunlight. And once again there are many tools set out in the courtyard and field—watering cans, barrels and pails, and a stool whose shape is deceptively similar to the initials that Albrecht Dürer stamped on his prints. And then there's the yard-barn-workshop-cowshed, many things in one, enclosed in a square of walls, through which we can see everything, a rooster as well as a small nanny-goat, and a ladder with a hen at the top, and many other creatures besides, so many things called into happy coexistence in one inclusive cluster.

The spirit of universal exhibition that mingles with all the other spirits moving through Europe during the second half of the nineteenth century imposes a catalogization, a museification—it aestheticizes the world. The proliferation of the visible becomes one of the projects of modernity, a project that has not been exhausted to this day. There is still much to say on this topic, and we will look inside many more times to come, slipping unseen through a broken window, into the Crystal Palace.

Cover Your Tracks

Erase all traces, or more precisely, "Cover your tracks"—this is the refrain in the poem that opens Bertolt Brecht's *Reader for Those Who Live in Cities*.[64] Walter Benjamin quotes from it in his essay "Experience and Poverty," later bringing up the name of Paul Scheerbart, a name I can never get used to because it sounds so unwriterly, so befitting an engineer or technician, with that double *e* and repeated *r*, as technical as what ultimately became his most famous work, *Glasarchitektur* (*Glass Architecture*, 1914), technical in both title and content, and yet, as we will see in a moment, not a book about construction alone. It's also about the absence of traces, about a space where it's difficult to find them, about a city that would push its glassiness all the way up to the sky, that would keep moving ahead (for one must imagine the march of the city), that would be a stratum of space unmoored in time, its present always pressed into the future, because every moment in this city would clarify the next and never be lost, never fade into vapor trails, streaks of dirt, chips of stone, shadows—into all the usual traces left by the disintegration of what was once cohesive. The city, and perhaps half the world along with it, roads, gardens, pure and transparent, a glass *tabula rasa* on which nothing is ever written for good, the city a shield defending its residents from gloominess, from the accumulation of objects, from the compulsion to suppress their thoughts, to horde them, to collect objects, to never let them go, to heap all these thoughts and objects in the corners, in the dark recesses of their souls and apartments—one of many such cities imagined over hundreds of years, cities of gold and silver, cities whose contours we could never quite make out, the city as light, the city of colorful glass exposing itself as if to be photographed, captivating, sparkling, so that the only thing that matters is the glare that penetrates your memory, that erases the traces, that lights us up, brightens, overwhelms our faces, and makes it so that we do not endure, do not pass away, but only become.

What was it about Brecht's poem and Scheerbart's city that attracted Benjamin? What did he like about the idea of erasing traces, which he saw in Scheerbart's text and then elaborated? He himself lived in other, imagined, ethereal cities whose graphic equivalent he scratched out in tiny handwriting on small pieces of paper. He was interested in the connection between architecture and manuscript, the handwriting of manuscripts, *écriture manuscrite*. He mentions this connection in several brief theses on graphology, for he opposed the purely characterological interpretation of handwriting; through a comparison with architecture, graphological interpretation could slip free of narrow psychology, since it would no longer be concerned merely with tracking the graphic impulses that were supposed to be the immediate expression of various psychic tensions or ongoing conflicts, but with the whole model of writing, the analogue of which is construction. Benjamin believed that this "physiognomy" of handwriting told us more about the imagination of a given person than his way of walking, his facial expressions, or his gestures. The letters that he himself made were indeed remarkably small; few writers could produce such a radically minuscule scrawl before the advent of the computer; among renowned writers, surely Robert Walser was the only one capable of writing on a more microscopic scale, but what can you do: he was Swiss, Swiss and allegedly insane—like Rousseau. Benjamin wrote not only in German, but in French; in a reproduction of a page from his papers, a single ten-centimeter line contains around ninety letters in French, about twenty words in all. The letters don't run into each other, aren't packed too close; every one is, despite its reduction, separate and distinct, thousands of swarming gnats rubbing unaggressively against one another. In sum, they create somewhat uneven, gently waving lines, a city of squished houses, though sometimes of taller ones too, separated from time to time by narrow alleys, the whiteness of which creates a different, secondary network within the city, a secure labyrinth that allows you to navigate it at your leisure, to move at will around the walls, between them, with nowhere to go, no downtown to rush off toward.

Benjamin was fond of Baudelaire's wanderings around Paris, his haphazard, melancholic, exceptionally melancholic routes, whose irregularity led Benjamin to the idea of handwriting as personal architecture, corresponding to the architecture of Baudelaire's city. Did Scheerbart's glass city intrigue him as a challenge to the other, underdeveloped side of the imagination, as a disquieting, foreign, alien, as yet unknown, entirely different space, or was it just a spatial expression of the social ideas Benjamin held dear? Or perhaps the glass city had simply grown out of the flipside of melancholy, its dark side, the delectable shape of utopia, the kind of utopia every melancholic dreams of at least once, for there is no utopia or ideal city not enamored of transparency, that would not dissolve therein whatever has come before, the now-superfluous past; that would not wish, if only for a moment, to forget loss, to erase its intolerable traces, and the dark stains of grief it's left in us.

Benjamin is a hero of melancholy, but I also think of him as yet another quiet hero of transparency, and I can't rid myself of the image of September 26, 1940, the day he died, about which we know next to nothing aside from the fact, unverified, that after having swallowed poison and destroyed the manuscript of nobody-knows-what, perhaps some great treatise or, as some like to believe, a novel, he might yet have been saved, had he allowed the administration of a purgative, which he refused. He is alleged to rest—for he rests anonymously, without a trace, without the slightest trace—like Antoni Malczewski, author of *Marija*, the Polish language's most beautiful novel-in-verse about the disappearance of traces, who lies in an unmarked grave, without a stone of any kind, without words, without family, without a memorial in Warsaw's Powązki Cemetery—in the cemetery in Portbou, on the Spanish border, perched on a rock wall several dozen meters above the Mediterranean, a small square cut into the barren earth, black on gray, with azure below.

On that last day, then, Benjamin was walking out of a little French town, the last in a small procession of a few other people, a departing shadow, he a shell gleaming in our eyes as we, on another day, in another September, headed across the hills along the coastline, and the heat of the relentlessly sweltering summer drowned out every thought, reducing our naïve, foolish, imitative journey to embers, following his last trail, all the way to the Spanish border, and erasing that trace in our memory so thoroughly that we suddenly found ourselves not knowing why we'd come, our bodies burning, overexposed to the sun, and we saw only this thickness of light, in which there was nothing to hold on to, nothing left of memory. We were following him, following everything, the irresistible illusion of traces, hypnotized by our own clarity, moving toward the light, toward the noonday sun, toward a light that was getting stronger all the time, more and more light, and our backpacks were cutting into our shoulders, and there was nothing more we could do for him, or for that matter for ourselves, at most we could feel the gravity of each step, the effort needed to force oneself through the air, higher and higher, toward a border that tore itself from the sea in a gentle arc and climbed at an increasingly violent grade along the long drop until it finally hit you in the eye. We stood there: the crumbling rock along the border indicated the way through, and the sky was all sun at its peak, where everything was dying away, as if the last hour had arrived for the living and the dead. Why hadn't the border guard let him through? Had he just been joking when he started to ask questions, when he started to blackmail them, just fooling around, so that they would look at each other, start to panic? Or perhaps he really did want to deliver them to the Gestapo and the French police. We turned back.

The town was sleepy, quiet, and foreign; till morning it had seemed as if the air were being sucked out of the one-story houses, leaving just a few atoms to live on, and now was circulating unencumbered, refreshed, through the empty streets. The kind of foreign town he once wrote about, speaking of the light. As many as three times in his notebooks he repeated this same, brief fragment, "Light," with very few changes, beginning with the following words: "For the first time, alone with the beloved, in a foreign town."[65] Then, waiting for his beloved, he spots a light suspended ever so low among the trees. He goes somewhere else, strolls along the little streets, waiting the whole time, and turns back, intrigued as to how he can have seen this same low light three times between the trunks. No, it's not a big deal, it finally turns out to be the light of the moon, which slowly, eventually spills out over the treetops. But why note this on three occasions? What has grabbed him here—amorous anticipation, emptiness, hidden light like a polestar, a feeling, fulfillment; all of this together? Is it the impression of the glassiness of the moon itself, Democritus having been the first to write about it as consisting of a glassy substance, which allowed the dark zones of the cosmic sea to pass through its surface? At night, in the nearly deserted campground, we drank the local wine, like all nomads. The sea was sleeping peacefully right next to us, as if the day had worn it out; we stirred it with our bare feet until it finally issued lazy waves, one at a time. In Paul Valéry's poem "The Lost Wine," which I have never understood, he speaks of making a sacrifice to the sea, an "offering to oblivion," the poet says.[66] The drops of wine he casts into the water, not really knowing why (Valéry wonders too), perhaps instead of drops of blood, instead of the ultimate sacrifice, are, he feels, like transparency immersed in transparency; the transparency of the wine is saturated by the transparency of the water, lost in its purity, and the pure water absorbs the wine, and from its depths "forms unfathomed" surface and rise into the air. I was standing at the edge of the sea, Olga was reading something in the tent, and the bright bluish circle of her flashlight quivered in the distance, beneath the linen, and I was thinking about the day, about our march, about that moment of light that we wanted to give as an offering to Benjamin, though it ended up being to our own unease, and now, over the water's surface, under the September night sky, almost bright with moonlight, forms unfathomed were rising, emerging plain as day from the water, much as this place did, the end-point of our day's journey, and in the light the forms reflected on the water it became clear that there was nowhere else to go, that they constituted a barrier upon the impenetrable face of the water, and yet it was equally clear that they hadn't crept out from the depths of any one private life, from a time of which they were now the only residue; they flickered over the water like the cosmic candles at the ends of the earth, mythic lights at the world's edge—beyond which *ubi leones*—now suspended quite nearby, within arm's reach.

"Cover your tracks," Benjamin repeated, after Brecht, to the city-dwellers, and as his first, best example he cited the difficulty of life in a bourgeois apartment at the end of the nineteenth century: so much furniture, so much bric-a-brac, and then there was André Gide's point about how every object we want to possess becomes opaque, and then there are so many fabrics, bedspreads, and novelties that all we have to do is set foot inside to get the distinct impression that "There is truly nothing for us here!" There is no room in which *not* to leave a trace of oneself, in which not to leave some permanent mark, and God forbid something should get broken! Immediately the host feels as though—Benjamin quotes *Faust*—"someone had obliterated 'the traces of his days on earth.'"[67] And yet that's no big deal (a shattered vase! a broken railing!), so Benjamin reaches quickly for the most important words, "culture," "heritage," even "humanity." But most of all he quotes Scheerbart: "You are all so tired, just because you have failed to concentrate your thoughts on a simple but ambitious plan."[68]

We are all so tired, Benjamin repeats, exhausted not only by "the endless complications of everyday living," but by the entire experience we are carrying within ourselves: weary of 1933, when Benjamin wrote "Experience and Poverty"; weary of our illusions of "culture" and "heritage"; weary of the *démenti* that inflation has inflicted on our experience of money, that hunger has inflicted on our bodily experience, that the ruling classes have inflicted on our moral experience, that the experience of war has inflicted on the experience of peace; tired of constant degradation in the face of technology's march forward and even of those heights that have already been attained; tired of the fact that "economic crisis is at the door, and behind it is the shadow of the approaching war."[69] And it remains today, in our own time, as it was then, for we are also tired, so tired, still so very tired. Tired, and cast into new misery, Benjamin says, or else into new poverty—poverty, because experience has lost its causative potential, its ability to spur us toward creation, or at least toward re-creation. A poverty of transience, which people guard themselves from having to recognize by holding on to exotic, magical ideas, astrology and yoga, the Church of Scientology, chiromancy and gnosis. Or else bungee jumping, wine collecting, or survival courses.

Experience, the past's baggage, much like the objects we possess, darkens our lives, demands that we outrun them, ridding ourselves of the anecdotal, marginal encumbrances of thought, leaving our heritage to the pawnbroker. To exchange our poverty for a new and positive concept, for a kind of beneficial barbarism that would allow us "to start from scratch; to make a new start; to make a little go a long way; to begin with a little and build up further, looking neither left nor right"—it is with such an act, with such a rush of verbs that Benjamin lifts himself up and appends the names of the merciless minds whose work began with wiping the slate clean.[70] Descartes, of course, and then Einstein, Klee, and Scheerbart. Scheerbart, with his text—the best known out of his prolific output—dedicated entirely to glass architecture, but also to the fantastic topography in his cosmic, long-forgotten science fiction novel, *Lesabendio*, in which people speak a new kind of language and have new kinds of names: Peka, Labu, Sofanti. Or, just as well, Ogla and Merak.

Glasarchitektur

Obviously, the first thing to tackle is something quickly done. To start with, therefore, the veranda can be transformed. It is easy to enlarge it, and to surround it on three sides with double glass walls. Both these walls will be ornamentally colored and, with the light between them, the effect of the veranda in the evening, inside and out, will be most impressive. If a view of the garden is to be provided, this can be achieved by using transparent window-panes. But it is better not to fit window-type panes. Ventilators are better for admitting air.

In a modest way, it is thus comparatively easy for any villa-owner to create "glass architecture." The first step is very simple and convenient.[71]

This is how Paul Scheerbart introduces his practical advice. For the person not looking for anything complicated, just a little glass, a bit of light, and first of all as many glass walls as possible: whole walls, floor to ceiling, and then more of the same. The hardest part might be the wanting. Because even when the changes aren't so complicated technically, one still has to know that the future, the entire future, will follow a different track. "The new environment," Scheerbart writes in the passages that open his collection, "must bring us a new culture."[72] What will this new civilization be like? Beautiful, according to Scheerbart. His eighteenth fragment is entitled "The beauty of the Earth, when glass architecture is everywhere." Here we read:

> The face of the earth would be much altered if brick architecture were ousted everywhere by glass architecture. It would be as if the earth were adorned with sparkling jewels and enamels. Such glory is unimaginable. All over the world it would be as splendid as in the gardens of the Arabian Nights. We should then have a paradise on earth, and no need to watch in longing expectation for the paradise in heaven.[73]

Scheerbart's entire collection, consisting of brief, numbered fragments in keeping with the German convention, each one a small, self-contained whole furnished with a title, mixes sometimes technical—and occasionally rather technological—descriptions and suggestions with infrequent comments on cultural transformation and the new, glass, heaven on earth. This utopia—it may occasionally feel as if there's an undercurrent of humor, so practical are the suggestions, so general and chimerical the visionary beliefs—painted in unusually modest brushstrokes that nevertheless fundamentally alter how the world looks (without euphoria, nor with concrete details as to how its governments, or indeed anything else, will work), contrary to other utopias, dispenses with metaphysics and its corresponding reorientation of the soul, makes do without spiritual and social regulation, without feverish prophesying. It erects its space, which is rather urban, appealing exclusively to the industrial possibilities of construction, to the physical characteristics of its materials. Scheerbart is interested in matter, not idea; it may be that this shift in our approach to construction will eventually produce a new metaphysics—what kind, we'll have to wait and see—but not the other way around.

More than with other utopians, this connects Scheerbart with painters whose eyes, like a hawk's, like photographic film, are especially sensitive to any quivering of air, to any modulation of color. His project seems devoid of sharp socio-political pronouncements exploiting our enchantment with glass, seeing it as a demand for a universal transparency that would encompass all spheres of life, public and private. This is not a project of total control over reality, leaving the rest of us behind, stuck in the landscape we've known till now, with its darkness and confinement; it is the dream of a writer so sensitive to contrasts, to light, that he regards its self-evidence as the unacknowledged—more light!— self-evidence of the world. This is why someone like Edward Hopper is closer to Scheerbart than is Tommaso Campanella or other makers of cities of the sun—Hopper who, I will mention again, by his own admission, observed "only and exclusively" the presence of light. Indeed, Scheerbart cultivates a particular pedagogy of light, the effect of which is supposed to be an improvement of life, however one wants to interpret that, an improvement so essential that one could even call it revolutionary; but this enlightenment is predicated on physical observations, knowledge of the positive impact of particular phenomena of light. *Particular* phenomena: Scheerbart's objective isn't an open shower of light, but an opening toward such light as might be subtly modulated, the gleaming of which would produce a nuanced range, vibrant veils, of color. Then everything will look different, because even cars will have more windows, specially tinted, through which light will appear in its new aspect. In his fifty-sixth fragment, "Nature in another light," Scheerbart writes:

> After the introduction of glass architecture, the whole of nature in all cultural regions will appear to us in quite a different light. The wealth of colored glass is bound to give nature another hue, as if a new light were shed over the entire natural world. There will be no need to look at nature through a colored piece of glass. With all this colored glass everywhere in buildings, and in speeding cars and air- and water-craft, so much new light will undoubtedly emanate from the glass colors that we may well be able to claim that nature appears in another light.[74]

The glass architecture that Scheerbart extols appears as an intermediate form between pure, primal nature and its utterly unbounded, directly and openly accessible, and sometimes dazzling light on one side, and on the other, the civilization that it makes accessible to us, one that operates within its own dark constructions, which may even conceal further darkness. (Don't such "obscure" buildings—a castle, say—recall civilization as Kafka imagined it?) Daniel Payot assigns Scheerbart the splendid moniker of "sober barbarian."[75] A barbarian (as Walter Benjamin had already called him) because he wants to bring about the destruction of the old order. Sober because his vision seeks out a particular *media res*, a golden mean that would allow him to evade the inherent violence and rapacity of nature (following the model of German Romantics, Scheerbart sees nature as ambivalent, not just as a benign setting for life, nor a mill that simply grinds lives up), and with it the violence of a society whose architecture of shadow and brick masses is itself a cause of injustice. This is also where we get a romanticizing return to the idea of the Gothic cathedral. "The whole of glass architecture," Scheerbart writes in the sixty-sixth fragment, "Churches and temples," "stems from the Gothic cathedrals. Without them it would be unthinkable; the Gothic cathedral is the prelude."[76] For Scheerbart, the Gothic prepared space to receive light, to unburden walls, to fill interiors with pure air filtered through color. Without iron at its disposal, forever condemned to stone, the Gothic could not bring its inhalation of great emptiness—the inspiration of lightness that had been lurking for centuries on the invisible side of the world—to its logical end, not until Scheerbart summoned it from the shadows in order to exhibit it, rearranged.

A Digression in the Cathedral

This is an idiosyncratic reading of the Gothic and of its cathedrals, situating them beyond grandeur, beyond admiration for their loftiness of spirit and matter, a reading built—or rather fixed—on the technical relations between the building material and the undeveloped site, between the walls and the freedom of empty space and light. Among ancient representations of cathedrals and churches, the closest to Scheerbart might be the paintings and sketches of the Dutch "minor master" Pieter Saenredam, whose works often confront us with minute silhouettes of people—starlings crouched on the floor—at the bottom of the enormous abysses of the churches towering over them, so expansive and cavernous that they nearly efface all human presence.

Roland Barthes, who, particularly fascinated, devoted a bit of attention to these interiors, writes that in Saenredam there is admittedly none of the *horror vacui* that one might find in other Dutch masters, but there is something more "modern"—the absurd:

> Never has nothingness been so confident. [. . .] Saenredam is in effect a painter of the absurd; he has achieved a privative state of the subject, more insidious than the dislocations of our contemporaries. To paint so lovingly these meaningless surfaces, and to paint nothing else—that is already a "modern" aesthetic of silence.[77]

Yet one need only examine Saenredam's interiors through the experimental, slightly colored glasses we have borrowed from

Scheerbart to see another, perhaps less neutral and negative building. The kind in which what is human is subject only to delimitation and, certainly, to being silenced, and yet is not reduced to absurd emptiness. And we will discern, for just the time being—before the advent, before our subsequent pages are illuminated by the glass houses of Bruno Taut (who would find his inspiration in Scheerbart), Ludwig Mies van der Rohe (who knew Taut well before the Second World War), or Philip Johnson (who had been a pupil of van der Rohe after the war)—the possibility of glass architecture *avant la lettre*, of the mood and luminosity toward which it would later apply its plate windows and partitions, and with it we will see a space one can dream, arrange, give a utopian clarity, chisel like crystal, a *camera non obscura*, a pocket of light and air, the kind that Scheerbart, and later others besides, would eventually open completely, releasing it like a pearl from its chitinous cell.

Religious concentration vanishes in these airy expanses, but architecture sinks away as well; walls and ceilings absorb the air, and their function of lifting and holding becomes less pronounced—and Scheerbart's visions, or rather his postulates, are even more emphatic about this Gothic lightness, stressing the complete unburdening of the walls, relieving them, thanks to the use of steel and iron supports, of the odium of weight and darkness. As Jean-Louis Schefer beautifully puts it, Gothic churches (especially in Saenredam) are "a slight insistence on the obvious"—more than a space, but an act resulting in light: frozen, enclosed, packed in, slightly colored, which becomes the substance and quality of space.[78] It continues here, indispensible and indubitable, a little insistent, and does not so much illuminate as belong, intensely, independent of the dramas of weather, to the moods of the day.

Looking at these church interiors, in which people have settled to the bottom like grains of sand in an hourglass, or else have crouched there as if drowned in light, may call to mind, as much by force of historical association as through direct impression, still lifes in which the light behind translucent glass (there a chalice, a goblet, a crystal ball, here an invisible screen, or else the glass wall right in front of our faces), absorbs—into its eternal immobility, into its reflections, into its slight thickness—that which it encompasses and penetrates (there: wine, a book left open, the flesh of a lemon; here: human marionettes). Even if we take the term "still life" to heart, however, we can hear, as Barthes did, an inviolable silence—it pushes nothing forward, it ends nothing.

All glass architecture is composed and arranged as still life, as a multidimensional, spacious *bodegón* where objects are suspended in uncertainty as to whether they will continue to exist, whether they will harden in their immanence. It is an exhibition in which no one knows when he himself is on display, when he is drawing attention—and the eyes of others—to himself. The lesson of the Gothic, so dear to Scheerbart, and especially of the Gothic in the kind of interpretation of Saenredam I would here ascribe to Scheerbart, speaks to the fact that light does not so much envelope and stifle as it quivers and imparts a certain vitality. No one knows what it's urging us toward, not even Scheerbart, who, through his visions, does nothing more than prepare, bring about a certain state of readiness, arranging space for a new, happier beginning, without specifying its content. He believes that this reshaping will bring transformation in itself, that it is a promise, and maybe even—secretly—its fulfillment. How far that transformation goes, what it brings about, what kinds of activities, what kinds of social behaviors, what kinds of political expectations and choices, he does not say. Glass and light, properly arranged, are enough to spark a reaction, to bring about this spaciousness—which Barthes, referring to Saenredam, perhaps too harshly called a meaningless nothingness—to emit, well, what? Pleasure? Joy? Scheerbart says more than once that the effect will please many, that it will delight the majority of people. In Saenredam, however, looking at these figures deprived (like the anonymous future inhabitants of Scheerbart's glass houses) of all function, meaning, status, and social role, one can discard any such sense of optimism. "A sliver of community passes by," Schefer writes, "breaking to pieces, washing away, as it were, in the weightlessness of a light that allows nothing to exist, but freezes, slows, [. . .] and suspends all things": a sliver of fragmented community, existing here in its dormancy, in the creamy mildness of a light that seems to bring solace.[79]

The New Hygiene

This unexpected warmth in the Gothic, the readiness to take in light, seems to have struck a chord with Scheerbart; he himself protested against descriptions of his architecture as cold. At the same time, glass architecture, unencumbered, liberated from brick, will not so much serve to minimize its own presence or reduce clutter (which Scheerbart also liked about the Gothic) as give rise to a new reality. It would not be possible, you see, to hang decorations on the glass walls or to cover them with furnishings: one would not be able to add or accumulate. Lighting is to play the essential role, which will heighten the role of the filter constituted by the glass itself; the whole, combining glass and lighting, creates in Scheerbart's vision an ingenious fantasia that works the same in the day as at night and fosters the fundamental experience of the residents of Scheerbart's cities: enchantment and gentility. Many years after the fact, George Herbert's aphorism continues to ring true: "Whose house is of glass, must not throw stones at another."

In general, Scheerbart's vision rests more on the creation of the new than on the removal of the old. There appear innumerable formulations in his collection that can, given our historical knowledge, disturb us, a posteriori, summoning unpleasant associations. "That in a glass house, if properly built, vermin must be unknown, needs no further comment," we read in the forty-fourth fragment, which is of course called "Vanquishing vermin."[80] Yet we must, at least for the time being, discern in these comments nothing more than the mania for hygiene that had then been growing across Europe for a decade or more. The very word "hygiene" in today's broad usage (no longer referring just to spiritual or bodily discipline, as it had for Jean-Jacques, but also to so-called public health) made its appearance in the second half of the nineteenth century. Hygiene was associated with glass, creating an indivisible, symbiotic pairing; in many testimonials from the period one may note how the new obsession with microbes calmed its anxieties only in greenhouses and glass buildings. In his 1894 manifesto,

Jules Henrivaux, another promoter of glass architecture, emphasizes the ease of cleaning glass walls, particularly in the rooms of the sick; after cleansing and drying the apartments' glass surfaces and windows, there is no risk that any life-threatening damp will remain ("the damp" being the turn-of-the-century's subsequent bugaboo; in Polish literature, Stefan Żeromski showed himself to be especially sensitive to it): "Air, light, visible cleaning, these are the things which only the use of glass allows us to achieve and which clearly indicate the role that glass can and should play as the principal hygienic agent and aid."[81] Thirty-seven years later, a glass silhouette of a man, made of what was called "cellon," a transparent synthetic, would present its charms at the entrance to the International Hygiene Exhibition in Dresden, smooth, clean, with organs exposed beneath its transparent skin gleaming in all their obviousness and arousing our horror no longer. And now, this complete body, without a hint of impurity (free of both germs and hair), without secrets, was at last ready to shoulder the worst ideological fantasies—but before it was burdened with fascist obsessions, it showed us the ideal inhabitant of the ideal glass house; this body, freed from its own entanglements, poses no obstacles and is open to the objective and improved laws of the future.

In Scheerbart, hygienic concern for cleanliness, for minimizing contact with what is underneath, with what is dense and earthy (for it is from the earth that vermin force their way to the surface), highlights the desired lightness, the airiness, of the construction. In Scheerbart's aversion to depth, his intention to eliminate it reaches all the way to mirrors: he does not allow any reflections, mirroring echoes, the dangerous play of doubling, which, one might think, restrains the freedom of the imagination, its expansion toward a new perspective on sight, liberated from subjectivity. Typical too is the concern for removing all fire hazards, which is supposed to be accomplished by the strict use of only nonflammable materials; fire, an earth element, despite being so closely connected with the production of glass, has the menacing power to destroy this utopia. For glass does not hatch, Phoenix-like, from metaphors of burning and rebirth. Rather, it is the result of a delicate process of swapping, of replacement, of a kind of gentle levitation. Life as it has been seems more illuminated than suddenly transplanted and violently shifted onto another track; the swapping is predicated on the methodical, by no means violent, erasure of the past and its material forms. Scheerbart's lexicon is indeed revolutionary, yet it does not deal in images of destruction. The word "new" appears often, and sometimes there is talk of "battle," of "the difficult battle with the old, which has taken hold everywhere," but there is no smell of blood, no one is *a priori* better or worse, no social group has precedence over another, nor will one gain this sometime in the future; glass architecture is the product of the universal emancipation of all humanity. And "the first step is simple and easy."

It was Walter Benjamin who sharpened Scheerbart's tone, his smooth-as-glass phrases, by introducing the word "revolution": "To live in a glass house is a revolutionary virtue par excellence."[82] He had become interested in Scheerbart right after the First World War, in 1919, as we find in his letters to Gershom Scholem, and he returned to Scheerbart (his enthusiasm later cooled) in the aforementioned 1933 essay "Experience and Poverty," where he identified with him by intuiting a historical coincidence: Scheerbart, a Berliner, had recorded his views on the eve of the Great War, while Benjamin, also a Berliner, was commenting on them in what might be a comparable historical moment, before a new catastrophe. He begins by asserting the end of the topos of experience, of knowledge transmitted from generation to generation; the war has undermined the status of experience, which has returned from it without story, without words, "[n]ot richer but poorer in communicable experience."[83] In this deprivation, in this poverty of experience, signs of a deeper crisis of culture, one must, for the sake of survival—no longer survival of culture or civilization, but of humankind—succumb to barbarism, to what was then called "positive" barbarism: the kind that would make it possible to rebuild from scratch, from almost nothing. There were several exemplary architects in this millenary period, which had been condemned to such a fundamental loss of experience, and at the same time a loss generalized to a sense of universal emptiness: Adolf Loos, Le Corbusier, a bit later the Bauhaus, which likewise "created rooms in which it is hard to leave traces," and Scheerbart, the precursor who chose glass as his raw building material, pure in itself, poor, a sort of eternal zero among other materials, the most amenable to purification, to a new beginning, to building under conditions of loss, when one must make do with only fleeting pleasures.[84]

Glass, Benjamin says, is devoid of "aura"—and he says so in sudden rapture, he who, in his writings on the transformations undergone by nineteenth-century Paris, grumbled about the blow already being dealt to objects by mass reproduction, depriving them of their particular "aura," their individual existence.[85] But now, in the face of its necessary impoverishment, even the "aura"—which, rooted in time, emerges from the accumulation of experience, from the creation of value over long periods of time—no longer enchanted its czar; the logic of the new demands the performance of a barbaric gesture, stripping things of their depth and contenting oneself with having only one dimension. "Glass," Benjamin says, "is, in general, the enemy of secrets. It is also the enemy of possession."[86] Glass does not support anything, and in this sense it is the raw material that holds off accumulation, capitalist consumption, which, under these new societal conditions, would merely signify the empty imitation of past gestures and habits, and with them of material symbols (those sumptuous nineteenth-century bourgeois apartments, that splendor of objects, piling them up, capitalizing, collecting: the pointless accumulation!) that no longer have any weight or any role to play. Positive barbarism depends, Benjamin would put it still another way, on the preference for exterior structure over interior life. This last comparison refers precisely to the drawings of Paul Klee, in which facial expressions submit to the former (structure) more than to the latter (the riches of psychology)—this too responding to a general idea of the new "poverty." Contained within it is a notion that will have to be battered in the flour of words to come, all the way to the end, the notion of construction's precedence over what is hidden, of the obvious over the supposed, the precedence of the mechanical over the spiritual, of surface over depth, of the transparent over the knotty. Once again, as few traces as possible, no traces at all, a glass wall within us, behind which nothing is hidden, and which should not be, need not be, cannot be adorned. As few traces, as few things as possible, as few images of oneself, of one's own actions; yet this minimum, this new minimum is not the result of any reduction to essence, of the purging of superstitions and foreign influences, of the search for some durable foundation in one's own spirituality. Barbarism exceeds such processes of autoreflection and phenomenology: it concerns only what can still happen, not what might yet be saved.

Walter Benjamin wrote "Experience and Poverty" a few years before a new world war, in a fit of Cassandran premonition. Again, "economic crisis is at the door, and behind it is the shadow of the approaching war."[87] This is a document of hysteria, not in the sense of its expression or style, but in the starkness of its comparisons and its catastrophic tone. It arises from a powerful, traumatic experience of loss, identified here, much as it is in Rousseau, with the disintegration of experience as the backbone of culture. Scheerbart supplants this melancholy, which uncovers a suddenly horrifying emptiness (in culture, in society, in humanity), with another, positive emptiness. Daniel Payot, the best of Scheerbart's commentators, notes:

> Accepting and celebrating light, he creates emptiness, though this is not the cold, deadly emptiness of some asceticism that might ultimately re-sacralize past experience, but the beneficial emptiness of the new space, thanks to which its inhabitants, liberated from stifling accumulations, from their own treasures, will discover, once their things have been removed, the conditions by which they can once again take in the air and regain their freedom.[88]

Emptiness changes its color—in Scheerbart, quite literally—it sparkles with various hues and even contains a bit of garishness;

the sequins and trinkets that arouse childish delight in people turn the world into a sort of enchanted aquarium. In Scheerbart, Benjamin found, for a certain time, an open space, unrefracted, creaseless, radically and quite happily free of the burden of accumulation. Melancholy given over to hysteria—to the experience of suffocation and darkness in a place with no exit, no longer capable of taking on any new loss, which would leave only scattered traces—knows the grace of revision. Repudiating further rumination, further submission to the process of mourning, so as not to become a paroxysm, it illuminates itself and suddenly wipes away the path toward transparency, which has already given melancholy the slip, which slips out from within melancholy, from its emptiness, to revive itself by building a new home, or at least a bunker.

Melancholia and the City

Of course, if glassmakers and architects hadn't invented transparency, the melancholics would have. Looking through a windowpane is a textbook embodiment of the melancholic condition, in which "seeing without having" leads to other, worse verbs: refusing, departing, dying. One needs, for example, the city. Not nature, in which there are so few of the veils, of the potential strategies of obliqueness so essential for melancholy. Melancholy is predicated on its rejection of pantheism, among other things. It weakens the boundary between ourselves and the world, certainly, but it is anything but pantheistic. And nature encourages a pantheistic existence, it encourages us to lose ourselves in itself, for good or for ill.

Today, melancholy is connected first of all with the city, for it is the city that has constituted its true landscape for the last century and a half. And in the city, what is natural, what is naturally given, in rivers, woods, mountains, cannot be expressed, cannot find its own form. For one does not know how to hide, to escape, to curl up in urban spaces. Nature in general is, for the melancholic, horribly unambiguous; either it's a mill that grinds everything up, or else it looms before us in all its cold, dull indifference. Melancholy, meanwhile, seeks a simultaneous duality, being and nonbeing at the same time. Melancholy never settles down once and for all into a sense of complete absence, nor does it break out into a feeling of complete presence, but hangs between these states like a glass wall. In the city, it has all its necessary little recesses, passageways, hideouts, vagaries, irregularities—the whole, noose-knotted route to which Baudelaire and Benjamin, and Rétif de la Bretonne before them, have lent their names. The city lives erratically, and here melancholy can find its desired contrast, it can meander, it can hide. The city gives the melancholic a sense of being alien to the life clambering all around him. He associates it with the machinery that keeps the world turning; it keeps going full steam, thousands of coffees, teas, and sandwiches served to keep the life of the planet moving forward, while he sneaks off on the side, hides, and yet remains.

Windows, the windows of the city, stained-glass windows—these externalize this duality, becoming, from the nineteenth century on, the emblem of melancholic existence and the oft-described pleasure of the *flâneur*, the urban wanderer who sneaks between the letters of the apartment buildings. Pausing before stained glass, he enacts the spectacle of his own subdued desire, which commands him to stare into the world without reaching for it, to regard it both in detail and as an abstraction, in all its expansiveness; this is the gaze of Captain Nemo, only without the delight and interest that communication pays us for our efforts. Behind the windows of stores, cafés, and bars, something is freezing, crystallizing, people and things are holding still in a solid mass, and who can say whether it's an accumulation of inaccessible wealth or an inventory of decay? There's no way of accessing these people and things, they exist beyond us, and the gap between their time and ours is the characteristic interval of melancholy, which doesn't count its own seconds, and requires comparison, juxtaposition with another sort of duration in order to define and take hold of itself.

What will soon serve to summon the wanton eye of the consumer—a shimmering collision of sight and frustration ("There's something I don't have!"), the production of which is the basic strategy of advertising—turns out also to satisfy the melancholic's imagination, enamored as he is of this passive gesture of immobilizing and crystallizing things behind glass, out of reach. City windows—as Baudrillard defined it, "glass exists at a sort of zero level of matter: glass is to matter as a vacuum is to air"—create a veil separating the melancholic eye from the world, and at the same time they sharpen his vision; he is part wildcat, part falcon, a super-focused lens, attaining the photographic resolution that, for artists such as Hopper, will clarify a space and enclose it securely in a frame, sharpening it to the highest focus.[89] What a moment earlier had been an aimlessly wandering gaze suddenly drills into the one place where the image (in the eye, on the canvas) will arise; the lines of sight are ablaze, all the more for their being unsupported by any gesture of intrusion: here, it is only the eye that plays the role of the outstretched hand. There's nothing to welcome here, anyway, nothing to engage in; whatever life has been seized almost haphazardly in the frame was never for us—we ourselves were just passing by, and happened to stop. So what if the image was well composed: those yellow plates in the window paired nicely with that green tablecloth, those movements, so calm and careful, of the spoons with their soup, minestrone or tomato, and bringing it to mouths speaking inaudible words—"How is it?" "I'm going to the Cape next weekend. Want to come?"—filling space so well, flitting so fittingly around those inclined heads, everything so charming, but it had all coagulated in its own time, inaccessible to us, now walking on, stamping out each successive moment like a cigarette.

But the city holds yet another vision for the melancholic: the upward gaze, directed toward the sky, shooting out above and beyond the city—the city, from which there is indeed no escape; the buses just keep taking you in a circle (like Warsaw's #100), while the sidewalks lead only to themselves. Thus, melancholy is consumed by divergent ways of seeing. By the arrested gaze and the gaze that reaches beyond, moving out past the city, looking through, *trans-*. We keep walking, and all of a sudden the city spreads out and gains depth. As if the houses had grown another floor, a couple of floors deeper, as if they'd leaned back and unveiled the sky. As if the blade of our vision had sliced the view across its middle. The city has collapsed, cringed, hunkered into its underground garages, shrunken down toward the pebbles under our feet, darkened into the shadows cast at the corner of the eye, and our line of sight has become the starting line from which we will speed away, higher and higher. This is not the Assumption;

we're just looking. Somewhere over the rooftops the gaze discovers a layer of air that dazzles with its clarity; it's not from here, not from there, neither entirely of the city, nor bestowed by the horizon; it unfolds like a cocoon enveloping the earth, enclosing us in the finitude of its space and at the same time drawing us in with its infinite transparency.

Melancholy, melancholia in the city, knows this kind of broken, aborted transcendence. The moment *trans-*, the movement through, cannot be performed, the feet cannot keep up with the head, above which the azure unfurls its distant dome. It unfurls ironically, as Baudelaire writes in "The Swan":

> I see it still, inevitable myth,
>
> Like Daedalus dead-set against the sky—
> the sky quite blue and blank and unconcerned—
> that straining neck and that voracious beak,
> as if the swan were castigating God![90]

It unfurls cruelly, triumphantly, as Stéphane Mallarmé writes in his famous poem, "The Azure":

> But vainly! The Azure triumphs and I hear it sing
> In bells. Dear Soul, it turns into a voice the more
> To fright us by its wicked victory, and springs
> Blue Angelus, out of the living metal core.
>
> It travels ancient through the fog, and penetrates
> Like an unerring blade your native agony;

Where flee in my revolt so useless and depraved?
For I am haunted! The Sky! The Sky! The Sky! The Sky![91]

Baudelaire's swan found no haven in the azure. Can we still discern something of this azure, of this always crystalline blue, in melancholic space? Can we take hold of any part of it? Melancholy will never be transcendence, but—at its limit, in the last circle of its experience—one might approach another passage, a different *trans-*. Let's call it not transcendence, but transparence, a readiness to forget oneself—oneself, the loss one lives by—sheltered under the clear azure. Might something still happen there? Something other than melancholy? Might the future flash across this bare sky, what the poet Piotr Matywiecki calls "the fabric of our eyes"? Is something going to start climbing up toward it? Will some form, some new figure—of place, of time, of life—emerge from that sky, from that infinite transparency, like "a sea of glass like unto crystal" (Revelation 4:6)? No, perhaps not Blake's *Jerusalem*, something smaller, not necessarily everlasting, a small sort of architecture, a quiet and timid utopia, a timid mini-cathedral, a fleeting house of glass. As in Matywiecki's poem, "Cathedral":

I lie, transparent cross,
on earthen, dirty pain—
how am I to trust eternity?

Though from this ground
a cathedral starts to rise,
perhaps never to be completed.[92]

Perhaps never to finish rising, to reach its goal: at every turn, it's unclear whether it's a solid building going up or a little crystal palace that will grow out of the city's melancholia—or perhaps some other new structure.

Crystal Palace (1)

The window broken, you can go right in. And inside, as in that initial drawing from 1851, hundreds of people are standing. It's the grand opening—that's Queen Victoria speaking from the dais between the pavilions marked "India" and "Persia." The view is grand, the palace ending somewhere far in the distance, in the depths, whereas here, in the central hall, you can't even see the ceiling, but only clouds, if those are clouds, past the dome's network of tiny windows. The people, little people, their small silhouettes, crowded not only below but also on balconies, do not manage to fill the space, to cover the trees (they even have palm trees, real ones) pressing in along the sides. The candelabras, the enormous chandeliers, everything's a speck in the enormity of this world, closed fast and at the same time illuminated from within. In other drawings, flags are waving, strange, intricate altars rise up in the middle of the hall, statues are looking all around, and over here— this sculpture dominates the others—an Amazon is being attacked by wolves, the work of a certain *nomen omen* Professor Kiss.

This is how things look in the east wing, and next to the United States exposition, statues, enormous volcanic rocks, a gigantic eagle beneath the vault, a Blackfoot totem pole, a child at its lowest segment, wearing a headdress, staring at something, or else looking out over the entire exhibition, all this stuff, and he with his whole life ahead of him. I really love the drawing with the transept (that's what they called it) down the length of the enormous Hindu pavilion; in the middle, a mighty glass fountain by Follett Osler, palms behind it, and behind them a tall tree stretching out, perhaps of Eastern origin, and to the right a statue of the maharajah on horseback, and farther down the passageway a multitude of smaller white statues, the majority of them nudes, a few angels among them, and above them large, mysterious black creatures in broad robes, difficult to identify in the drawing, stone statues or cloth scarecrows, idols, hobgoblins, belphegors—phantoms of the Louvre.

"The hall is so enormous that the smallest detail assumes the dimensions of an elephant's foot." It's true, the journalist who wrote these words is quite correct, in such enormity of space each detail seems insignificant and, at the same time, highlighted, enlarged. The journalist, by the way, is still alive: he was just here in Warsaw, in March 2006, before the opening of the skyscraper called Rondo I, and he described what he saw in a photo-essay for the newspaper. It just happens that the quotation fits the Crystal Palace to a T, for there is also a great deal of similarity between the plates of the Palace and these newer photographs. A wonderful *déjà vu,* and look at this winter garden, too—you could transport the entire thing from one space to the other— you could water each with the same water.

The Warsaw journalist was delighted by Rondo I and its winter garden, just as its visitors were delighted by the Crystal Palace. Immediately following his visit, a Parisian journalist wrote:

> Imagine a Winter Garden as large as the Tuileries. Here are the enormous, thick trees of Europe, which stretch their crowns beneath transparent vaults, and there a cluster of palm and bamboo bespeaking the Orient [. . .], the Golden Land of the *1001 Nights* [. . .]. Imagine the long miles of carpet, the splendorous crystals, the insanely sumptuous furnishings, bronze, velour, porcelain, fabrics of silver and pearl, jewels worthy of Cleopatra, and all these marvels exhibited in a transparent palace supported by scarcely noticeable columns, and the light, such light, bathing these glittering jewels, those glittering materials, those whispering fountains, and the armies of sculpture [...].

Seventy-four thousand square meters, or four times larger than the footprint of Saint Peter's Basilica in Rome, with seventeen thousand exhibitioners; here was an auspicious building, both in the place where it was erected, in Hyde Park, and on the other end of London, on Sydenham Hill, where it was transported thirty years later. One of its most ecstatic depictions, and at the same time one of its coldest, we owe to Lothar Bucher, a German revolutionary, later a refugee, and later still—as Marshall Berman, a great contemporary admirer of the Crystal Palace, takes pleasure in informing us—an agent for Prussian intelligence, who attempted, unsuccessfully, to bring Karl Marx into the secret service.

Bucher was one of those little people who, in the contemporaneous prints representing the Crystal Palace, is staring from down below into the roof-enclosed sky:

> We see a delicate network of lines, without any clue by means of which we might judge their distance from the eye or their real size. The side walls are too far apart to be embraced in a single glance. Instead of moving from the wall at one end to the wall at the other, the eye sweeps along an unending perspective that fades into the horizon. We cannot tell if this structure towers a hundred or a thousand feet above us, or whether the roof is a flat structure or built to form a succession of ridges, for there is no play of shadows to enable our optic nerves to gauge the measurements.[93]

An art critic visiting the Glass House in Connecticut, designed by Philip Johnson nearly half a century later, would note a similar absence of shadow, but for now we must keep looking straight ahead. Bucher continues:

> If we let our gaze travel downward it encounters the blue-painted lattice girders. At first these occur only at wide intervals; then they range closer and closer together until they are interrupted by a dazzling band of light—the transept—which dissolves into a distant background where all materiality is blended into the atmosphere.[94]

This is a convincing description, a technical description of ascending materials. Perhaps this very process of beatifying engineering—a process because it's thanks to the invasion of light that the Crystal Palace didn't so much exist as become, revealing itself each time anew to those who entered its space—is what brought out such enthusiasm. The building seemed thoroughly innovative, nothing but steel and cast iron woven into a lightweight structure, and right away its novelty underwent its apotheosis—almost literally, since an interior band of light created an aureole within. The innovation consisted of, among other things, keeping architectonic forms to a minimum, instead favoring forms from engineering. Paxton had been a landscape painter, just a bit of an engineer, but essentially a specialist in hothouses and landscape architecture, and in any event he was not an architect per se. What interested him was the project's pure technical challenge, which was then stripped of its formal architectonic complications. Berman writes wonderfully of the Crystal Palace as a "lyrical expression of the potentialities of the industrial age."[95] The slender construction, supported by a scarcely visible scaffolding, with its gently aerodynamic forms, light, ready to take flight, the sky's distant relative, the sky's shimmering lens, the azure's filter and dispenser, gave an impression of poetic ethereality, not of epic durability. From the very beginning, the Palace was supposed to have been a temporary structure, one that took less than four months to build, and like a soap bubble it was only supposed to last a short while, not an eternity, and this is more or less how it went: it lasted quite a bit longer than its creator had designed it for, but it was just a blink of the eye in historical terms. The bubble burst forever in a mysterious fire in 1936, and its vanishing off the face of the earth, when compared with the misadventures, turmoil, and catastrophe that would follow, is an argument that speaks on behalf of the Palace and the relatively pleasant flavor of its demise. Before it perished in flames, however, it traveled. Roberto Salvadori compares it nicely to the "steel castle" in Ariosto's *Orlando Furioso,* which had the magical ability to appear in different places. The Palace itself was moved to another neighborhood of London, and a couple of different versions of it were realized (or not really, since there were many designs) outside of England, one in New York that even shared the same name (1853), one a year later in Munich known as the *Glaspalast.*

The delighted response to the Palace, then, was universal; tourists and architects alike made pilgrimages to the first Crystal Palace in both its locations. The aforementioned Bucher wrote that "the impression [the building] produced on those who saw it was of such romantic beauty that reproductions of it were seen hanging on the cottage walls of remote German villages."[96] Those must have been beautiful visions, if it's true, bright splashes on the rain-saturated Prussian walls, but it was by an entirely different door that the Crystal Palace entered cultural history as an artifact, as a symbol, as a founding site for new utopias, as an invitation to dystopia, as the *genius loci* of modernity—and this door was Russian. This brings us to what is widely known as the great intellectual argument between Fyodor Dostoevsky and Nikolai Chernyshevsky, and it arose due to their conflicting interpretations of the London building. Dostoevsky wrote about it in 1864, in *Notes from Underground,* immediately entering into a polemic with Chernyshevsky, who had written about it in his novel *What Is To Be Done?,* published the previous year. Half a century later, before the First World War, and particularly before its conclusion, the Crystal Palace, as the first construction in which glass, light, and air met in transparent unity, as the first full realization of the glass house, would become almost common currency as the image of a new world, the one that was supposed to arise, since it was no longer possible to go on living like this.

The Crystal Palace's ascendance in the imagination quickly met the needs of modern utopia. As early as Fourier's model of the phalanstery, utopian buildings have been seen as connected by glass galleries. The transparency of form, not merely as an allegory, but as a real material fact, expresses the great millenarian dream of the total reconstruction of the world, of passing into, of jumping into, a new society. It resolves the dichotomy of center and periphery posed in Romantic thought, the dichotomies of multiplicity and particularity, of the masses and the individual, best formulated by Baudelaire and highlighted in Benjamin's reading of his works. In the world of the mass versus discrete units, transparency, which suggests immediate omnipresence, presence both here and there, of myself and the Other, achieves the joining of the whole and the individual, allowing us, as it were, to hammer out a new unity of being in the face of this new vision of vastness.

Chernyshevsky visited the Crystal Palace in 1859, Dostoevsky traveled to London in 1862, and it is likely that both saw the construction once it had already been moved to Sydenham Hill, somewhat larger now, relative to the original (though some argue that Dostoevsky visited an inferior, uglier, much heavier version of the Palace in South Kensington), and both found in it a particular *imago mundi*. For Dostoevsky, it was the image of Western civilization in its already fixed form, almost at its apogee; for Chernyshevsky, it was an image of the civilization to come, heralding the new man. Dostoevsky brought bad news back with him from London and derided the Palace; Chernyshevsky floated away, enraptured. Perhaps we had better begin with the good news.

In his prophesy or dream of the future, Chernyshevsky multiplies the Crystal Palace into hundreds of copies, placed every couple of miles, separated by meadows and woods, creating a new, essentially non-urban space. The cities that had been around up till then would lie somewhere on the sidelines, and authentic, dynamic life would be shifted from those metropolises to these crystal-natural "megastructures," as Berman calls them, neither urban, nor really rural, and highly developed. This vision, in *What Is to Be Done?*, recorded in Vera Pavlovna's dream, opens with the invasion of light proclaimed in Goethe's "May Song": "How bright, how splendid / Is everything! / How the sun shines down, / How the meadows sing!"[97] Things might just be better then, "translucent clouds," "fields glimmering with gold," "the brilliant azure of the sky," and the best words fell to the experiences of the people themselves: "joy," "love," "bliss."[98] There's a lot going on here, a summary of the old times, the history of woman and man, until finally Vera is shown "how people will live," and where they will live.[99]

But this building—what on earth is it? What style of architecture? There's nothing at all like it now. No, there is one building that hints at it—the palace at Sydenham: cast iron and crystal, crystal and cast iron—nothing else. No, that's not all; it's merely the shell of the building, its external façade. Inside there's a real house, a colossal one, surrounded by this crystal and cast-iron edifice as if by a sheath, forming broad galleries around it on every floor. What graceful architecture in the inner house! What narrow spaces between the windows! The windows themselves are huge, wide, and stretch the entire height of each floor. [. . .] There are flowers and trees everywhere. The entire house is a huge winter garden. [. . .] In the dome there hangs a large pane of frosted glass through which light pours into the room.[100]

In these bright spots (for the earth is awash in bright spots) people dance in a thousand pairs, and on "just an ordinary weekday evening" at that, to the music of a one-hundred piece orchestra; they dance briskly, for they are eternally young—in the crystal houses people age slowly or not at all—and they eat together at "splendid place settings" of "aluminum and crystal," and while they're all eating the same thing there are five courses, and they're always served hot.[101] Sure, people work; Chernyshevsky's utopia is social to the core, so people do farm work, with singing, but the labor is a pleasure and doesn't sap you of energy, since from day to day (and this might be the author's most utopian notion, more so than the five hot courses) one is never short of the desire to twist and spin—I can only hope that we're not talking tango here—late into the night in each of these crystal palaces, each having its own separate collective.

This ultra-pastoral utopia, a harbinger of the kolkhoz and the state farm (well, you can forget about the five hot courses every evening), is regarded, despite its rural, anti-urban flavor, as an expression of modernity, of modernity *à la russe*. Transplanting the modern architecture of the West into the territory of the "New Russia," and with it the ethos that one must be, as Rimbaud said, "absolutely modern," Chernyshevsky skipped over the phase of urban capitalism (that is, the developed kind, as he said, in "Parises" and "Londons," or else the sluggish kind, as in "Petersburgs") and immediately created a Russia that was benignly collectivized, naturally happy and technically advanced, at the very forefront of modernism. And one that was not, it happens, so far from the notions of the new West that surrounded the visionary architects of the 1920s. Le Corbusier wrote of the Van Nelle tobacco factory, stretched out across Dutch meadows, as if he were copying his images out of Chernyshevsky:

> The glass begins at sidewalk or lawn level and continues upwards unbroken until it meets the clean line of the sky. The serenity of the place is total. Everything is open to the side. [. . .] [I]nside we find a poem of light. An immaculate lyricism. Dazzling vision of order. The very atmosphere of honesty. Everything is transparent; everyone can see and be seen as he works. [. . .] The male and female workers are clean, in cream-colored overalls and blouses, their hair combed. I found it fascinating to observe the faces of those factory girls. Each one of them was an expression of the life within: joy or the opposite, a reflection of their passions or their difficulties. But, there is no proletariat here. Simply a graduated hierarchy,

clearly established and respected. This atmosphere of a well-run, diligent hive is attained by means of a universal and voluntary respect for order, regularity, punctuality, justice and kindness.[102]

Dostoevsky wasn't fond of the Crystal Palace. It so happens that he wasn't fond of many of the things that he encountered during his travels to the West—not even of Cologne Cathedral. Far from the sense of mystery and infinitude pulsating in Lothar Bucher's description, full of fascination, his impressions, transposed into *Notes from Underground,* seem to address a different building: they are utterly saturated with skepticism, and they speak not about openings, but closings, not about infinitude, but limitation. The Underground Man is horrified by the thought that the "crystal edifice" is "forever indestructible," that eternity has somehow already begun within it, and that there's no longer any way of turning it back; there's no escape, he's already locked inside, where "one can neither put out one's tongue on the sly nor make a fig in the pocket."[103] In fact, the novel's hero only says a few words regarding the building itself, but from them critics have drawn conclusions as to some of Dostoevsky's fundamental social ideas, upon which they have erected entire mental constructs.

Perhaps the most powerful additions to the Underground Man's confessions are offered by Peter Sloterdijk, to whom I have already entrusted a couple of pages, and my dear Jean-Jacques, now that I've washed my hands of him. So before I ask Sloterdijk to speak again, we should recall the watered-down, customary, textbook interpretation of the words Dostoevsky devoted to the

Palace. On the most basic level, it posits a sense of the totalizing, if not totalitarian, nature of Chernyshevsky's utopia, of the eternal inviolability of its laws:

> And it is then—this is still you speaking—that new economic relations will come, quite ready-made, and also calculated with mathematical precision, so that all possible questions will vanish in an instant, essentially because they will have been given all possible answers. Then the crystal palace will get built.[104]

The modernity projected by Chernyshevsky abandons all questioning once and for all, eliminates conflicts and doubts, dismisses the unknown. It assumes an innocent expression of universal purity, which can in no way be disturbed, and which cannot be cast aside. *Consummatum est*, nothing else can happen beyond the eternal return of the same, this self-fulfilling perfection. In Dostoevsky's critique of the Crystal Palace—aimed directly at the relevant passages in *What Is To Be Done?*—we can frequently discern a critique of modernity as such, both in the Russian socialist version promulgated by Chernyshevsky, emphasizing its ultimate achievement, as well as in its occidental, vulgarly rational, mechanistic, and materialistic incarnation. In Dostoevsky's eyes, the Crystal Palace was meant to personify both of these misfortunes of modernity, the plenitude of utopia and the soullessness of rationalism.

For Marshall Berman, Dostoevsky is both right and wrong. He is mistaken "about the Western reality of modernization, which is full of dissonance and conflict, but right about the Russian fantasy of modernization as an end to dissonance and conflict."[105] Dostoevsky's critique of the Crystal Palace is aimed straight at the Russian future; it foresees the coming Soviet totalitarianism and, we might add, is one of the first to present the specter of transparency as enabling almost unlimited political surveillance. The tradition of this alternative critique of transparency as a source of total control continues uninterrupted, parallel to the history of the specter itself, and, begging the patience of Berman and Sloterdijk, I would like to take a moment to note a few facts and examples important for that critique.

The Laboratories of Power

I have already mentioned Milan Kundera's sharp critique of transparency. When he wrote about it twenty years ago, the system of visual control now extant was still in its embryonic stage, and the widespread monitoring of our cities, of streets and the interiors of buildings, was not yet in force. There were not, as there are today in Great Britain (for example), four million cameras installed throughout the country, or one camera for every thirteen people; there was not yet the possibility, devised in one of London's so-called working-class districts, of local residents using the Internet to follow what was happening on neighborhood streets and squares and to inform the police when they noticed something suspicious. Nor was there the intelligent camera we can expect to be available soon, capable of analyzing what takes place within its field of vision, and, if the computer deems it necessary, sound an alarm. For example, if an individual is observed loitering for too long in a particular place, in front of a bank, in the hall of some institution.

But we should take a minute to rewind about two hundred years and return to the first system of universal control based on complete visibility, that is, to the panopticon dreamed up by the philosopher Jeremy Bentham. Eighteenth-century transparency, as existential as it was for the likes of Jean-Jacques, immediately acquired, as they would say, a social function. What would seem a harmless sort of dream becomes embroiled in a concrete project for organizing social life, one in which the ruler can completely control the ruled. Shortly after Rousseau would pronounce his ideal of the utopian, primal clarity of human hearts, and Sterne his metaphor of a glass pane replacing skin, allowing one to see the interior life of other people in all its honesty, Bentham would sketch his vision of the panopticon, an architectonic construct (primarily a prison, perhaps, but also a school and hospital) affording complete visibility of those present inside. This project spatializes the notion of transparency not only by using a large amount of glass—obviously important as a building material—but by the strategic geometry of the design itself, with a central observation tower and the special arrangement of the windows at both ends of each cell. This creates a space that is open (unlike those in a traditional prison, these prisoners are not hidden in the solitude of their cells and deprived of light) and at the same time completely controlled; its basis is the production of complete, unobstructed visibility. Michel Foucault would call it a "laboratory of power," light, bright, and effective.[106] The name, Bentham's unusual invention, was, according to Foucault, a way of "dissociating the see/being seen dyad."[107] In the panopticon, one imagines the eyes that are looking in, but they are never visible to the object of that gaze. The observed person never knows when he is being watched, which makes him feel as though he were being scrutinized all the time and behave as though there were always someone's eyes on him; this essentially fosters constant self-control. Another essential idea for Bentham is that of automatizing the system of visual control: anyone can assume the role of the seeing eye, power becomes anonymous, one employee can replace another. And, finally, a third idea: the system allows for control at multiple levels—the prison is visible, but so too is the guard who enters the cell, and whoever's watching the guard from the central tower may be visible as well. This notion seems to approach something from Kafka's novels, but today it would suffice to enter a modern office, where the walls have been replaced by open spaces, by glass partitions, or where there is at least a rule that you should work with your door open, to be convinced (in the blink of an eye) that Bentham's panopticon is emerging in later democratic spaces.

In Russia, glass houses, as spaces for an impossible existence, would appear in Yevgeny Zamyatin's dystopian novel *We,* and transparency itself would appear as the imperative of the police state in another dystopia, Nabokov's *Invitation to a Beheading,* written in 1934 and published in book form in 1938. The novel is set in the not-too-distant, but decadent, future of a world edging toward collapse, and Nabokov's diagnosis of this society, in which its hero, Cincinnatus C., is being investigated for a lack of transparency, surely refers not only to Russia, but to all of the totalitarian regimes that took power in Europe following the First World War. Cincinnatus C. is therefore locked in a fortress and sentenced to death, because, in contrast to all the citizens who are transparent (and more homogenized, barely distinguishable, nearly interchangeable, and thus extremely automatized), he, the victim of "gnostical turpitude," poses an obstacle, is impenetrable, "impervious to the rays of others"; he casts a shadow and therefore gives "a bizarre impression, as of a lone dark obstacle in this world of souls transparent to one another."[108] This has been going on since he was a child, as if caused by some genetic flaw: "In the midst of the excitement of a game his coevals would suddenly forsake him, as if they had sensed that his lucid gaze and the azure of his temples were but a crafty deception and that actually Cincinnatus was opaque."[109] At the same time, he alone seems alive in this meager, shoddy world (everything here is so-so: not just the people, but the furnishings too), and he alone is conscious of this fact: "I am the one among you who is alive—not only are my eyes different, and my hearing, and my sense of taste—not only is my sense of smell like a deer's, my sense of touch like a bat's— but, most important, I have the capacity to conjoin all of this in one point [. . .]."[110] At the moment of his execution, death seems to afflict this entire "transparent world" just as it does Cincinnatus himself. Everything collapses, the gale scatters the ruins and scraps, and at that point, "amidst the dust, and the falling things, and the flapping scenery, Cincinnatus made his way in that direction where, to judge by the voices, stood beings akin to him."[111]

Which is no doubt to say non-transparent, authentic, individual beings, not embroiled in some destructive community of openness. Cincinnatus reaches his own kind; the transparent nightmare ends with his death or sleep (it's not actually clear whether he has perished or not). Anyone who discerns in transparency one of those most horrifying phantasms that support fascism, communism, or other more or less authoritarian forms of government or social organization will find it unmasked relatively early in Nabokov.

In Nabokov, we do not have glass buildings, but glass souls. At the time he was writing his novel, however, such buildings were already standing in the cities, already sprouting up in books and gleaming in movies. There was no need of the kind of visionary recognition of danger that the imperative or notion of transparency brings; all one needed was to visit one of those buildings. One of them, also from the early thirties, the work of Pierre Chareau (we'll spend more time there soon), looked completely innocent when it was quietly erected off the Rue Saint-Guillaume in Paris. And yet after his first visit to the building in 1934, Pierre Vago, a correspondent for *L'architecture d'aujourd'hui*, wrote:

> Does the man of the twentieth century really have to spend his days and leisure time in a glass box, among scattered columns, in a laboratory open on all sides, under the eye of the nurse (the servant, the secretary) following us from her glass cage; to receive his roast from a cart that slides down, to take a moving ladder up to his bedroom, to admit daylight through a partition made of

glass bricks, through which the bluest sky and the loveliest weather become tarnished and gray?[112]

In 1926, two years after Żeromski had, in his novel *The Coming Spring*, presented the protagonists' utopian dream of living in glass houses, Sergei Eisenstein wrote his screenplay for a film called just that, *The Glass House*. The idea allegedly came to him while he was living in Berlin, a city where glass architecture had established important footholds; Eisenstein wanted to film in the Hotel Hassler, where glass had been used as a basic building material. The film was never made; all we have are a few sketches. In them, one can see silhouettes sitting in glass squares, rooms or cages. Ivor Montagu, Eisenstein's friend at the time, wrote:

> The idea was this [. . .]. People live, work and have their being in a glass house. In this great building it is possible to see all around you: above, below, sideways, slanting, in any direction unless, of course, a carpet, a desk, a picture or something like that should interrupt your line of sight.
>
> Possible, I have said—but in fact people do not so see, because it never occurs to them to look. [. . .] Then, suddenly, something occurs to them to make them look, to make them conscious of their exposure. They become furtive, suspicious, inquisitive, terrified.[113]

Eisenstein wanted to show that life dies in an environment of extreme transparency, unnoticeably, slowly, but absolutely. A note to the last, sixth section reads: "impossibility of going on without demolishing the glass house."[114]

The Crystal Palace (2)

It's interesting that, as a new architectural material, glass serves two utterly contradictory political systems both in Eisenstein's time and later. In *Architecture and Democracy,* Claude Bragdon concludes that glass architecture makes an excellent contribution to strengthening democracy. In the spirit of Chernyshevsky, and especially of Scheerbart, he argues that illuminating buildings through large panoramic windows fosters a sense of togetherness, of fraternity among people. The greater visibility fostered by large windows and abundant light augments the democratic process; the light that comes through the windows to the interior of offices and apartments arouses a need for transparency in our dealings with each other, the atmosphere in which democracy is supposed to flourish. Literal visibility promotes figurative visibility, the social kind, in the workings of the state, the administrative system, finance, and so on.

But let's return to Berman and his interpretation of *Notes from Underground.* Ultimately, he concludes that Dostoevsky objected solely to "a modernization of trouble-free but deadening routines"—one that washes away all negation, suffering, and doubt—but that he was not opposed to and did not condemn the entire package of modernity, understood as a risky venture.[115] If he had only taken a good look at the West (instead of blindly attacking the Crystal Palace), he would have seen that it was free of all routine, as were the uncrystallized yet undeniable cities that Chernyshevsky shoved to the margins, like Dostoevsky's beloved Saint Petersburg, whose irregular, sprawling construction, cut through by a river and bridges, happily lent itself to the notion of unification through glass. In arguing for Dostoevsky's ambivalent relationship to modernity, accepting it as adventure but rejecting it as routine, Berman refers us to the words of the Underground Man:

> Man loves to create and build roads, that is beyond dispute. But may it not be that he is instinctively afraid of attaining his goal and completing the edifice he is constructing? How do you know, perhaps he only likes that edifice from a distance and not at close range, perhaps he only wants to build it, and does not want to live in it.[116]

In these words, the Crystal Palace finds justification as a new form through whose conception man develops, throws himself into unknown, dangerous adventures, and at the same time is condemned, if the only, ultimate result is to be the Palace itself.

Dostoevsky's utopia interested him, maybe even hypnotized him, like an evil basilisk whose gaze one must ward off. And he did ward it off: he read Fourier, admitted his system's "beauty" and "rigor," but also its "unrealizeable" and, ultimately, "killingly funny" character.[117] In *Notes from the House of the Dead*—in one of the later-discovered drafts—he formulates the allegory of a palace made of marble and gold where, despite all its luxuries, one cannot live, simply because one cannot leave. Later, the theme of the Golden Age would return in his novels with redoubled force, revealing its own ambivalent power. Dosto-evsky never stopped being tormented by the question of free-dom hidden within utopias, even the most enticing of them. For the aforementioned Sloterdijk, however, there is no ambivalence in Dostoevsky. The most important thing in his rejection of the Crystal Palace is his premonition of "the end of history" that oc-curs in Western civilization at the moment it sets off on the path of violent industrialization, and which shapes highly developed capitalist society; there's no room here for tolerance and nuance, for admiring the daring in the construction; you board the train to utopia solely by your will to analyze evil, not by dreaming of five hot meals a day.

For Sloterdijk reading Dostoevsky, or else for Dostoevsky as read by Sloterdijk, the Crystal Palace personifies—it quite liter-ally embodies, as a space/accumulation—the hyper-consumer spirit of the West. It is "an emblem for the final ambitions of modernity," the logic of which inevitably entails "the world's coming into the world," pinning it down to a single time and place, generalized and generally accessible.[118] Chernyshevsky's pre-communist utopia is essentially conducive to the project of fulfillment contained in modern consumer society. "The vision-aries of the nineteenth century," Sloterdijk writes, "like the com-munists in the twentieth century, had already understood that social life after the end of combatant history could only play out in an extensive interior, an interior space ordered like a house and endowed with an artificial climate."[119] Sloterdijk plays a bit with Dostoevsky's thinking, turning the latter's diagnoses into theories when, for Dostoevsky, there had been concrete and not too conceptual experience; for example, Sloterdijk blithely calls Dostoevsky's internment in a labor camp, what Dostoevsky calls an "enclosed palace" in *Notes from the House of the Dead*, a "thought experiment" (Małgorzata Łukasiewicz, Sloterdijk's Polish translator, admitted that she was furious at having to render those words), as if Dostoevsky then, and Sloterdijk now, were experimenting with thought in an equal and comparable way.[120] No, Dostoevsky knew hard labor firsthand, in the closed space of a prison camp; he was not experimenting but seeing, and wanting to survive. The traumas of what he had lived through in Siberia must have crept into his diagnosis of the Crystal Palace; in this sense, it was surely no mere intellectual speculation, but also, indirectly, a repeat broadcast from the house of the dead. Admittedly, it has by now lost the gravity of suffering, but, tempered accordingly, it has gained intellectual acuity, especially in its deep, prophetic understanding of historical process.

The Crystal Palace serves, then, as the architectural materialization of both ideas: the humanistic-sentimental commune (under Chernyshevsky's pen), as well as—and this most of all—Western consumer culture, whose bases for existence Dostoevsky managed, here, to foresee. This is why Dostoevsky's thinking about fulfillment and limitation, which accompany his description at every turn, whether in *Notes from Underground* or, we might add, in his "notes" from his trip to London, can be so easily related to the twentieth-century thematics of post-historicism. Here Dostoevsky writes:

> Yes, the Exposition is striking. You feel a terrible force that has united all these people here, who come from all over the world, into a single herd; you become aware of

a gigantic idea; you feel that here something has already been achieved [. . .]. No matter how independent you might be, for some reason you become terrified. "Hasn't the ideal in fact been achieved here?" you think. "Isn't this the ultimate, isn't it in fact the 'one fold'?"[121]

The ultimate, the fulfillment, the achievement of one's goal: the language of enclosure maps out Dostoevsky's underlying experience and his interpretation of the Crystal Palace. Sloterdijk writes:

> This gigantic hothouse of detente is dedicated to a cheerful and hectic cult of Baal, for which the 20th century has proposed the term consumerism. The capitalistic Baal, which Dostoyevsky thought he had recognized in the shocking sight of the World Exhibition Palace and the London pleasure-seeking masses, did not take shape any less in the building itself than in the hedonistic turbulence that dominated its interior. Here, a new doctrine of Final Things is formulated as a dogmatics of consumption. [. . .] [T]he enormous Crystal Palace—the valid prophetic building form of the nineteenth century (which was immediately copied around the world)—already pointed to an integral, experience-oriented, popular capitalism, in which nothing less was at stake than the complete absorption of the outer world into an inner space that was calculated through and through.[122]

In other words, the *indoors,* which in the twentieth century will, to an ever-increasing degree, replace outdoor space and concentrate life—especially since the 1950s, when the first shopping malls, huge mercantile centers, and closed arcades, started to appear in the United States—first everyday life, then athletic and artistic life, and then every life.

Here I could toss Sloterdijk the description—proof of crypto-colonialism, of the super-smooth pacification of the whole world, of the replacement of transcendence with mood—of yet another glass palace, one that was illuminated especially powerfully, the one that served as home to the 1900 World's Fair. Paul-Armand Silvestre wrote at the time:

> A quintuple polychrome vision awaits the spectator to whom appears in different directions Europe, which the rosy fires of dawn tint; Asia, where the gold dust of the dogstar burns; Africa, where the sun dies in a red wave of blood; America, lost in the vapor of pale hyacinths and violets of the twilight; Oceanica, finally, where the moon plunges as it were into the sparkling and at the same time somber dust of the lapis lazuli. Thus the Old World and the New will revive in their plastic evocation what I might call the five ages of light.[123]

In a novel published a little earlier, Emile Zola took great delight in describing a visit to the trade gallery, the *grand magasin,* the harbinger of today's shopping malls:

> The architect, who happened to be an intelligent one, a young man enchanted with the new age, had used stone only for the basements and the pillars at the corners, other-

wise constructing the whole framework of iron, with columns supporting the assemblage of beams and joists. [...] Space had been gained everywhere, air and light entered freely, and the public wandered around at ease beneath the bold vaults of the widely spaced trusses. [. . .] And all this cast iron beneath the white light of the glass roof composed an airy architecture of complicated lacework which let the daylight through—a modern version of a dream palace, a Tower of Babel with storey upon storey and rooms expanding, opening on vistas of other storeys and other rooms reaching to infinity.[124]

A contemporaneous ad for glass houses, mass-produced by a certain construction firm, takes up the idea of the happy interior that sucks the outside world in: "Live as if in a garden, near to nature, and experience in full the charms of every season, all the while without forgoing the comforts of the modern interior: here is the new version of Heaven on Earth, furnished entirely by glass houses."

Sloterdijk has also adapted the metaphor of the Crystal Palace to the new historical situation of Poland as a member of the European Union. He has remarked (in conversation with Maciej Nowicki) that Poles, too, "will find their happiness there," happiness according to the model of Western democracy, guaranteed by separation, produced by the wall removing it from what is outside (that is, the non-Western, peripheral, impoverished, flipside world).[125] *Intra muros,* inside the Palace, the wonderland of consumerism will be achieved, for Poles too, exchanging their old metaphysical desires for physical desires, their discourse of infinitude (of the soul, of the cosmos) for the discourse of infinite fulfillment, of endless consumption. In this exchange we see the advance of Western nations, those that first formulated the "great culture of metaphysical fulfillment" through which consumer desires only developed all the more easily—though the Palace's newer guests will also succumb to them in due course.

In his remarks on the Crystal Palace, Sloterdijk develops his theory of the "capitalist interior," its foundations laid by Benjamin. But Sloterdijk faults Benjamin for not having realized the philosophical-historical potential of the metaphor of the Crystal Palace, so enthusiastically did he interpret the Parisian arcades as a key to understanding "the capitalist state of the world." He believes that Benjamin chose his architectural space poorly, yet it was on the basis of that choice that he worked out the laws governing capitalist society. The arcades themselves didn't have this prophetic power; their forms were already inscribed in the past. Indeed, visited today, the arcades of Paris, which happen to be increasingly empty, off the path of tourists and locals alike, as well as the arcades that imitate them, such as those in Bucharest, reek of nostalgia and the past. They are overrun with little antique shops, used books, century-old postcards, knickknacks, coffee served in wavy, delicate china. Then and now, in Baudelaire's lifetime and later Benjamin's, in our modern time, time flows backwards in these arcades, it withdraws along the pins of music boxes, it floats away on the pendulums of old clocks. But do we really want to recognize today's shopping malls as the last, ultimate incarnation of the Crystal Palace? The comparison is enticing, and the arcades' interiors so inviting, so manifold and warm, a paradise on earth, the Lord's own aquarium, packed so seductively with all the goods of the world, with colorful flavors and images, objects that open themselves to the touch, leave little more to add, little more to obtain. On a Saturday afternoon, among hundreds of people wandering the galleries, sitting at one of the many cafés there, each next-door to the other, eager and at ease, with abandon, we surrender to the hypnosis of this space, which draws us in so magically, so welcomingly, making its dome into a new sky, a fairytale constellation, the roof of the world lowered to our horizons. Leave the cosmos on the outside, leave that other life out there as well, we no longer wish to leave, we pass from one storefront to the next, here's Banana Republic, there's H&M, and yet another café, we'll soak up the atmosphere that's been installed here, just another feature of the design, cramming the whole world under one dome.

But then it was Scheerbart and Benjamin who said: as much light as possible, but as few *things*—this calls for a new project. And Maeterlink, in his famous poem "Hothouse," is simultaneously enraptured and terrified by his vision of a world enclosed once and for all; he is spellbound and, at the same time, enchanted by the hothouse made of glass:

> A hothouse deep in the woods,
> doors forever sealed. Analogies:
> everything under that glass dome,
> everything under my soul.

Thoughts of a starving princess,
a sailor marooned in the desert,
fanfares at hospital windows. [. . .]

[. . .] cripples halted in the fields
on a day of sunshine, the smell of ether.

My God, when will the rain come,
and the snow, and the wind, to this glass house![126]

Three Houses

Throughout the world, many houses have been built that have been given the "glass" label, most often Glass House, *maison de verre*, *Glashaus*, *Glasbau*. For them, the Crystal Palace remains a mythic, foundational inspiration, the matrix from which these glass progeny have arisen; at a certain point in architectural history, the glass house became a sort of challenge, a test of one's technical and artistic skill, like the still life in painting. The first generations of twentieth-century architects enthusiastically tackled glass projects as a universal challenge to the imagination, and their struggle with glass continues, taken up by subsequent generations, to this day, fought first on computer screens in successive versions of programs like AutoCAD and ArchiCAD, and then, unfortunately, on the streets of our cities. They are still tormenting us: glass has become a material so facile, accessible, and workable that, deprived of Scheerbart-esque inspiration, instead of opening and constructing a new world for us, it has begun to exchange its ideals and ideas for commercial banalities. Only a few of these buildings support all the words I've expended here and ennoble their meek syllables.

One of the first realizations of glass architecture, a classic today, was the *Glasbau*—the Glass Pavilion—in Cologne, the work of Bruno Taut, a member of the group *Die Gläserne Kette*—The Glass Chain—designed and constructed shortly after the appearance of Paul Scheerbart's book, which he had dedicated to Taut. Bruno Taut, also known by the nickname "Glas," adorned his building with aphorisms from Scheerbart, such as: "glass initiates a new era," "without a Glass Palace life becomes a burden," "colored glass triumphs over hatred," "light needs crystal," "the culture of brick arouses our compassion," and the aforementioned "in a glass house . . . vermin must be unknown." Besides the Cologne pavilion, the story of transparency—our version of it, at least—includes the designs for the crystal mountain, *der Kristallberg*, which form part of Taut's beautifully titled book, *Alpine Architecture*. Rising above the wooded slopes of the Alps, it looks like a structure made of transparent polyhedrons, the shape of the highest of these immediately calling to mind the polyhedron from Dürer's *Melancholia I*. Both Dürer's image and Taut's buildings, connected by the similarity of their ostensible material and traversing the opposition between nature and culture, participate in erecting "the lofty cathedral of the future," an idea that Bruno Taut borrowed from Scheerbart and further poeticized, socialized, and anarchized.

Le Corbusier would soon design his own particular, if less glassy, versions of glass houses, and their emergent aesthetic would also be used often by the architects and artists of the group called Bauhaus, among whom we must mention the name of Walter Gropius, the co-creator of, among other things, the half-glass Fagus factory (1911, with Adolf Meyer) and the famous building simply called "Bauhaus." Gropius was riding the same wave of enthusiasm as Scheerbart and Taut when he announced:

> Together let us desire, conceive, and create the new structure of the future, which will embrace architecture and sculpture and painting in one unity and which will one day rise toward heaven from the hands of a million workers like the crystal symbol of a new faith.[127]

One of the most distinguished glass buildings, the first of our three, stands to this day in Paris and was erected in the early thirties by Pierre Chareau, Le Corbusier's pupil and sometime adversary, an architect of interiors assisted by the Dutch architect Bernard Bijvoet. Today, though it remains occupied and has been designated a cultural landmark by UNESCO, it is only open to a small number of visitors capriciously selected after many letters and recommendations. "Dear Sir: I have a Hopper reproduction on my wall; in light of same, would you consider inviting me into your home . . .?" The house provoked strong reactions from the start, and during the war it became famous for the fact that the German command, attracted by its renown, wanted to set up offices there but had to abandon this plan on account of the need to black the building out in case of an air raid, which Chareau's design made impossible.

Chareau did not refer to Scheerbart as Taut had, but he did express himself in the same spirit, ascribing a new function to architecture, that of leading society into the future. "An Architect cannot create," he wrote in 1936, "if he does not listen to and understand the voices of millions of people, if he does not suffer their hardships, if he does not fight to free them from hardship."[128] French-American architect Paul Nelson spoke of Chareau's house as the first example of modern architecture, in that it becomes its own meaning, its own basis, and not just a necessity or ornament. Nelson underscores that Chareau introduces the fourth dimension—time. His house is not still or photographic, but cinematographic; thanks to the play of transparency and translucence (the walls, both interior and exterior, consist partially of panes of "Colorado" glass, more translucent than transparent), there is a dynamic effect that gives a sense of movement, of being transferred from one frame of film to another. Someone once called Chareau's house "a light-making machine." When artificial light beams from inside to outside, the house transforms into a magical nightlight; and when subsequently illuminated by the floodlights installed in the courtyard, the interior becomes engulfed in a polar night. The transparency here was never literal, never a given. Chareau himself even compared his translucent walls to tent canvas—that of nomads. Here, transparency is an "architectural membrane," as architecture folks say, a means for modulating light, for directing it. Its use doesn't eliminate spheres of darkness, recesses, shadows, doesn't indicate a boundary between interior and exterior.

In Chareau's house, the space is partially open, but it is delicately and precisely appointed, and it operates on such ingenious angles of perception that it seems to shift under your feet like a moveable walkway, a zone for continuous walking, if only so that one might always view the whole from a new perspective. Seen from outside, it can even be surprising that the Chareau house counts as glass architecture, but it earns this designation through the interior's use of transparent walls and by the interplay of its floors.

Yes, from the outside, the Chareau house is, in spite of everything, not so alluring, not enough to blow all those millions on, even when you enter through the gate and finally reach the façade, itself "normal," nothing special. It's only the interior, between the floor and the ceiling, the kitchen and the corridor, that reveals its intelligence and taste, that lets the space breathe, that takes in the full light from outside while still hiding a bit from the light itself. Whatever one thinks about the ideas of its creator, it is nevertheless functional, clever, sharp, despite being forced into the cramped Parisian landscape, blocked in to left and right by other buildings; it seems a bit like an artificial paradise, around which the monotonous daily grind is pulsating, people with shadows for faces zipping into the metro, errant hobos making camp for the night and rolling their empty bottles up to the gate.

To get to our second glass house, you have to sail across the ocean, move quickly over some meadows, take Route 61, then head along the border of oaks and one sequoia that Ponus Ridge Road twists around, and then a few meters later, on the right, or maybe it's the left, the town called New Canaan emerges—New Canaan, as if we're starting life all over again. Groups of sightseers used to make pilgrimages there, stopping traffic with their long Pontiacs with Statues of Liberty and nude mermaids on their hoods; even today, there's no lack of visitors. Philip Johnson started constructing the Glass House, quite famous within the genre of glass houses, toward the end of the 1940s, and it took a long time, into the following decade. Canaan wasn't built in a day, and neither was New Canaan. One day, when Frank Lloyd Wright came to pay a visit, he is alleged to have asked "whether he should take his hat off or leave it on."[129]

Although Johnson started his work later than the prewar glass avant-garde, he regarded himself as continuing their legacy, as a reader of Scheerbart, an admirer of Taut, a pupil of the great Ludwig Mies van der Rohe, the symbolic father he had to exorcise from within himself and, of course—more on this a little later—obliterate. Unlike Chareau, who was more focused on the practical side of his design, Johnson subordinates functionality to art; the Glass House quickly became an object around which there was much heated discussion regarding architectural form as a source of beauty and form as a source of meaning and practical use. The house sometimes looks like an unpopulated glass island in a sea of green, an abstract Aphrodite made of colorless chlorophyll; sometimes like a glassy, undissolved ice cube, a block that dropped out of some strange space odyssey. Even today it remains a bone—a bone fragment—of contention, one of those places that become catalysts for architects formulating their own understanding of their profession and interpretation of their own work.

In Johnson's house—his own house (he came here, lived here, worked here)—material transparency—literal transparency—

receives distinct emphasis over virtual, conceptual transparency. One of the most famous and beautiful pictures of the Glass House shows Johnson's small silhouette from behind, sitting at a desk, itself ultra-thin, as if designed by Giacometti (it happens that a Giacometti sculpture was the first prop installed there), while all around glass surfaces rise up high, broad, three-dimensional, interpenetrating, casting mirror images onto each other, absorbing the surrounding trees as amber does insects. They are joined together by numerous glass echoes, by so many reflections that we no longer know where this house, where this box, one hundred and sixty-seven square meters and seventeen meters long, begins and ends, where the trees are growing, where their roots are planted, where to find the roof of this world—in glass, or in the sky. Johnson called his house—or once called his house, for how many times can one revisit such a metaphor—"a celestial elevator in which when it snows, you seem to be going up because everything is coming down."[130] There's nothing pantheistic about this obvious lightness, however: nothing melts here, nothing loses its contours, nothing goes *au natural.*

Crucial for Johnson's entire project is the gaze—and not only in winter—from inside, from that purified space without walls or partitions, not counting the brick cylinder concealing the bathroom. Through the panoramic window-façades, one sees the landscape all around, a wooded garden, well maintained, carefully arranged. And one has the impression (as Paul Goldberger did) that this is a perfectly enclosed space, with nothing beyond it. Then there's a strange illusion of enormity and, at the same time, of finitude. It's not just that you can simply leave this house and move out into the world, but that it seems when we are looking through the windows that the house was created precisely to be left, that it was built in order to make our departure into its surroundings, which promise a magnificent adventure somewhere beyond, that much smoother, that much simpler. At the same time, one gets a counter-impression that arrests this expansion: as you stare into it more deeply, this outside world seems increasingly fictional, sketched out, over-designed, like the elegant furniture inside the house. More than the house's shapes and overall appearance, the detractors of Johnson's design faulted him for the appearance of the grounds, precisely arranged, "manicured," composed. But this is perhaps how it had to be, or how we would have wanted it. Sculpting the terrain, drawing it into view, recalls the arrangement of an aquarium, that is, the miniaturization of the world, making it enchanting, slipping it into the palm of the hand.

The enchanted world, the bewitched visitors: when you're picturing this house through others' eyes, when you drop in at an ideal hour—one moment walking through Skaryszewski Park, a moment later sailing across the ocean—you get the impression that you could live there, sitting in Giacometti's chairs and staring out the windows at the maples and the lawns, at that lone sequoia, an epiphany of transparency that, in a moment or two (because you have to cross back over the ocean: dusk is falling on the park), will have gathered, will have essentially condensed all of its bliss, permitted itself to be saturated with it, allowed it to flow into your pupils. Then the house will seem a new *Nautilus,* a ship half-made of air, levitating among the scraps of time, as if Chronos were puffing them languidly from a pipe. Fine, then—we're talking about the impression that the house won't endure, but rather gently vibrates and leads us somewhere, which seems to answer Johnson's intention not so much to outline a space, as he puts it, as to organize it, to introduce it into a "temporal or spatial succession," which he himself calls "procession."[131]

Johnson's Glass House started to take shape shortly after Mies van der Rohe constructed the third—ours and his own—glass house, called Farnsworth House, in Illinois. Van der Rohe—the leading figure in pre- and postwar architecture, one of the first great promoters of glass as a building material, already the creator of undulating glass walls and roofs in glass skyscrapers in the twenties and thirties, as well as the author of the fantastic design for a glass skyscraper at Berlin's Friedrichstrasse Station (1921), and then the German Pavilion in Barcelona, a kind of Doric glass temple, and the model for the "Glass Room" displayed in Stuttgart in 1927.

Somewhat narrower than the house by Johnson, his pupil, barely twenty-three meters by nine, but standing on pilings to protect it from flooding, the Farnsworth House seems more elegant, more purist; constructed according to van der Rohe's famous adage that "less is more," it was to give the impression of being the quintessence of the minimum, a rigorous lack. Different people have described the house differently: for example, as a crystal etui, or as a clean geometric object, or as "practically nothing" suspended in space. Its proponents praise its extreme minimalist aesthetic, which later vanished from Johnson's version. In their judgment, Johnson gave van der Rohe's "cultural vision of constructive structure" a formalist, or rather a decorative, interpretation; this especially concerns the load-bearing elements. For these critics,

Johnson's house is "dead mannerism," "a stylistic exercise," devoid of Mies's metaphysics. They would have surely said the same of Robert Konieczny's design for the glass house near Opole that in 2006 won the prestigious House of the Year Award from *World Architectural News* and was nominated for Europe's highest architectural honor, named for, *nomen omen*, Mies van der Rohe; at any rate, Mies's legacy weighs heavily on Konieczny's work, as it did also on Johnson's design.

Yet, as attested by many who have visited and compared them, van der Rohe's house is much less attractive and inviting than Johnson's. Indeed, as the noted sociologist and architecture critic Richard Sennett has described his visit, the severity of the surroundings, not to mention the snakes in the mud by the eight steel piles, quickly arouse the desire to climb into the house and to hide there, but once inside, the feeling of being sheltered doesn't last long; there, it seems that the presence of people is entirely accidental, that nothing could actually live there. This sense of the building's solitude and alienation flows from the impression that the white Farnsworth House is a sculpted form that has been placed in nature, whereas Johnson's darker house seems a part of it. Otherwise, in Sennett's opinion—he having rushed inside to get away from the snakes—because of the unusual height of the glass walls in Mies's house, because of the peculiar interplay of the proportion between them and the wooden pedestal, of how furnishings have been arranged, it's impossible to imagine anybody dozing off or indulging in reading the newspaper while scarfing down bacon-flavored potato chips, sitting on the armchairs that stand there so proudly. Such everyday gestures of domestic life strike him as quite obscene here. "It is a modern expression of the sublime," Sennett concludes.[132]

This is why Sennett believes that Mies van der Rohe went too far; he created a work that was purist, clean, elegant, but so isolated that none of these merits could redeem that seclusion. Anyway, Mies had done it before, as he was designing his first skyscrapers, imagining them as isolated, closed towers, alone on the horizon. Though he regarded himself as an innovator utterly outside of tradition, he essentially remained, *volens nolens*, a Romantic, a dark Romantic, in the sense that he sanctioned the division between an artist, the lonely passerby enclosed within his own interior journey, as well as his collective, social surroundings (on the one hand)—and inhospitable, hostile, threatening nature (on the other). He availed himself of modern building materials, but he reenacted Romantic oppositions, the incommensurability of interior and external life. This kind of isolation produces an architecture of spiritual solitude, a cold aesthetic; it has something of the inhuman, of the inaccessible.

We will not argue with Sennett over whether van der Rohe was a closet Romantic; we might just as well think of the second half of the nineteenth century, of the hermetic poetry of Mallarmé, of his idea of the poem-crystal, to which no one has access, not even the author; this closed poem, transparent on all sides, is composed of words crystallized from language like coal from plant matter. And we can see Mies van der Rohe's house as an extract of transparency, which he drew from its invisibility and framed, that it might not withdraw back into its sanctuary, into the hidden *diaphanes*, into its sleepy existence in the substance of all things.

Mies did not create so much as he issued decrees; in his interiors, every change, the shifting of so much as a single element, destabilizes the entire arrangement and all proportion. The house itself, which Sennett calls "solipsism of incomparable elegance," was, through the use of transparent glass, supposed to remove the opposition between interior and exterior. But, according to Sennett, Mies fell victim to his own purity; proclaiming the unity of space, he deepened its division. In his building, there is something excessively dramatic, overwhelming, but in its "inhumanity" there is something sacral and thus, in its own way, religious (as someone else might say of Parnassus): even a work that rose up from the depths of solitary experience assumes objective qualities, is inhuman, does not belong to us, is already inviolable, beyond any potential for participation or intervention. This is why the Farnsworth House, while so similar to Johnson's Glass House in its exterior form, achieves a completely different level of focus—it is a foreign, sublime body in nature, a kind of architectural monad, magical and hypnotic, encased securely in glass.

To Mies van der Rohe's "Romantic" (and, I would say, still thinking of Mallarmé's poetry, "symbolic") use of glass in the Farnsworth House, Sennett opposes his own understanding of "modern" glass. He was helped in this less by terminology than by whiskey. One evening, he had gone to a reception on Chicago's Lake Shore Drive, to the glass skyscraper designed by van der Rohe. On an upper floor, among glass walls that also served as windows, the reception was getting off to a slow start, it was still mostly empty, and Sennett was feeling, as always, uneasy in Mies's space. Until eventually things became noisy and so crowded that he found himself pressed against the walls, the dark masses of Lake Michigan swirling in the abyss below. If anyone else showed up, he thought, he'd be seized with terror of falling into the void; visually, there was nothing there to protect him. But he soon noticed that, like a mirror, the glass reflected the quivering wave of guests, and his anxiety passed; after all, Sennett was himself a part of this wave. He recalled (third whiskey) Baudelaire's notion that it is only in feeling exposed to danger that we feel alive. And then (fourth whiskey or second Manhattan) he felt at home in Mies's space. The pane was both a window and a mirror at the same time; through the experience of defeat, of terror, Mies's space took on another dimension. And Sennett (third Manhattan or first screwdriver) grasped the modern and, at the same time, positive meaning of glass. It is bound up with the ambiguity inscribed inside it, with the fact that it's a site of exchange between inside and outside, a place where space is violated and defeated, but also a place worthy of marking a boundary and defending it. "And I suppose this is why plate glass is so interesting," Sennett writes, "now a window on nothing, a mirror of solitude, its possibilities have yet to be explored in the practice of an unambiguous, permeable, violating, warm, and thus truly modern art."[133] Here is the perhaps too synthetic perspective that brings together the merits of our three houses and smooths out, somewhat, the differences between them, between their three desires.

For if we were to place our three houses on the same imaginary street, somewhere between Skaryszewski Park and Abbey Road, we would have our pick, well, not of the litter, but of transparency in all its stages. Mies van der Rohe's house, an aesthetic of disappearance, hermetic, a form unknown to life, an inaccessible monad in which one can seal oneself up, best of all on a Sunday when a sudden emptiness steals into even the most complicated existence, to seal itself up there and go on in the essence of its own desire, at the zenith of its own obsession, in the pure crystal of abstraction, at the world's edge, beyond any social or biographical "I." Philip Johnson's house, born of a similar aesthetic, but entering into a dialogue with space, ultimately belonging to this world, installing its transparency within as its *modus vivendi*, not *absendi*, separating itself from its surroundings so as to be more a part of them, a terrestrial *Nautilus*, fascinated but friendly, a warm observer. Chareau's house, wound like a snail into its own shell, but exposing to the world its innumerable watchful eyes, a well-managed space, perfect for spinning yarns about glass before stepping out for a baguette or to do some shopping at the little market a few steps away. Which should we choose, all of them so lovely. "Let's just go for a walk," Olga says, and slips on her shoes. The construction firm Warbud S.A. is building something new down by the park again—there will be verandas facing out toward the lake, we'll have to take a good look. How many years can you go on living in the same cluttered little hole in old Grochów?

Rowe and Slutzky

On this note, having brought up these three houses and Warbud S.A. (or perhaps J.W. Construction or Budimex Inc.), I must mention what is perhaps the most important text on transparency for theoreticians of architecture. It comes to us from the silver pens of Colin Rowe and Robert Slutzky. It is entitled "Transparency: Literal and Phenomenal," and by the very arrangement of its title it explains that there are other dimensions of glass architecture, more difficult to discern—literally invisible at first glance.

Rowe and Slutzky tell us that the majority of people, including art historians, associate transparency in architecture solely with the transparency of the materials used, whereas no less essential, though less obvious, and perhaps even deeper, though it is the default condition, is phenomenal transparency, which refers to the kind that emerges from the structure, that shows through in the layering of one plane atop another. A design's individual planes allow it to pass between them, submit to it, are strung along it as though on a beam of light. One can find such a configuration in Cubist painting, and Picasso's paintings, such as *L'Arlésienne*, are among the best examples; Picasso (as well as Léger, and Braque, or Gris, or Ozenfant) painted successive surfaces one on top of the other, and they look as if they're made of celluloid; no given surface is inert or frozen—the viewer may come away with the impression that he's looking straight through them.

We get a similar impression, Rowe and Slutzy tell us, when we stand before certain constructions by the Bauhaus or Le Corbusier, for whom it is the appropriate layering of planes, and not the glass itself, that produces transparency. Several of Le Corbusier's realized projects have the very same structural characteristics as Léger's canvases, as for example in his painting *Three Faces*, in which we see three such planes superimposed. It is not the windows, then, but the interpenetration of layers producing an effect of depth that gives us this non-literal, harder-to-attain transparency, at times more intellectual than sensual (although here intellect is not an essential criterion), which no longer emerges from the inert surface of a windowpane or from any other material, but from the particular structuring of space. Rowe and Slutzky believe that the aesthetically richer and truly interesting transparency, as much in art as in architecture, is not that of the material, but of the plane: a transparency that is not literal, but phenomenal, not passive, but dynamic. This is why they prize the transparency of Cubist painting, in which the plane is always active, and call for the creation of a comparable transparency in architecture, one that would not arise exclusively from the nature of the material used—that is, in most cases, glass.

Transparency in architecture joins both poles, the literal and the phenomenal (to stick with those murderous characterizations); in the ideal construction, it draws the gaze deep within and pushes it back out, up until the moment—so I imagine it to myself—when transparency explodes from all corners like a single, sudden illumination, forever lost on the inattentive observer. To hell with the word "phenomenal," anyway: transparency described in this way has the lightness of true discovery, of a flash that reaches out from underneath bodies and things like the flickering robes of phantoms (the best are those in Andrzej Wajda's film *The Wedding*), like a reality that's been hidden till now and is suddenly so obvious and—Scheerbart would have liked this point—emancipatory. Its discovery then recalls the optic trick, fashionable a couple of decades back, of trying to discern an image concealed among thousands of colorful dots painted by a special process. It wasn't easy; before you stood a multicolored, inscrutable wall of tiny dots, but just when all seemed for naught, it looked as though, unexpectedly, in one fairytale instant, the tiny dots dissipated (for me faster than for anyone else, I'm proud to say) like a curtain suddenly drawn aside, and there appeared a three-dimensional interior, a cat prowling in the garden, a path leading into a forest, a little boat on a silver lake, and perhaps you, Olga, spotted suddenly deep in the hospital corridor, in your green scrubs: a chlorophyllic being among the specks and spots of pajamas and gray sweaters, among the swishing pants and pitiful plastic bags in their hands, standing motionless with some test tube in your hand, about to go through the door beyond which the blood was pulsing along into the first bypasses cobbled together by your hands, to ensure that those hearts were still clenching and releasing in their eternal yes-no.

In his reflections on Futurism, Guillaume Apollinaire opposes it to Cubism as an unusually transparent and pure art. But Cubism, and later Surrealism, produce a different, still more modern concept of transparency than Futurism, which appeals more immediately, as in Scheerbart, to glass materials. On the one hand, Cubism is bound up with an idealization of the interior. In his manifestos, André Breton speaks of artists as "recording instruments," or else as transparent photographic film that captures interior reality.[134] He writes about the diamondlike purity and hardness of the work of art, and in *Nadja* he develops this alternative vision of the glass house as an analogue for the interior transparency that liberates the artist from all psychology:

I myself shall continue living in my glass house where you can always see who comes to call; where everything hanging from the ceiling and on the walls stays where it is as if by magic, where I sleep nights in a glass bed, under glass sheets, where *who I am* will sooner or later appear etched by a diamond.[135]

Francis Picabia, introducing his *Transparences,* linking transparency in a similar manner with the seat of existence, with the expression of the powerful "I," nevertheless writes that his aesthetics "are derived, at present, from the kind of boredom that summons within me a vision of pictures that seem frozen on an immobile surface, far from the affairs of man [. . .]. This third dimension of mine, these transparencies, did not arise from light and shadow; transparencies, with their forgotten corners, allow me to express myself in the likeness of my inner will."

On the other hand, Cubist, Surrealist, and also Futurist conceptions, when they are concerned with speed and the dynamics of motion, discover that the relationships among forms, things, and objects are, albeit only for the skilled imagination, transparent. Breton speaks of the "unrestrained, super-clear" connection that settles in between one thing and another, and that the common mind is not capable of grasping. It is said of Cubism that it collapsed the *pareti di vetro,* the already hackneyed—yet ever-enduring in the history of art—glass wall of Leonardo da Vinci, through which the viewer enters a three-dimensional space that recalls the world to such a degree that the painted surface seems to disappear. Instead of a static and faithful representation (as well as what is simply transparent: glass balls, veils, cloths), the modern painter strives to present the very perception of things and the dynamic relationship between them.

In this new optics, transparency can now burst out from dark objects or from what connects them; no longer is transparency merely the medium through which one sees but the potential that emerges from the transformation of all objects (or colors, as in Delaunay or Malevich) and their shifting into an infinite number of relationships. For an example—and here I am following Sophie Thompson's lead—we can point to Giacomo Balla's *Swifts: Paths of Movement + Dynamic Sequence* (1913). The birds' flight, observed from behind a window, is presented in time and space in such a way as to render it impossible to differentiate one swift from another or, for that matter, this side from that. The whole seems like a series of superimposed photographs that shine from underneath and through each other. The Futurist assertion that "movement and light destroy the materiality of bodies" is exemplified in this case by virtue of the medium of transparency, which resolves the formal paradox that obtains between the presentation of immaterial motion and the static durability of the painted surface.[136] Transparency does not consist, then, of a single, stable form, but arises on the edges of forms, in points of contact between their auras, in their interpenetration, in dynamic exchanges, during which tertiary forms are created; transparency here becomes a field of possibility, that phenomenality that Rowe and Slutzky speak of in reference to architecture.

The example of André Breton, about whom I spoke a moment ago, provides a good illustration of the ambiguity of transparency, the oscillation between its straightforward and literal appearance, on the one hand, and its immediate realization, closer perhaps to Rowe and Slutzky, on the other. Breton, dreaming of a "House insanely glazed in the wide open sky the wide open earth," quickly grew bored with the new glass architecture that made open and literal use of glass, since it turned out to be excessively functionalized and, ultimately, as far as Surrealist projects were concerned, barren and aseptic.[137] Sure, it mixed the exterior and interior in such a way that it must have inspired the surreal imagination, since it heralded spatial recreation, but it ultimately fell into functionality and design, it held back the endless march through forms, the surreal imagination's joyful parade.

Rowe and Slutzky, and independently of them the Cubists and Surrealists, suggest that there are transparencies that are deeper or more shallow, better or worse, and maybe even good or evil. Transparencies that please us with their self-evidence and that quickly, too quickly, become static decorations, spectacular or handy, miserably bourgeois, as Breton would say, because they serve trivial forms of stabilization, existential and material; even glass houses, which turn into spaces of accumulation, spectacular, yet safe and passive and, as we would say today, hyper-technological. Whereas the kind of transparency that arises from the difficult layering and linking of things and that flickers only before the eyes—this is where we're trying to get, this is why we break through obstacles and steal through spaces to find its hiding place, where it reveals itself in its meaningless, useless splendor, like a mineral discovered in mines of air.

Transparent Things

We now return from constructed forms to words and to things. That is, to a few additional literary portraits with transparency in their blood or in their background. A moment ago I was speaking about the architectural transparency of forms as understood by Rowe and Slutzky, something close to the Cubist imagination. In Vladimir Nabokov's novel *Transparent Things* we find a related idea about the transparent surface of existence, the penetration of which opens before the trained eye, and first of all before the eye of the narrator, layers of time other than the present moment, allowing one to see other objects and forms, to move away from what is immediately visible. "Now we have to bring into focus the main street of Witt as it was on Thursday," Nabokov opens one of the early chapters. "It teems with transparent people and processes, into which and through which we might sink with an angel's or author's delight, but we have to single out for this report only one Person."[138] The short theory of transparency contained in this novel sets up an opposition between the transparent surface and the hidden depth. In people, deeds, and things, the past shines through, if we only know how to see the transparency on the surface. "A thin veneer of immediate reality is spread over natural and artificial matter," the narrator tells us, and this veneer should not be disturbed if we do not wish "to break its tension film" and fall out of "the now."[139] When we do so wish, however, there's nothing to stop us:

> When *we* concentrate on a material object, whatever its situation, the very act of attention may lead to our invol-

untarily sinking into the history of that object. Novices must learn to skim over matter if they want matter to stay at the exact level of the moment. Transparent things, through which the past shines![140]

Nabokov's narrator would have us understand that his narrative, spotted beneath its transparent surface, could go another way, farther, deeper: it could take a detour, penetrate other transparencies, in different directions, such that it would encompass a different—and maybe even an entire—past, or all of history. If a narrative is ultimately presented here somehow, it is because the narrator holds back from sinking too deep and returns to the surface, if only to keep from disappearing completely from view. But Nabokov's narrator is no novice: he knows what it means to descend and how to move "among staring fish," whereas the beginner—clearly among those who discern this transparent membrane, which no longer takes any great expertise—can easily get lost in these depths.[141]

But the expertise vaunted by the narrator is not, in spite of appearances, a gift of the chosen—of writers, for example; the way is not open to all of them. Nabokov's novel, skillfully but mysteriously constructed, gives us to understand that penetrating the surface of things, as well as speaking about it, is the province rather of the dead than of the living—Leszek Engelking has written on this—and that the narrator, for at least the greater part of the novel, is no longer of this world. The Beyond seems to be one of the most important themes in Nabokov's writing, but closer to my current interest is the idea of a veneer (a membrane, a glass crust) covering things. Is this great mine of the past—which in

Nabokov descends down many shafts, sometimes into his protagonists' very bowels, passing what remains of recent meals, and sometimes into the pasts of stones along the way, into their prehistory—is it accessible to the living, to their probing gazes, to the eyes of their souls and imaginations? Or else it really may be that we are supposed to take from Nabokov's novel about the literary agent Hugh Person, about his father, his wives, among them the brunette Amanda, the notion suggested therein, that in life we do not rush forward into any finite histories, that the past is not an aquarium into which we can, so long as we are alive, set our gazes, that the past and transparency are a mismatched pair, a juggling act whenever we try to link them together. Though it is a source of pure, purified, transparent (and "apparent," like a light turning on in a dark room) images, it does not seem a good source of transparency itself. Memory is merely a hallucination of transparency, a hole in the head, through which our being trickles out. And transparency is that which can always happen. It is better to move toward transparency, and thus it would be better not to believe in the transparency of things past, to jettison memory and to think instead of transparency, *transparence, transparencia*—may it come, may it finally make us speak.

Icy Meditations

So far, I haven't once used the word "transparent" according to its basic dictionary definition: clear, easy to understand. For instance, in all of the multifaceted examples I have mentioned, which elude the immediately given experience of clarity and visibility, transparency flows out, and sometimes bursts out, from a particular perspective, suddenly discovered or attained with great difficulty, revealing the world in a new and different order. Transparency always contains at least a trace of sweetness, the fruit of revelation, epiphanies about which it is in no way easy to speak clearly. Those who dream of it, touched by their sudden discovery, unexpectedly discern a new principle governing space and their own way of seeing, which, without warning, arranges everything differently and gives space itself a new shape.

At the same time, as it is currently understood in everyday usage, the concepts "lucid" and "transparent" are most often associated with the clarity of a conclusion, with an easily comprehensible transmission. Italo Calvino devoted one of the renowned lectures he would have delivered in the United States (had he not died shortly before his planned departure) to just this kind of clear-cut transparency. He chose it together with other concepts (lightness, quickness, exactitude, multiplicity) as "values, qualities, or peculiarities of literature that are very close to my heart."[142] The lecture on transparency—on "visibility"—is essentially a lecture on imagination. In it, Calvino refers to visibility metaphorically as "the power of bringing visions into focus with our eyes shut, of bringing forth forms and colors from the lines of black letters on a white page," the power of effective "thinking" in images, which is under threat, considering our increasingly chaotic multimedia civilization—the lecture was written in the mid-1980s—which bombards us with countless representations visualizing, in an insane manner, everything.[143] Thus Calvino's call for a kind of education in visibility, which "would accustom us to control our own inner vision without suffocating it or letting it fall, on the other hand, into confused, ephemeral daydreams, but would enable the images to crystallize into a well-defined, memorable, and self-sufficient form, the *icastic* form."[144]

Calvino also posits visibility as a state that evens everything out; he gives the concept of visibility an unambiguously positive and safe value. It is the term he applies to imaginative equilibrium, or to a balanced imagination, in which the freedom to fantasize is legible and controlled. Transparency as a quality of imagination enables one to put the brakes on the frenetic pace imposed on it by the millions of images cloned on screens all over the world. In the homeostasis he presents, in this vital equilibrium, there is none of the extremity one typically finds in the many other texts with transparency or translucence in the title, in the table of contents, in the illustrations, or in their overall concept. It is a hygiene of the imagination, a happy *media res* protecting us from chaotic excess in that dark and gloomy forest of swirling images whose ruins accumulate in us like, in Calvino's words, "a stock of death."

But in literature the theme of transparency rarely has such a therapeutic, harmonious, and rational dimension, and it is rarely understood strictly as a conscious regulator of form that keeps watch over its clarity. It appears in various ways, sometimes directly, as in the many descriptions of glass architecture I've already cited, in the houses, palaces, domes, and arcades packed into the prose of the second half of the nineteenth century and the beginning of the twentieth. Perhaps one can find it even more frequently in melancholic dispositions and depictions, where quietude creeps in, where the end draws near and life's turmoil grows still—and it's surely because it is not an exclusively rational demand, but an obsession, that one can write about it beyond just writing articles and conference papers. Visibility comes to us from the direction of death, from the direction of an indifferent nature, from the cold sky. It is hypnotic, yet it seems no longer entirely of this world. It is bound up with how we imagine the end, death, departure, silence. As a challenge for the writer's imagination, it wanders through the centuries, bringing together authors who are completely different from one another, of greater or lesser caliber, the contemporary and the ancient, meeting here momentarily on the stage of a single paragraph, related by virtue of the shared striving for pure light noted in their texts, their striving for emptiness, for silence, by their abandoning the real, the concrete, the perceptible, the living, in favor of the motionless, the hardened, the fading, the falling silent.

For example, of all the (poetic-metaphysical) images of the Polish novelist Andrzej Stasiuk, whose descriptions of global landscapes with minimal human activity the melancholic imagination laps up like fresh water, I am most moved by that contained in his afterword to someone else's novel, Sten Nadolny's *The Discovery of Slowness,* which concerns John Franklin's tragic expedition to the Northwest Passage. That afterword ends as follows:

> We can only imagine how ice made its way into every recess, every fiber. [. . .] We can imagine how the crew's movements became slower and slower, and time gradu-

ally drew out like a tensed chord, until it finally broke and stopped still halfway through some activity, at the beginning of some gesture. We can imagine how John Franklin observed his own motionless body, then the dying, ever slower flow of his thoughts. All that remained in the end was the movement of the air, the polar wind blowing from time before the world's creation to time beyond the end of history.

Following Stasiuk, then, I imagine this painted image (though it should be a film instead, shot with a motionless, patient camera), this ice covering bodies and tools like white amber on the arctic shore, though in fact I don't have to imagine it, since Caspar David Friedrich presents it in his famous canvas *The Wreck of Hope*, also called *The Sea of Ice*, which shows a polar landscape in which the sea has forever imprisoned what remains of a small ship.

In his "Elegy" on the death of Joseph Brodsky, which fell on a white, snowy December day in New York, Stasiuk sets up a similar polar climate. It is so cold that time hardens, "the air has the transparency of glass," the soul "turns into an icicle through which everything is as clear as in the palm of the hand," it becomes "as transparent as a sliver of ice in the cold-clarified air." Here, too, death serves, as it were, a purifying function, it becomes a kind of cold X-ray, through which life loses its physical non-transparency and comes to resemble the kind of aura in which it will continue, glassed-in, dead, but not entirely extinct, just as the figure of John Franklin has not vanished from the ice of the Arctic. One can imagine, if we were to embellish this elegy, a cocoon hovering around the entire earth, and through which the indifferent universe peers down; our souls freeze within it, arrested in their journey beyond: let us repeat, a transcendence that has become transparence. Transparency absorbs human history and exchanges it for the frosty heavens, it draws it into the cold reality of the cosmos, for which earthly destinies are a fleeting commotion, now encased in eternal vastness. In Stasiuk's prose, the narrator's eye often drives toward those elemental things that precede creation, and to those that come after history, on the other side of the edge of all instances, where events have no turns left, and life has either not gotten going or has already been extinguished. This is a kind of cold, negative idealism, transparency as the idea organizing the cosmos, its eternal background, from which existence grows, and to which it ultimately returns.

The theme of cold death that one finds in Stasiuk's peculiar, poetic cosmogony was born in early Romanticism and inspired by three complexes of the imagination: the alpine, the polar, and the Siberian—or, more broadly, the Russian. The specter of the Russian "cold hell," primarily the creation of Polish literature about the experience of exiles, continues to this day in the Polish imaginary (as evidenced so many years after Mickiewicz, so many years after Słowacki's play *Anhelli*, by Eustachy Rylski's 2005 novel *Warunek* (The Condition)), as well as in French literature following Napoleon's defeat in the snows of Russia, a trauma that remains a part of France's culture and collective imagination and that belongs to the cruelest, harshest visions of death.

The alpine and polar complexes also bring a certain mildness to thanatotic imagery; they create an atmosphere fit for melancholic

freezing, for a soft, white meditation. This is how Antoni Malczewski, the first Polish alpinist and author of the Polish language's
most beautiful epic poem, contemplated the white and azure atop
Mont Blanc in 1818. Whatever I'm writing, he comes to mind.
When he reached the summit, climbing up to, in his own words,
"death's country," a country of snow and ice, from that height he
saw that history and human affairs are a modest aside to the elemental, cosmic silence, and he "thought himself witness to the
creation of things at the moment that God gave shape to chaos."
We find similar descriptions in Chateaubriand's *Memoirs from Beyond the Grave,* in which, among many images of disappearance,
of falling into eternal silence, into absolute quietude, of descending into the grave, we find descriptions of Antarctic landscapes, of
death in transparent settings:

> The mountains clothed with snow, the valleys covered
> with white mosses, on which the reindeer browse, the
> seas alive with whales, and speckled over with floating
> ice, form a most brilliant scene, illuminated at the same
> time by the glowing light of the west, and the splendours
> of the Aurora; it is difficult to know if one is present at the
> creation or at the end of the world.[145]

This is how the theme of transparency is presented in what may
be its most magical and immediate version. This melancholic, cold
transparency demystifies reality, the solidity of its forms, just as it
demystified the entire life of Gabriel Conroy and, more, the whole
world as he knew it, and even more still, the whole world as it is.

But in doing so, it perhaps mystifies it all over again, secretly, covering it in a layer of eternal ice and snow, again, as amber covers a fly. Motionless landscapes saturated with light, the cold dome of the sky, whose emptiness flattens terrestrial forms: when melancholy drives us from our own time, how easy it is to cross into a state of half-being, and how hard it is to tear ourselves away from that cold magic. I sometimes think of these landscapes as special, cold counterparts to the crystal palaces, as arctic or cosmic hothouses where the warm and sultry air has been replaced by frost. If life has its own utopia, perhaps nothingness does too. It is that other side of transparency, its mortal, magical charm—if only of surrendering to the sweetness of immobility, to the dream of crystallization. You have to get out of there quickly if you want to say a few more words about silence in poetry and prose.

The Silent Way

The writer Julien Gracq, who died in 2007 at the age of ninety-seven, described Chateaubriand's work as "a world reduced under his gaze to pure, dreamy transparency, squeezed wonderfully into the nothingness between what has been and what will be." Behind these cold landscapes, behind this love for slowing the pace of life, behind this "dreamy transparency," there is also the secret dream of writing free of form, avoiding clarity, descending into free digression, finally flirting with silence. Chateaubriand is constantly departing from the main line of his text, weakening it, diluting its meanings, leveling them with one another, dissolving them in ob-scurity. Saint-Beuve, his contemporary, was already getting irri-tated: "At the most crucial, decisive moments he indulges himself, he freezes, he starts to chat up the ravens on the trees by the road," he stares uninterrupted into the empty sky (a frequent image in this prose), he gets lost in thought. The socialist priest Lamennais determined at the same time that Chateaubriand was a tree nour-ished by its leaves, not by the earth. As perhaps the only exemplar of the poetics of disappearance he regarded and distinguished Joubert, Chateaubriand's friend whom I mentioned several dozen pages back, himself touched by the magic of transparency, who dreamed, we will recall, of writing that could "represent with air," that "ranges over great, empty, transparent spaces." The mute space of transparency, discovered in this way, also encompasses the text itself, pours into it as into a form, not so much to fill it as to thin it out, to clarify it, to silence it.

Most essential to this view of self-absenting is Chateaubriand's last book, written shortly before his death: *The Life of Rancé*, on a Trappist monk who founded an order that observed an unusually ascetic vow of silence. I would like to pause for a moment to take in Roland Barthes's reading of this text. Barthes is intent on com-pletely dismantling the causal links within Chateaubriand's last bit of prose. The speech of literature appears as an enormous and delectable ruin, Barthes tells us, a scrap of Atlantis, where words, feeding on colors, flavors, forms, and thus on properties rather than on ideas, glow like shreds of immediate, unthought-of light, undisrupted and unencumbered by any logic. In Chateaubriand, as Barthes reads him, there is a general slackening of connections and contingencies, a dismantling of mutual references; metaphor does not serve to bring things closer, but splits them apart, removing them from one another; logic once was the curtain that concealed the license and caprice of the chosen words, but now it's vanished, and the writer has a free hand. This lawlessness, this free associative play, is accompanied by the abandonment of any overarching thought. *"The Life of Rancé* is a destructive look at everything that had desired to situate History within certainty"; it is "a book of history written by a historian who no longer believes in History, nor in narrative." Everything comes undone; thought meanders from word to word, from image to image, as if along islands, linking them into loose archipelagoes, and from beyond them, through their diaphanous contours, pure time shines through, that with which Chateaubriand so frequently identified his own existence.

Earlier, as he was writing his great autobiographical opus, *Memoirs from Beyond the Grave,* narrating his own life had a particular dynamic, it rolled along without unnecessary stops, supported by the kind of project of spiritual immortality that Chateaubriand harbored, speaking in the voice of the deceased genius, an eternal voice, for posterity and the dead alike. The future, longed for, planned, stretched the narrative of the past like a canvas, made it taut; this walk along the traces of the past contained no groans of nostalgia, none of that claustrophobic scrutinizing of family affairs. When the work was completed, it was necessary to invent a new future, which now became the freedom and possibility of silence; any further intercourse with the past would only amount to lament; one had to liberate oneself from one's own biography.

On this note, Barthes wrote in reference to *The Life of Rancé* that "literature is no different from a branching path on which we get lost; literature divides, it leads us astray." In Chateaubriand, Barthes discovers a model for (and perhaps an ideal of) literature approaching the edge of silence and self-suspension, a lacework literature that bleaches away the gravity of its own constructions and sentences yet presses ever forward in the motion of its own disappearance, giving all it has to avail itself of a language that is essentially superfluous. Transparency is here connected with an imperative to be silent, to whitewash meaning; it is the looming background, an absence coming gradually to the fore.

One cannot write blithely about transparency without writing about writing itself. We know that even the appearance of words can be an object of reverie, that every style erects a partition, this one opaque, this one transparent, that silence peeps out through texts like a subterranean stream and often turns those texts into nothing more than a lacework bridge of words. For this reason, Chateaubriand's final opus is often read in the context of Maurice Blanchot, that great theoretician of silence, as announcing the latter's powerful move toward introducing the authority of silence into literature, toward achieving a moment in literature that would elude all narrative. The word "transparency" appears often in the studies of those critics and philosophers who have written on Blanchot, and Blanchot's work clearly calls for it. In Blanchot, as Georges Poulet writes, for example, "gaze, word, thought reduce beings to such transparency that no cognitive activity can encompass them. They call to mind certain fish, so wondrously transparent that no one knows what to do to keep them in view. The gaze moves past them." The basic gesture of Blanchot the writer, though also of Blanchot the critic (for he was also an outstanding literary critic), would seem to be departure, absenting oneself, creating a distance, a sense of separation. Poulet writes:

> The kind of critic Blanchot embodies is one who finds himself on the other side of the window, one who asks without hearing an answer, one who also does not expect an answer [. . .]. In this way, the basic effect of such criticism is to reveal the zones of absolute solitude that surround every human life. Never before in criticism have beings and people been thrust into so merciless a distance. But this distancing occurs in the most transparent atmosphere. The gaze sees from a distance, clearly and surely. It is this greatest transparency that shines on Blanchot's pages, a species of desperate understanding accessible to him who has abandoned everything and who, in absence, finds the only possibility of intimacy.

As he reads them, Blanchot puts his authors to the test of just such a purifying filter. Those who make it through the filter to the other side are those who leave as few traces as possible, as little as possible on that built-up, obscure side. Robbe-Grillet, for example, author of the novel *The Voyeur,* in which, as Blanchot writes, transparency lurks behind everything and every face, squeezes in between two sentences, between adjacent paragraphs, and becomes so intense that "time [. . .] [is] incessantly transformed in the shining presence of space, the place of deployment of pure visibility."[146] Similarly, Blanchot's books of literary prose do not aim to tell stories, to invent events, scenes, or psychologically compelling characters. One can compare the Blanchotian novel, as has been written, to "a machine for the production of vacuum and transparency." As in negative theology, this purified space is not supposed to be a void of nothingness, but a site of consciousness from which all markers of individual existence have been removed, a kind of formal asceticism whose action removes all that is secondary, transitory, temporary, in order to reveal, to lay bare a feeling of existence as if unperturbed, anonymous, of "impersonal neutrality."[147]

In a related system of thought, transparency also appears when one is speaking of writing as a striving toward a different, peculiar coolness, the coolness of style. This is how Barthes wrote, for example, about Camus's *The Stranger*, referring to its "transparent form of speech."[148] He also speaks about language that is "neutral," "innocent," "basic," and, in an expression that has become his most famous, "the zero degree of writing."[149] About the kind of writing, then, in which style assumes a total (artistic, metaphysical) neutrality, devoid of any individual qualities, of a particular character. Devoid of all affect, emotion, of a particular rhythm, it seems to create—like white monochrome in painting—a space in which, insofar as it is possible, all traces are erased, and a new beginning takes shape, if it can. But for the time being, there is just the one, even voice that, like air, remains elusive, minimal, quiet, but lively. It is, Barthes writes, silence's alternate mode of existence; the writer casts off all ornament, fluidity, particularity of expression, and finds himself in a new situation, that of someone who exists and creates beyond Literature. "The zero degree of literature," however, as Barthes adds incisively, and as his reading of *The Stranger* years later proves, quickly produces its own automatisms, replacing freedom with repetition. It reproduces itself, turning into a monotonous *perpetuum mobile* that overturns style; if one imagines this style-without-style chromatically, as neutral or transparent, repetition covers it in grayness. This is why we have to press farther in our search for transparent words, to Mallarmé.

A Spider, Poor Devil

I wanted to add something about Mallarmé and, before that, about Octavio Paz, but it all fell apart because of that cyclist. Of course, it wasn't a big deal, notwithstanding all those wasted hours and many hundreds of dollars needlessly spent; it was a trifle, though a trifle that swelled like a grain of rice, cast a pall over the entire day, grew fat on the whole world. A spider on a spiderweb, poor little devil, weaving before my very eyes, wove himself into the windshield. A glass cobweb in the car, born from a single blow.

It was a nice day, sunny all morning, even my coffee tasted better than usual, I was driving out of town, in a good mood, I was coming around a bend and all of a sudden I'm on top of this cyclist, suicidal, he braked hard, nothing serious happened, I gestured to him that he was nuts, he'd get himself killed if he didn't get his head out of the clouds. So I drove off, and in the rearview I saw him chasing after me, yelling. I stopped, he ran up to me, hobbling and screaming, and banged on the windshield, the jerk, he must have had brass knuckles or just really hard bones in his hand, he looked me in the eye and then ran back to his bike. I drove off in a daze, stunned; the spider was sitting in his glass web off to the side, over the right wiper, and I pretended not to see him, pretended he was just a stain that the next good rain would wash away, or a sponge would do the trick, with some chemical concentrate, but no, he was already inside me, already growing inside me. I stopped a couple miles down the road, I had to do some shopping, to look around the store; I grabbed a cart like nothing had happened, as usual it resisted, jammed into the others, I got to the first sale shelf, but already I felt a fog reaching up from my stomach toward my head, wisps of nausea that overpowered my will. The spider was growing inside me, building a wall between things and myself. I saw cans, bottles, jars, but I no longer saw what they were; I saw long aisles dividing the shelves, but I didn't understand what kind of space they sketched out here, where they led, I saw people lolling about with the future content of their stomachs on wheels: they seemed like apparitions from a ghost dance, gliding like mannequins across a strange and mysterious stage. I understood that I wasn't going to buy anything, I wasn't even going to touch anything, I wasn't going to read any labels or check expiration dates; I spent a long time walking like the guy on the emergency-exit sign, abandoned the now-forever-empty cart, and walked, one foot in front of the other, not knowing where I was going or why, past the produce, past the fish and the meats, and got to the shirts and socks before turning around, the fog had spread out everywhere, I was blind, and what sprouted out and upward in front of my eyes, all those products and shelves, now belonged to some alien vision dreamed up by God-knows-who, all those juices, boxes of tea, those motley inscriptions coming together into a meaningless, haphazard mosaic, colors splashed in all directions from the same overturned box. I walked, and I kept walking, and I don't know when or how I left the store, the parking lot was empty, I went from one white square to the next, to a third, to a fourth, the security guard must have thought I was waiting for someone, pacing so patiently along the rows, walking up to the chain-link fence and turning around, and then finally I got in my car and drove off, it was agony just shifting the gears. I drove down the highway on the outskirts of town, full of billboards and gas stations, auto shops and service centers, everything dirty and cramped, I passed more big-box stores and couldn't understand why people go to these places, pushing their carts so carefully, and every motion seemed excessive, and the changing light seemed like my heart palpitating, the spider dug in deeper on the right, gave increasing clarity to its presence, I locked myself in the house, couldn't eat, poured myself some juice, which tasted to me like swamp water, the pear turned out to have no fragrance, the chocolate no flavor. The voices of people outside the window sounded like screams and curses as a prelude to murder, the reverberation of cars parking recalled the landing of blows, the music on the radio disintegrated into isolated, hideous tones, a nonsensical plucking of strings, the idiotic banging of drums. I tried to snap out of it, to concentrate, but in vain: it seemed a waste that the lines in my book should blacken the white, I didn't bother to turn on the TV, I sat still in the deepening night, the spiderweb in me held strong like a chain-link fence, no, there was no longer anything beyond the premonition of continuous disaster oozing out from everywhere, from the walls of the room, from the outline of the houses outside, from the bricks of the looming world, from my interiority.

Aerofanie

Octavio Paz speaks of *aerofanie*, a particular (and primarily poetic) art of cultivating transparency. And, speaking poetically, of the mining of, as he describes it, rock crystal, a bright star, from the surrounding darkness of time, the world, and language. *Aerofanie* (we will now use this word to refer to the effort to attain transparency through literature) attracted and sometimes utterly enchanted no small number of authors; one could assemble an impressive anthology consisting entirely of aerofanic passages. Among them we find fragments both mystic and mystifying, since the transparency that poetry reaches for is often translated into quietude, it amounts to silence and remains metaphysically bound up with the absolute, drawn very quickly in the direction of ultimate questions, to the very crux of reflection upon what it means to be literature, what the text is that is now being written.

The aforementioned Octavio Paz, for example, for whom the concept of transparency serves as the thematic basis for a meditation on his own writing, laid out his own creative path in his commentary on one of his poems:

> As I wrote, the path to Galta grew blurred or else I lost my own bearings and went astray in the trackless wilds. Again and again I was obliged to return to the starting point. Instead of advancing, the text circled about itself. At each turn the text opened out into another one, at once its translation and its transposition: a spiral of repetitions and reiterations that have dissolved into a negation of writing as a path. Today I realize that my text was not going anywhere—except to meet itself.[150]

Initially, one has to choke down the boredom or irritation brought on by yet another autothematic authorial reflection—though when Paz wrote these words it hadn't yet become the rage. We, at least, do not want to read texts, and especially novels, about how a writer can't write a novel, the complaints he's writing about not writing. (Though it won François Weyergans the Prix Goncourt in 2005, an award he earned for exquisitely eating his own tail.)

But the somewhat tautological concept of the text, which ultimately mirrors itself and contains a reflection of itself, which approaches the limit of its own potential and thereby creates a definition of its own being, which in turn becomes the definition of being as such, is inscribed in all writing. And one has to give it a chance. The silence contained somewhere at the end of every text is an interpretation of the world; quietude, limit, void—these have always accompanied literature, serving as its ultimate horizon. In the literary work, whether poetry or prose, there is always the potential for silence; beneath the surface of words, a quiet is perched, an emptiness, what Mallarmé would call a purity, *le Pur*. Some, like Paz, and Mallarmé especially, take a specific interest in this, or, more, are hypnotized to such an extent that it becomes the object of all their desires, indeed the horizon of their entire poetic and metaphysical project.

For Paz, this is *blanco*, the text's ultimate goal—ultimate, but inexpressible. He also calls it "universal transparency," or sometimes the "adorable azure."[151] Paz is essentially a cheerful poet; reaching universal transparency allows him to reveal the great unity of the world, the happy and general law of analogy that governs it. "Analogy: universal transparency: seeing this in that."[152] This fundamental, primal transparency, the only one that remains and lasts and might just save the world, cannot be expressed directly. It is, rather, eternal non-expression. The task of poetry consists in— well, among other things—in revealing it, in what Paz describes as an "impartial clarity [...] in which things become presences and coincide with themselves."[153] This is why the poet must struggle with his own language, strip people and things of the burden of names. Paz speaks of making things transparent, so that "names grow thinner and thinner, to the point of transparency, of evaporation."[154] He wants his poems to be "crystallizations of the universal play of analogy, transparent objects which, as they reproduce the mechanism and rotary motion of analogy, are waterspouts of new analogies."[155] He pictures the poem as a crystalline shell or a transparent chamber in which all time and all images gather in an "incorporeal appearance," as a resonance chamber (in Paul-Henri

Giraud's reading of Paz) gathers sounds in order to release them purified, with greater force.[156]

Paz employs many artistic means to realize his poetic project, including, for instance, cryptograms. Speaking of them would also seem to demand recourse to Eastern thought, to Tantrism and Buddhism. In Buddhism, as Giuseppe Tucci reminds us, the diamond "symbolizes Supreme Cognition, *bodhi,* Illumination, Absolute Essence, Cosmic Consciousness, which, once it has been attained, is never again lost."[157] Buddha sits on a diamond throne that endures beyond time and space, an image that even transfixed Mallarmé, who nevertheless erected his own transparent verse chambers in solitude, ultimately beyond the notion of the world's primal unity and similar zero points connecting things with their modes of existence; Buddhism turned out to be a passing fancy. And while Mallarmé was an idealist, he sought his absolute not only beyond transcendence, but beyond any sphere of signification. With words detached from their meanings he wanted to build "a pure, transparent block" (*bloc pur et transparent*)—a Book, Poem, or Sentence that comes into being only as words lose their contact with any point of reference.

The terms "pure" and "transparent," which are supposed to express the nature of this sort of poetry, are as much metaphors as they are the spaces that delineate poems' physical dimension. The poem as the effect of striving toward crystal purity seems like a geometric solid that, like a diamond, grants no access. Not even the poet can access it; it clears the way for him, but in the end it does not let him all the way in. The poem (or poetic prose), purified of everything, contains nothing of the poet; it is supposed to be perfectly impersonal, constructed from sounds that the poet has lumped together, stepping back swiftly so as not to sully them further with his human presence. "The hour of my leaving has sounded," the narrator of *Igitur* says, "the purity of the mirror will be established, without this character, a vision of myself [. . .]."[158] Everything has been fulfilled, "the Dream has agonized in this glass flask, purity which encloses the substance of Nothingness."[159] Francis Ponge (1899–1988), another great poet who remained under the influence of Mallarmé's poems, speaks of "the growth of crystals: a formative will, and the impossibility of adopting *any other way*."[160] For Mallarmé, this is absolutely imperative, obvious, in effect an objective law, and not an imaginative caprice.

The Pure, *le Pur* (Mallarmé admired the syllable's drawn-out sound), is not given to us in advance; it appears only at the end of the line. Mallarmé, much as Paz would do later, sets out on a journey of the imagination based here on the sometimes desperate and impossible struggle against an obstacle, on persevering through darknesses, stripping off veils, smashing windows, clawing out toward daylight, the unblemished azure, the cruel ideal— for it is mercilessly alluring and transfixing. One after another, the heroes of his poems—Igitur, Herodiade—are afflicted with the disease of idealism, as Mallarmé himself would eventually call it; they grapple with adversities and make particular journeys of initiation, the end of which is the Absolute. The only problem is that this Absolute has no concrete features, it neither arranges nor expresses anything; it is, according to the poet, "an empty pause." Sometimes, of course, it serves as a gap, through which one can see the cosmos, but at other times it is sealed within itself, creating an uninhabited *Château de la Pureté*. A place so uncompromisingly pure and transparent that it isn't always distinguishable from nothingness. Now attaining a paradoxical clarity—"Nothingness having departed," the narrator of *Igitur* tells us, "there remains the castle of purity"—later losing its distinctiveness, dissolving in non-being.[161]

Mallarmé, describing himself as a specialist in the Absolute, inexpert in anything else, perhaps seems to be searching for a purely abstract transparency. But the devotee of transparency must place him higher than Paz. Though less artful a poet, Mallarmé was a genius of the phrase: to a greater degree than Paz, he was a dreamer of transparency, not a conceptualist of it. There is something architectural, theatrical, about his poetic imagination; transparency and purity are exposed to view, extracted, chiseled like ice cubes; one can come away with the impression that ice, the azure, the cold, the polar fantasies we spoke of earlier, overtake this imagination and light it like the blade of a dagger, which is to cut through the gloom. When Mallarmé departs from his too-abstract poetry to write poems "now barely colored by the Absolute" (which is the most appropriate measure of a thing), they might gain in materiality, but they remain an Arctic to the rest of the world, somewhere at the poles of memory, occasionally coming into view and then once again dormant in the background.

Roland Barthes calls Mallarmé "the Hamlet of writing," someone who leads literary language to the level of the sublime only "to sing the necessity of its death."[162] He wants to take literature to the gates of the Promised Land, that is, a world now without literature, to which the poet will still manage to bear witness. The word, freed from the ring of clichés, from social contexts, assuming no responsibility for any new contexts in which it might now take root, becomes "a light, a void, a murder, a freedom."[163] In "Bobo's Metamorphosis," Czesław Miłosz writes, "I liked him as he did not look for an ideal object. / When he heard: 'Only the object which does not exist / Is perfect and pure,' he blushed and turned away."[164]

I will defend Mallarmé, albeit unsuccessfully, from Barthes's perspicacity and Bobo's lack of enthusiasm, which is unwavering (that suspicious purity, that flawlessness, that quasi-absence)—and I will do so with a spatial, architectural argument, for it would seem that there really is a lyric object in Mallarmé, one that has been carved out of ice, glass, frost, the azure. Pure, perfect, yet full—not of void, but the substance of transparency. "There is transparency": recalling Aristotle's words, I imagine that Mallarmé's own words are like the things in the former's treatise *On the Soul*, with their dormant portion of transparency. So dormant that the poet cannot make them shine, cannot make them reveal themselves in the light that transparency sets in motion. On the contrary, he removes the concrete, he waters things down, reduces the words' meaning to sounds or order to see "all that transparency." This, too, is why he pushes the lyric "I" into a corner; words have been summoned, they no longer accommodate personal confessions, appeals, or emotions: here I am, a pure and transparent block. One surely cannot go on writing in this manner, least of all when the dreamer of transparency hews this transparency into a diamond for himself, the ideal image not so much of a poem as of dreaming: when he has tired of himself, having written so many pages already, exhausted by the burden of his own "I," by having to bear the cross of constantly eking out some stylistic flourish, Mallarmé's voice seems to come from a siren, luring us to her mysterious and illusory "maybe," her trans-transparent depths.

Hysteria

Hysteria arrived one morning, almost at noon, and stayed. But it must have been hovering nearby earlier on, in her younger days (there was that awful keening that one day, and that time she tore away from the preschool, running straight ahead, wherever her legs would take her), looking for points of entry, a hatch into Olga's body, a crack in the fragile ice of imagination: her sensitivity to cold, that quiver in her throat before what she knew would be a long time apart, her readiness to cry whenever she saw the dirty, the broken faces of men on display on the street, in archways, and in front of stores, or else as she was waiting, even then, all of eight years old, for a phone call, for her father to come home, for a movie on television that had been delayed, for Christmas dinner, which was never ready—for anything.

Her hysteria was most often connected with loss. Someone had to disappear, irretrievably, once and for all, and in her tears and convulsions compassion for those who were leaving mingled with her love for them. But in the worst of her screaming, when she would bury her face in the pillow and throw herself on the blanket, as if there were a grenade in there that was about to go off, when she was so shaken with its trembling that she felt like a flat, vibrating sheet of paper, so flat that there was nothing to take hold of, no way to stop her shaking, it became clear, with a clarity that was not conscious, but that hit you straight from that trembling sheet of paper, that her compassion and even her love were rattled in those initial sobs, and that here, on the blanket, on these pillows, she was left alone, quivering, that hysteria consisted in that trembling, in that howl, in that dance of hers beneath the vault of heaven, that this was a matter strictly between her and the empty space of the air around her, between her and universality, between her life and her death.

Real hysteria, then, struck quite hard when it finally arrived, as a test run, that morning, almost noon. Her father was in the hospital, a few days had passed since his operation, successful, the first of many, things were fine and calm, then one day, the fifth or sixth since she had stopped her daily visits, she was surprised by how much she liked the taste of her morning coffee and croissant and the jam smeared on its side with half-firm chunks that pleasantly tickled the tongue. In the evening she called the hospital, a friend from school was on duty, and her father came to the phone and told her about his sudden fever, nothing to worry about, he might have to stay three, maybe four days longer. She slept, woke up before dawn, and in the darkness her father's words split into two sounds, down divergent paths, the first calm, humming monotonously, the other an undertone, the bass of calm resignation in which, deeper still, there was nevertheless a note of dread, metallic, like the watch glimmering on her wrist in the hollow it made in the pillow. That note came back around noon and split apart into a thousand chords; Olga lay down, felt her heart beating faster, saw the whitened knuckles of her fingers, the first convulsion came from her feet, the second from within her chest, but after that she was crying quietly, no longer wailing; her father called in the early afternoon, he felt fine, the fever had abated, and Olga ran into the kitchen to make herself spaghetti fit for a queen (*for a queen*, she repeated, and she smiled at herself in a spoon).

It happened again a couple of years later, right after her last conversation with Krzysztof. They had agreed to meet in front of the church at Three Crosses Square, it had gotten dark, and she knew that the emptiness of that Sunday evening, stretched like plastic wrap over the entire square, was a sad warning from her own city, from an ally that on good days lay down beneath her feet, embracing her gently with the arms of its buildings as she walked, full of joy or calm, to meetings, to the movies. They were supposed to have gone to some café, but Krzysztof was adamant. He shrank into himself, stuck to the sidewalk, and then there were the words "part ways," which, though she could already feel the lump in her throat, amused her with their unnaturalness: here was a child speaking grown-up words in a grown-up expression, words he had picked up somewhere. He brushed her shoes with the tip of his shoe, and that touch was itself a relocation; he no longer wanted to touch her hand, her shoulders, but he wanted to give her a sign, to comfort her, to be warm; he tapped her shoes as if checking whether she was still alive, he tapped her shoes as one would a dead mole or rat, and she was this mole, this ex-rat, swept from the path of some giant looming over the heap of her body, a giant church with a triumphant cross at its crown, leaning over for a moment longer before continuing on, toward the life to come, toward a future that would no longer be within her reach. She didn't yet know that it was happening, she got onto the bus, carefully punched her ticket, carefully chose one of the many vacant seats, halfway between the front and rear doors, opening the front of her coat and making sure it didn't touch the floor. The scream started to grow once she got home; it poured out as she was hanging up her coat. First she ran around the apartment, from room to room, to the kitchen and back, in one room she threw herself on the bed, but she couldn't lie there for longer than a minute, in another room she threw herself on the couch, she embraced it, and a minute later she ran to the kitchen, leaned against the sink, spat out the first wave of saliva, that top layer, returned to the first room in large, loping bounds, a wounded horse, then to the second, the third, threw herself on the bed, lay there briefly, more and more briefly, thirty seconds, then twenty, everything was moving along with stifling regularity, each station visited in order, bed, couch, sink, but quicker, more and more quickly, and when there finally wasn't any time left she threw herself on the rug, she convulsed as though her liver were being torn from her body, the first vomit spurted over the floor, she flopped into the bathroom, sat on the toilet, then felt a little better, it was warmer in there, homier, the door to the john touched her forehead in an almost friendly way, she got up, went out, barely limping now, standing up straight, brave, and then the second wave hit, this time not carrying her through the whole apartment but lifting her up, toward the light, toward the ceiling, toward the sun, somewhere up there, high up, until her throat cracked, until the sky opened, and Olga soared, screaming, howling, and threw a sweater over her head, blind, tall, and so high up, tall and blind, and collapsed again, now she was crawling, and the rug was the earth, the black earth she wanted to bury herself in, and she touched its Persian weave, its exposed patterns, with her lips, ravenously, clawing at the dust with her nails, she was digging up the clay, the sand that soon would cover her. The wave crashed, it subsided, so Olga got up, leaned against the sideboard, there was a bottle of vodka in the bar, she stuck its neck deep into her mouth and drank greedily, immediately feeling that it was coming back the other way, summoning the third wave, and now she was throwing up into the sink, and this is what she wanted, she wanted to spit herself out for as long as she could. She stopped screaming, now the pain reached from her feet all the way up to her nose, it stopped at her eyes and wound around her ears, toward the back of her skull, and once again she couldn't stand still, she walked, now taking smaller steps, through the whole apartment, she was wobbly, she was shuffling more and more, the new wave was crushing, it wanted to beat her, break her down, and Olga broke her steps into smaller and smaller segments, until finally she came to a stop, no longer able to move, and stuck there, stamping her feet against the floor. The pain was twisting away from her head toward her throat, it stopped there, allowed her to stand motionless; she was screaming more and more quietly, she started to whimper, to pant loudly, and again she was moving through the apartment, sniffing around, she was a dog sniffing around, breathing loudly through her nostrils, looking, yes, she was looking for something, she chose a couch in the middle room, lay down, covered herself with a blanket, the spasms subsided, after an hour she ran to the bathroom and had a long pee and was surprised at having to do so, then she went out and was immediately drawn back toward the couch. The phone rang, and she said, "Olga's not here, she'll be back tomorrow." And she was surprised that she knew how to speak, she waited a moment before she was able to put the phone down, three seconds passed unbearably, intolerably, and she threw herself on the couch with relief and pulled up the blanket, careful not to leave a shoulder exposed. It grew quiet, which was like an answer, Olga was listening to it, and then she was only hearing it, she drifted off for a moment, and in her sleep she felt her large, warm right hand cradling her left, squeezed into a little fist, as if the Great Lord were sheltering a tiny little planet in his palm.

A Pure, Transparent Block

Is it possible to picture Mallarmé's poems graphically or spatially? As he himself dreamed? As a *bloc pur et transparent*? A "pure, transparent block," a cuboid or polyhedron? If it's to be a polyhedron, I'd happily leave it to Albrecht Dürer. Let him slip it into his *Melancholia I*, in the place of the mass in the foreground, in front of the figure of the Angel. Instead of a dark, porous layer, pure walls of crystal. The etching's title would have to be altered slightly, however, for I would want this work to speak to more than just melancholy.

Or else I could imagine these glass monads as Mario Merz executed them in the seventies, his various clear igloos installed in diverse landscapes and museums, especially the one that remained just a design but was supposed to be an homage to Gaston Bachelard, author of books about the elements of imagination, in a hilltop forest in the Ardennes; after a week's journey, Merz finally found the ideal spot for what he called "my last igloo."

Or else Jaume Plensa, the Catalonian artist whose name has already flashed through here once before, could sculpt these sorts of things today. He produces shapes, blocks, and especially cuboids out of synthetic resin; their walls, whose transparency differs from that of glass, are covered with inscriptions. Like on the largest of them, *La Riva di Acheronte* (The Shore of Acheron). On four sides, nearly illegible, frosted words—transparency within transparency—scraps of words, glimmers of words, from Shakespeare, Baudelaire, Blake, Canetti, carved into this transparency, this translucence, illuminated with floodlights from above. Arrested in resin as though stuck on the path toward their goal, they could go no farther and shriveled on the shore. If you happen to approach them, they seem huddled before some obstacle. Which is why some viewers have come away with the impression that the words are imprisoned, stopped dead, bound by impossibility; rising up like fissures, they cannot be penetrated, and seen up close they look like nothing but grooves, cracks in those frozen, transparent sheets of resin. You can enter some of Plensa's blocks, you can stand there or even sit on benches inside. Sometimes Plensa also hangs transparent words on invisible strings, suspended from the ceiling like clear garlands of liana, the visitors pressing between them in their tropical forest.

What do we find, then, in this pure vacuum of the interior, beyond the shores of Acheron? Only that which is beyond the reach of words? Or else is it better to sense there, after Mallarmé, not so much the defeat as the emanation of words, to feel whatever can be extracted from them and united into shimmering vacancy? Something that appears over them before as a band of light providing no aid to meaning or understanding, and which has now been drawn out and concentrated? Jaume Plensa's transparent stairwell, *bloc pur et transparent*, a bright cuboid, stands somewhere at the edge of worlds, ours here and the other one out there. The transparency it contains—the last room of our abode, or else the beginning, the first room, of the other—concretizes Mallarmé, as well as my secret inquiry. Is it on this side, or is it exclusive to the other? Is it of this world (yes, I asked this earlier, and more than once), or that one?

Is this the limit that one must always approach in thinking about transparency? Surely, each of us, in our own existence, beats several thematic paths, follows the trail of several threads. It begins with a couple of related image-themes that cling to us, and through which we stare, in our solitude, at the world. Later, once we've reached adulthood, we discover that we can pool our imaginations together, that they've been with us since long ago, that they have been waiting to take root in still other imaginations, that they create collective experiences, sometimes adopting and developing these images, sometimes uncovering their completely unrealized, not infrequently negative, value, itself so different from what we had known. And as the next phase passes, the images that guide us free themselves—as they may do often enough—from the collective imaginary, from social applications, and return again to us, though they return a bit foreign, since we know by then that we have spent a chunk of time with them, that they have forced us toward our destiny, that is, to repeat the same thing. Is there any way out of this personal mythology, this mythic circle, in which we entangle ourselves, and which we ourselves forget? Or are there loopholes in there somewhere that lead out to the future, waiting to be discovered?

It very often happens that, whatever it is I'm discussing here in connection with transparency, I unwittingly approach the image of the edge, of the border; this image draws me in. All of the others interest me, each is fascinating in its own way, yet this is the one that returns most frequently. Space ends on this side, there is no way to go farther, yet we've gotten as far as this point, the last in that place where we live, where nothing is any more than it is; place ceases to be place, it leans into another time. But here the idea is not some melancholic desertion of being, but rather the experience of "the lightly hued Absolute," a placeless idyll that, far from any magic, mysticism, or ecstasy, from all wisdom, Buddhist or otherwise, from the possibility of something that speaks or satisfies itself, affords the sense that one has been liberated from his own biography, from the tangled layers of the past. This is no longer melancholic absence, but, as has so often been the case, melancholy avails itself gladly of the aesthetics of transparency and often wins us over with it; for a moment we become the ground of being, about which nothing can be said.

Beyond all other meanings—social, aesthetic—the most extreme experience of transparency I know (and there are so many!) leads us out from the depths of our psyche, releases us from the excess of the "I," from all holiday parties, into a winter night in Dublin. In

our lives, the transparency that is brought about by surveillance—
that of a neighbor, the police, the state, an institution—is surely
the pure negation of our person, violence against our intimacy. In
its favorable dimension, however, when we find ourselves experi-
encing it ourselves, of our own free will or imagination, from the
sudden flash of the moment or even the sudden touch of something we've read, we are seized by a sense of readiness, sunny or
cool, bright or cold, but always complete readiness. I won't say for
what, just that the pure, transparent block that has burst within us
is our "I" itself. Transparency speaks here essentially about time,
is a form of future time that cannot yet be spoken.

What, then, is the precise, absolute opposite of transparency?
Not opacity, not darkness, not mystery, not fog. Not that spider
on the windshield, the poor devil, a thin streak of shadow. Yet
an element dozing so lightly that a single brush of the spider's
leg, one spot of damp, a kiss of loss, one evil glance from Baron
d'Holbach—this is all that's needed for it to spring into action. I
call it hysteria. It's an approximate term, but let's stick with it.

Hysteria is narcotic and rapacious, and it is eternal return; it
seems to be an incurable affliction. It arises in us suddenly, and
it does not come from without, the way flu does; once aroused,
it can't be stopped until the moment the attack burns itself out.
The ogre then hides, buries itself deep away, and there's no telling
when it will awaken again, though it's there, ready to renew the
assault. Hysteria is summoned by a flaw in transparency, even a
slight one; the tiniest crack stirs it up. It's like a small spot in the
eye: there's simply nothing to be done about it. Which is why both
of these experiences, hysteria and transparency, come together,

forming the ends of the axis that spins in our beings. Some people are more susceptible to it, likely to succumb to pathological exaggeration, and in others it causes a barely noticeable tension, but as a pair, as a powerful opposition, they form what I sense is one of the formative features—to put what I have already suggested a little bit differently—of modern existence, modern not in the qualitative sense, but historically, starting with Jean-Jacques. The pattern evolves, but it goes on, embodied in both the great and in their quite mediocre copies (well-meaning sentimentalists, ludicrous figures), one of whom will now go on to say:

I'm setting aside psychological, somatic, and physical genealogies; surely no theory of hysteria, and there have been so many in medicine and psychoanalysis, makes a point of this reciprocal dependence, this perfect opposition between hysteria and transparency. Yet it is essentially a sisterly opposition, since both cases, if we were to take them to their ultimate extremes, would place their subject (or, let us say, their victim) in a comparable situation. Both the ideal, radical subject of transparency and the radical subject of hysteria are exposed to a similar realization of evacuation, deprivation, loss. They approach a limit that cannot be crossed. They no longer have anything that can belong to them; possession is a *lied* of the past. Everything has gone so suddenly, perhaps just for a moment, but it's still gone away, it's stopped being, stopped being here, being important, stopped counting for anything. Hysteria brings the experience of an unexpected, sometimes staggering encounter with an obstruction, and this obstruction is the "I" who has been robbed of any frame of reference: time no longer wishes to flow and becomes stale; people have departed, things have vanished or sealed themselves up in utter foreignness. What is one to do with this mass of selfhood once faced with so sudden an appearance of emptiness, with being face-to-face with one's own "I," now thrust into boundlessness? The only thing around us now is infinitude, the stifling substance of time, in which one must go on living, alone in the world, bearing oneself—but how, in what way? There's frenzy, convulsion; the hysterical subject, Saint Vitus, dances beneath the blue heavens. The victim of hysteria, much like the victim of transparency, discovers that what had been reality until now is slipping from under his feet—that the past no longer means anything, but he doesn't recognize this, and doesn't have the courage to cross into the pure, transparent block. Hysteria is quintessentially of this world, the revelation that there is indeed something beyond (what is it: emptiness? heaven? eternity? death?), but this vision surpasses us: after all, this is where we come from, this is where we had our lives, and then we were suddenly left with nothing, without those lives, holding nothing but our useless selves.

I look at Mario Merz's igloo, at Plensa's transparent sculptures, at their nomadic fluidity, their strange, unjustified presence within the world of shapes, their modest appearance, like a guest at the wrong wedding, at their squat forms in cities (for that's where they've been erected), I look at these cages stuck into streets like imprecise metaphors, at these blocks in nature, on meadows, glades, placed there like foreign bodies, substances from another planet, and at those that remain in museums too, focusing thoughts in abstract sublimation. One could still wander for a long time from one block to another, performing a glass pilgrimage, looking through the cities, girding subsequent pages with their views, because the history of transparency is after all just like the history of melancholy or the history of love: you can write about it without end. As opposed to one's own history, which doesn't have a surplus of time at its disposal, because the espresso machine is working fast, fast and steaming, and that strong coffee is flowing presently into two cups, one yellow, one blue.

Olga

One winter, Olga left for a two-month residency, actually an internship, in Krems an der Donau, in Austria. During its vacation period, the cardiology clinic there was eager to give work to fresh graduates from Poland, who for their part received an apartment and a little pocket money. She was glad to be near the Danube. So much bad stuff had happened before: her father had died, she didn't know how to get her bearings. The river might finally bring some solace to her sad life with its eternal flow, the collective childhood its water carried with it, which was embodied in the barges that floated along with its current and had all the majesty of time, which goes on forever, in the morning mists lifting around nine like curtains in a theater, unveiling the ancient stage of day. In her first week of enthusiasm she felt herself opening to that flow, so much that it would fill her with its trembling. But later, hour by hour, her alienation grew. She had an increasingly intense feeling that her time was peeling away from the time of the river, that it was returning to her, turning into a small, compact ball. The river purified everything, taking all of her blood along the way, and Olga, looking at it through the window of an empty house, froze—she was a small, dried-up brook with no outlet, a narrow trough of sand and stones, waterless, far from the ruthless, alien current. A few more days passed, and she felt the itch of emptiness in her veins all the more, she was constantly thirsty and she gulped down water, emptying glass after glass in a single draft, as if striving to replenish the stream of her life. She ate little; the itch descended to her gut so that food could no longer be held down and permeate her body. She struggled, she hydrated relentlessly, from time to time she had the impression that the brook was starting to flow again, that there was something there in the basin, trickling just enough for her to be able to make some plans, to read for about an hour, maybe an hour and a half, and later to do the shopping, perhaps a salad and some yogurt, perhaps that really good salami they have here, after which the thought faded away, the sand within her went dry and became hard all over again, and she only had the strength to go out, to walk through the depopulated streets of the old town, to move along in this way until night fell.

She came back to Poland after a month or two, she herself didn't know when, it wasn't important, and the following days were mashed together like pulp in overripe fruit. She worked in clinics, submitted her resignation, couldn't stand the sight of people imprisoned in the diving bells of their bodies, which they brought to her for repair. She traveled, registered for some conferences, pretended to herself that she was developing her specialization.

She went to Krynica for the next congress of cardiologists. On Saturday afternoon she went into the mountains. As she ran up to the hilltops, she saw an orb of light illuminating the meadows beneath her feet and the air over her head. She felt as though she were drinking that light in and, in return, giving up the whole superfluity of her body, all its excess, the way it leaned outward from her breasts, its extension in her arms, the way it exposed her materiality so obviously, all the idiotic muscularity and sinuousness of the backs of her thighs. She was like an X-ray film, light, as if all the inessentials had been removed from her outline. That evening, at the closing of the congress, she went dancing, found an old-school dancehall, and the tango was like a continuation of that light, of that "not-I" in the "I." A labyrinth with no exit, yet filled with light, that's how she thought of herself and of her body.

She awoke the following day differently from usual, not emerging slowly into waking life but surfacing from sleep violently and with such a feeling of purity within herself that it was as though she had never slept and didn't know what it meant to sleep, to have heavy eyelids. It must have been pretty late, the air was already hard on her legs, packed with warmth, and she entered it as if she were entering thick, hot water. The bed remained ashore with its pulled-down blanket and white pillowcase; the scattered hairpins were not expecting her return and seemed to be occupied by their own inscrutible shapes. She lit a cigarette, which trembled for a moment between her fingers and, with the first drag, it freed her from her silence: Good God, she said, and she felt that she wasn't speaking to herself. The light washed over her body, and she noticed that she was standing in a rectangle of yellow that colored the green floor along her shadow and rescued her silhouette from grayness. She spied the sun through the open window. It had already begun to escape beyond the doorframe, but three quarters of its sphere dispatched the day here, inside, and fed the rectangle with color. She leaned heavily on her feet, drew them slightly apart, and the muscles in her calves and thighs tensed beneath the skin in an emotive reflex of excitement, of amorphous anxiety. She brushed the hair from her forehead, slipped it behind her ears, grew fond of how it touched her neck. The lines on the yellow-green border smoothed out their corners, held the line of what might have been separation as much as cohesion, the way a comma both slices through the sentence and holds it together.

My life, she thought, my entire life. It was here, somewhere right here, it was this bright, sunny spot, this draft of transparency enclosed in a window frame, it was an object that you could hold in the palm of your hand, grip like a rock, a ball, a branch, my entire life, she thought, a little square that no one knows, a blade of grass spinning in space, which no one can discern, and which I have cut out with my own appearance, and which was issued by this seed of me, stuck into the soil, into this place of wholeness, of everything, glass, a shard framed in silhouette, visible only to myself, a shard that everyone carves out for herself and sees with her own gaze, a shard, a blade of grass, my emanation fished out of air, so poor, wretched, and whole, this form that I have created, and now it's closed, yes, almost sealed up, this scale, one little scale on the great fish of the world.

The cigarette's glow inched slowly toward her fingers and was like a warm Annunciation. She stood briefly under the shower;

she ran downstairs without makeup. The dining hall was nearly empty, as if it had opened for her alone, only further in, at the bar, the last guest was sitting on a stool, his back turned toward her, and wearing a hat despite the early hour. She felt hunger, the kind she hadn't known in a long time, and walking around the buffet she loaded up, we loaded up, on all the things set out there.

The Plural

"What's with the plural again? Your 'we' is irritating me. We loaded up. We were. And why don't you just stop talking about me? Stop it, you're bugging me. What is this?! I'm always hungry! And, anyway, it wasn't exactly like that. It was a little different. A whole lot different! For example, it wasn't my hysteria. It was yours. And I didn't know anyone named Krzysztof."

"That's true," I admitted. "I was a little embarrassed. I didn't know how to talk about it."

"Then stop already!" Olga's knuckles were white. She smashed a thin sheet of ice under her heel and shoved me with her elbow, giving me a good jolt.

A deeper frost had finally dug in the night before and had frozen the puddles; we went for our last long walk before the holidays. The air was bluish and so clear, unambiguous, and powerful that if one were to take away the walls, houses, and trees it would remain there like a solid mass, a cast pulled away from a concrete form, now, in this time, no longer needed, falling off to the side like a rocket tower after blastoff. Step by step, we reached the river, which moved swiftly and smoothly, only a crest reared up a bit beneath the crust of ice, tensed like a cat, and gleamed with an unusually dark gray light. Old sailboats leaned heavily against their sides, propped up on logs, in the half-open boathouses and in the yards before them, kayaks and boats lay deck-down, and it all looked like a minor catastrophe, something out of the history of a lackluster Atlantis that might yet come back to life, get itself together for spring. I looked at the river and breathed deeply, the cold of the air seeped in more and more forcefully, it erased all inscriptions, removed every sentence of the text in my head, and I suddenly wanted to be this pure ribbon encumbered by nothing, no letter, no shadow.

"Fine," I muttered, "have it your way. I'll stop."

"Why not just say something about yourself?" she suggested to smooth things over. "Where and when you were born, what happened after that first breakfast you opened with."

We were leaning against the spine of an old boat with a couple of punctures, and its shape at the stern and the yellow flecks of paint recalled a little cutter with a steep underbelly, yet another strange form of seafood dragged up from the depths.

"It must have been summer," I said. "A ripe time, more July than August, because it's quite warm in the room, but not a heat wave. The sense of being low, close to the floor, hands touching the parquet. Motes of dust in the air, a black dog runs past, maybe sits a few yards away, a moment later stretches out on its stomach. If he's panting, he's doing it quietly. He doesn't cozy up, doesn't bark: he's just there. Somebody else, crouching down, probably on hands and knees, is definitely scrubbing the floor with quick movements of the hand. It's a good thing there's someone there, though those movements are so odd, circular, repetitive, precise. Warm, nice, bright, with darker corners somewhere off to the side. There, on the left, a patch of sunlight on the wall, in outline, square. It's growing, and everything's so clean. The floor is shining, the window wide open. You can see everything. You can see everything so clearly now. Not out the window, but here in the room. No obstruction. A clear line of sight. Like through a screen, only without obstruction. Warm. Nice."

"And what else?"

"Nothing. That's it."

Names, barely legible, were written on several of the sailboats and small craft: Hannah, Anatole, Barbie: where were they now, what lands were they wandering, which streets did they follow, trying to get home before dark? They left their names, which went quiet over the water, faded like drawings on rocks, calling cards stripped from their bodies. Hannah, Anatole, Barbara: names that had come unglued, disappearing on plastic and wooden boards, in frozen air and the first flakes of snow, just about to cover this embankment of the Vistula.

Cake in Arcadia

Snow was falling all over some—damn, it's cold, and suddenly beautiful in the mounting white, had to buy something to go with the little Christmas tree in the little pot, because that was the best we could manage with all our other stuff—the herring, perhaps some pâté (at least partially rabbit, not pork-neck), and we were walking down an empty bike path along the river, which sucked down snowflakes like an hourglass does sand, but for how much longer, still a couple of hours, before the whiteness would win out over the current and overrun its swift flow.

"You know what?" I said. "I have a confession. I went dim then, too. I exuded darkness. I lied. It was my fault, not his. He was innocent. I was the one who ran into him. Even if it wasn't too hard. It shook him up, that's all."

"Who are you talking about?"

"That guy on the bike."

"Oh."

To our left we started to see the glow of bricks in the Mariensztat district, the red spots from the white Japanese flag, and at the Citadel we turned in the direction of the "Gdańsk" metro station, and there, now in the increasingly dense rows of passersby trudging faster and faster from one step to the next, metal filings pulled forward by the magnet of light and warmth, we reached Arcadia. We'd spent an ungodly length of time shopping, in the end we'd gone through several dozen checkout lines, only one third of which were open, and had looked in awe at all the fearless shoppers with their carts, which in this swirl and crush looked like junks on the Mekong Delta, and shortly thereafter we were sitting at a table in our favorite Sky Palace Café, with a view of the entranceway and the customer-service desk. I had a sense that the espresso was tasting especially good, and that, it being the middle of the week, the peach mixed unusually well with my ritual French pastry. I really loved coming here. Though I hated it at the same time. I was looking at Olga, who, having set her empty cup aside, was evidently waiting for something over her own ritual apple pie and two scoops of vanilla ice cream. I asked, "You don't like it today?"

Olga indicated with her head that, no, it tasted great. And suddenly she said, "If you want, I'll tell you a story too."

From the rear pocket of her baggy army pants she pulled out a rather long, white receipt, and unfolding it ceremoniously with both hands like a royal edict declaring a new tax, she examined it carefully under the light. All of a sudden she said, in too loud a voice: "Seventy-one zlotys, twenty-four grosz. VAT, twenty-two percent the cost of goods, seven or three percent for other purchases. Change for a hundred-zloty note. Thank you, and please come again. Remember: ten-percent discount for Carrefour cardholders. Refund only with original receipt. A fairly young woman, no older than thirty, thirty-four. Spent her first couple of years outside of Warsaw, in Błonie, then the rest of her childhood in the capital, where her father got a job at FSO Motors, shortly after they'd started production on the Polonez, the pride of the Gierek era. They moved to the Chomiczówka development, where the factory owned a building that offered cheap apartments, up to fifty-three meters for a family with children; after a few years you could buy the apartment from the cooperative. Spent the last seven months looking for work, receiving a little bit of unemployment money, and spent all that time on a mental rollercoaster, from initially relishing her freedom—you get up when you want, you sleep as much as you want—to depression that was treated, once it had drawn her close to the brink, with Prozac at first, and then with the new generation of psychopharmaceuticals. The medley of oriental and domestic herbs, called 'Serenity Garden,' purchased today for six fifty, is happily the last evidence of her blues, of that totally dark patch, as she put it herself—in a word, her illness, which resulted in her losing seven kilos, and what little money she had for food (if she ever ate anything, at the end of her long, pointless strolls through the city, she'd stop in at one of the last workers' cafeterias in the capital, on Marszałkowska) she re-purposed for medication. She'd been an experienced saleswoman before, having spent five years in the shoe departments of a luxury store in the Promenade Mall, the only one with pretty decent English. Sure, she hadn't learned much in school, and she spoke haltingly like everybody else, but her first serious boyfriend—I'm not talking about those little flings at vocational school—was British. He worked in the grocery department at Marks & Spencer, where he was responsible for pastries and cakes, and later, moving up quickly, for customer service, finally holding a position as 'brand manager.' They were together for over a year, but then he was transferred to Koszalin, where the company was putting up a new store. They had a weekend together, and then another, but you know how the express trains to Koszalin run, then a week at the seashore in September, then her birthday in Warsaw, and a phone call, and another, and it was over, drowned in the salty water. 'What a pity.'

"Sometime later she became involved with a man who was past fifty, one of those consumer types"—Olga drew a second receipt

from her pocket and examined it attentively under the light—
"easy to identify by their compilation of Bob Dylan's greatest hits
(twenty-four zlotys for a double CD). He does his basic shopping
at the MAKRO Cash and Carry, where certain items are tax-de-
ductible. He drops in here mostly for the occasional French goat
cheese (chavroux, cabichou), Italian pecorino, not to mention
Spanish manchego, which only recently appeared on our shelves,
promoted by an intensive ad campaign. Almost ninety decagrams
for seventy-nine zlotys, they're having guests, because, after all,
there's no way the kids would touch that stuff. But one thing at a
time. Childhood spent in Błonie, by no means picture-perfect, but
comfortable. His father, a regular Mr. Fix-It, had a civilian job in
the army. He was a regular party-member, and at home he mostly
just kept to himself. He fixed the private cars of all the big shots
in that smallish, yet quite hierarchical town, and when he had
stuff to fix (Polonezes! from FSO Motors!), and with his income
supplemented by the bank wages brought home by his wife, our
consumer-type's mother, this made for an abundance of meat on
the cutting board, regular vacations at army retreats in Masuria,
newly imported Czech furniture, and the annual blue jeans from
the newly-opened Pewex, which only accepted Western currency.
To these jeans, which were scrubbed down with pumice, they soon
added a guitar, on which the current consumer-type and sometime live-in boyfriend could play a dozen or so chords, graced
every Saturday by the soulful stylings of his then-girlfriend, Janka,
whose name, transformed into Jane, became the title of what we
would have to admit was the best of the two songs he managed to
compose. Just before Martial Law was declared, Janka left for Chi-

cago, and for the next few years she would send postcards from over there, signed with her better name. But with that I'll stop talking about him, because if you keep plucking a string, it'll just keep making the same sound.

"The hopeless romance between the consumer-type and our youngish woman didn't last long anyway; they'd met at the medical clinic during a two-hour wait, and they split up without much fuss three months later. They still run into each other in this or that mall: he gives her a nostalgic hello, she responds with a meaningless nod . . . Last year, the aforementioned shop our heroine works in took a big loss, and not its first. Dealing exclusively in a wide range of classic high-heeled shoes, which until now had held their own against changing fashions, and actually specializing in the most traditional, handmade heels, those that are least protective of the bones in the arches of the foot, they hadn't looked kindly on the invasion of thick soles. Where such soles came from, where they got their fantastic enormity, their width, no one could say for sure. Our leading weeklies, *Polityka*, *Wprost*, followed *Der Spiegel*, the London *Times*, and France's *Le Nouvel Observateur* in proclaiming the arrival of the 'philosophy of the thick sole'—all of these periodicals' front covers making this proclamation at precisely the same time, let us not forget, within thirty days of each other, giving the thick sole the imprimatur of a cultural event and indicating that it had become a new obligation, a material morality . . ."

"I remember that," I threw in, "I remember when the cover of the German *Stern* had Jesus Christ crucified in Adidases that were thicker than the cross itself; the nail barely got through the rubber to reach the wood. And then that image was back on the cover, this time painted as if by the brush of Holbein the Younger, a few months later, when the same popular and influential magazine named Christ its Person of the Year. And then the French weekly *L'Express*—which of course for its Person of the Year chose the soccer star Zidane, whom the entire population of France, from busboys to Jacques Chirac, calls by the childish nickname Zizou—on the very same day gave us the famous scene on the swing from Fragonard's painting. The young lady floating wispily on the wooden board is wearing high-tops with the laces undone, shielding her feet from the lustful gaze of the men, who are dressed in undershirts with a graffiti-style devil sprayed on the front, and they're pushing her and looking up from below—frankly, a little less playfully than in the original."

"That's it," Olga agreed. "It was those magazines and their talk of the 'philosophy of the thick sole,' first in quotation marks, and then without them, that connected the phenomenon with the New-Agey need to 'fly,' to take your body upward, to give it an altitude that'll also lift its spirit, now unburdened and joyful. This need was noticed, reinforced—rather, it was created—by great big shoe companies, which were bringing to bear their experience in manufacturing athletic shoes, especially for basketball players. Slowly, gradually, they started to make the soles thicker in sneakers and work shoes, running shoes and boat shoes, giving them cool-sounding names like Keds and Vans, like exotic vehicles. But as much as the fads connected with sports shoes—like leaving the laces, which were specially made for this purpose, nonchalantly untied, so that they'd slap happily against the sidewalk, embodying what earlier marketing and sociological research had defined as a sense of freedom, of carefree youth and rebellion; or the plastic baubles stuck in various spots around the shoe, which sent light signals into the reflectors on jackets and pants, not to mention on backpacks and school bags—needless to say, those baubles weren't stuck into the holes that were already features of footwear (How else could you *not* tie the short laces of your leather shoes?)—that's the extent to which the thick sole trampled the subtleties and crossed every Rubicon of shoe design. Every manufacturer in Asia and the Caribbean, as well as the small factories in Italy and Spain, to say nothing of those in Poland, all of them desperate to find a way into the market and ready to betray all tradition for even the most paltry return, threw themselves into the production of elevated dress shoes and mules, and then they released thick boat shoes with heels, and finally heels with thick rubber soles—the Polish slang term is 'pork bellies.' So, our client-slash-heroine's store missed its shot at new contracts with their suppliers, whom they happened to despise, they suffered serious losses, which is obvious when you consider their situation, and wanting to get into the black again as quickly as possible—and not by slowly winning their customers back—they made a drastic switch into selling cell phones and sunglasses. After three months of unemployment—and let me add that she went to pick up her unemployment check in person, despite the unimaginable lines, on the first day it was available, because in this uncertain psychological situation and under such never-ending stress she had no faith in tomorrow—today's customer, our heroine, unexpectedly found a job in the last bastion of the old shoe that is Chmielna Street, in the very center of town. She hasn't been working there long, and she's still uncertain about her future. Winter arrived today, snowy but beautiful, she has Thursday off, and in a surge of vague hopefulness our customer came in today for the first time to buy herself something at our store, which is located quite far from the neighborhood where she's been living alone for the past month, after her parents, already retired, returned to their first home in tiny Ożarów, to her still-living grandmother, to Maria Konopnicka Street, formerly Rosa Luxemburg Street. So she got in her ten-year-old Ford and came to do some shopping, as if she could get some guarantee, a seal of approval, yes, as if she'd gain some assurance from this ultimately not-terrible, well-regarded shopping mall, which, as it will sometimes dare to admit, did indeed want her and her money and finally accepted her alone in the money's stead. Note the orange marmalade, highest quality, imported from England, only recently available, which costs as much as eighteen zlotys. That's the day's most extravagant purchase: its balanced, elegant bitterness matches the bronze sheen of the best English leather from Lloyd's, whose goods, along with Italian shoes from Roberto Capucci, the girl sells, and spreading it on an evening baguette (1.50 zlotys) and a morning croissant (4.50 zlotys per pack), she will find the redemption of every employee, the visceral connection between life and work, she'll treat her everyday palate to an angelic flavor. The evening will be lonely, no wine, nor anything sweet for dessert, not even any olives, peanuts, or bacon snacks for an appetizer; this loneliness is also indicated by the absence of whipped cream for the little basket of Australian strawberries, which have a plastic flavor but introduce the pleasant foretaste of June into the whiteness of winter. Spaghetti, tomato sauce from a jar, a salad, fat-free yogurt: dinner doesn't promise to be interesting. Besides that, there was one of those lackluster instant coffees; some Tetley Earl Gray tea in round sachets, though you have to admit it's better than their lemon tea; olive oil made from olives grown in the European Union, cheap, but fairly decent, and approved by the Good Living Foundation and the Institute of Cardiology; and, finally, facial cream containing the newest, indeed revelatory formula called 'Skin Balance Essence.' After dinner she'll watch the movie advertised on the cover of *TV Week* (1.50 zlotys); if memory serves, today Channel 2 is premiering a new series set, as always, in a hospital, presumably a provincial one. The nurse's name is Zo, the surgeon's is Ron, and his beautiful wife, a cardiologist, is called Dor."

"What kind of names are those?" I snickered. "But, honestly. On the French hospital drama they're showing on cable now, the main character is an anesthesiologist named Jo, the on-call doctor is Bo, and the anesthesiologist's rival, a careerist resident, is called Den."

"Sadly, I'm afraid that our customer wouldn't make a good TV character. But about that cream—it's to be applied at night, for wrinkles, but I'll stop there. Because night is the mother of us all."

Olga crumpled up the receipt and, pleased with herself, tossed it into her coffee mug. She took another bite of apple pie. "It's good," she said, picking up the thread of calories that had been cut off by her story. "It's exceptionally delicious today."

With a little coaxing from me, she ordered a second slice, and we drank tea by the mugful, so as to carry its warmth with us for a while on the way back to our humble abode.

Jean-Jacques: A Suite

When writing *The Social Contract,* when writing *Discourse on the Arts and Sciences* or composing that awful *Letter to d'Alembert on Spectacles,* he's called Rousseau or Jean-Jacques Rousseau, though in Poland we call him Jan Jakub Rousseau (our Romantics simply wrote "Ruso"), and he stands politely in his place in the long line of philosophers and thinkers who litter textbooks like hens in a roost. But when leaning with dismay over the broken comb, when running with fire in his soul out of the room where Mlle Lambercier besmirched his honor and never even thought of believing him; when standing on the streets of Paris handing passersby his pamphlet "To All Frenchmen Who Still Love Justice and Truth," in which he employs every rhetorical and hysterical means to protest his innocence; when he is refused a public reading of the *Confessions* and flees somewhere far away, no longer feeling like a person among people; when he lays his next manuscript upon the altar of the Cathedral of Notre-Dame de Paris in the hope that, at the very least, the Lord will hear him out, but only gets as far as the locked grating that guards access to the altar, and he knows that, though he wants to, he no longer remembers how to cry out; then, then he becomes Jean-Jacques, a boy, a youth, or else a hunched, already old man who, in his odd skullcap, steals away through the trees in the park, flashes past the crowds at bus stops, waits in checkout lines, looks at billboards, at the cakes in shop windows, at morning on New World Street, later at the tiny Misianka Café in Skaryszewski Park, now on Francuska Street, and in a moment he'll come up to us holding that faded little folder, gripping it so tightly and awkwardly, and looking us straight in the eye he'll say, "I am alone, alone in the world."

"I am now alone on earth, no longer having any brother, neighbor, friend, or society other than myself."[165] Cars are flowing past, the bus waits a moment longer by the stop, a cell phone prods at someone with a Mozart minuet, and he moves on, pauses before the roses in a tall vase and talks to the florist, driving his gaze into her, and surely beyond, through her pupils, into an emptiness utterly devoid of people:

> People can no longer do good or evil to me here. I have nothing more to hope for or to fear in this world; and here I am, tranquil at the bottom of the abyss, a poor unfortunate mortal, but unperturbed, like God himself.
>
> Everything external is henceforth foreign to me. I no longer have neighbors, fellow creatures, or brothers in this world. I am on earth as though on a foreign planet onto which I have fallen from the one I inhabited.[166]

Alone in the world, alone yet again, as at that moment when, cast out of the interrogation room, he awaited his sentence. He was crying then as now, as he is standing hopeless today on the corner of Francuska and Waleczna, tomorrow somewhere in Ursynów, exposed to the surprised looks of passersby, and the tears fall from him quickly, as if they gushed from some primal place, washing his face of everything incidental and inessential. He was all alone with his transparency, with his heart of crystal, accessible to all eyes. He wanted to show it to everyone, he wanted everyone to show him theirs, that together they might brush off the veils that grow over people like calluses on skin. He did not succeed. This was his rebellion, a rebellion that demands neither destruction nor a new creation—no, one did not have to create the New Man from scratch, as Rousseau's epigones thought; it was enough to cast off the shadows, to finally look each other in the eye. He tried; the looks got bogged down along the way, never reaching our hearts. He himself began to doubt: transparency grew despondent, went hazy, frosted over with weariness. And yet it went on. He could not throw it out or sacrifice it to others, it remained in him alone like an undelivered gift. It's there, now cold, chilly, frozen, like the craters on that foreign planet: it is with him in that barren abyss, and he feels it there, a metallic disc thrust into his insides, an indifferent sadness, a thing no longer of this world that he brought here within himself and wants to keep carrying farther, as far from the earth as he can.

He wanders like the unburied. This is how Hölderlin wrote of him in his ode, and he, too, cried: "And like the unburied dead you wander / Unsettled and look for rest . . ."[167] In a loose tie, in an old, threadbare cap, he stops in at the bazaars, which have been open since six in the morning, and at the warm bakeries steaming with doughy bread, and that smell reminds him of something—but what? what was it?—and he peeks into the huge stores and shopping malls, into the cavernous interiors of the arcades, where the throngs of people carry him along, and he descends into the underground parking structures and says aloud to himself:

> Ten meters underground, as grain before the snow,
> The cars sit patiently, snug in their colored stalls,

And nature gleams metallic, muffles man-made calls,
A place where man's content to come and go.

From what God-given seeds could such a canopy sprout,
And where do rubber roots find water in this dark?
Philosophy comes second to recalling where you parked.
The columns split the space as buildings do the clouds.

Oh, I'll linger here a bit, I feel so elevated!
I pay no mind to cars, mere wheels grouped in fours.
I fear, and yet I feel desire unabated

To see a sea of steel, those transparent other shores.
Yes, I'm going there, my tongue with obols weighted,
To pay my way to another life: of things, and malls, and
stores.

Where did it come from, this transparency? Did it really co-
alesce into this sunny day from scattered flecks of light and penetrate him, Jean-Jacques, together with Mlle Lambercier's scream?
Did he spot it later, when he wanted to understand what goes on
between people, or was it something assigned to him from the
very beginning, in the crib, fluttering down like a strange bird and
brushing him with its wing? Did he bring it out from the depths of
a heart filled with longing and to which he is now returning, unac-
cepted, unchanged, only a thousand times more miserable, long
since relieved of any hope or joy he'd once had? Alone, with only
this inside him, face-to-face with this transparency, like a closed,
sealed monad, a seed whose parting shell has been clamped shut,

he prowls like a werewolf through an unfamiliar town and feels within himself the unsought, discarded crystal, now superfluous, yet very much his own, belonging to him alone, the pure lake he's gulped down, this other "I." Hegel said that Rousseau, now, I'll tell ya, there's a beautiful soul, one of those fellas for whom the object of thought is so "perfectly transparent" that all difference vanishes: the object becomes the same as the "I" that's contemplating it, redoubles it, and that whole transparency forces nothing more than barren repetition. He, however, the foreigner, is still here, is standing at the tram stop and passing up one tram after another, staring at each successive number, so inconsistent, 6 and 24, 4 and 36, and what can we call him, what name should we give this stranger?

> But a man like you, Rousseau,
> Whose soul had the strength to endure
> And grow invincible,
> Whose sense was sure,
> So gifted with powers of hearing
> And speaking that, like the winegod,
> He overflows and, divine and lawless
> In his folly, makes the language of the purest
> Accessible to the good, but justly blinds
> Those sacrilegious slaves who could not care,
> What name should I give this stranger?[168]

Hölderlin's question belonged to Jean-Jacques as well, was posed to himself and everyone else, and his answer was "a demigod," he should be called a demigod, "demigod" was what he replied to himself as well as to us, to those people at the tram stop and in the crosswalk: "It's demigods I think of now, / And there must be a way in which / I know them, so often has their life / Stirred my breast with longings."[169] And will not leave him alone: Hölderlin keeps coming back to Rousseau, and out of longing, out of disquiet, and sometime later, in another poem, he'll keep asking. Why, then, a demigod?

The messengers have found your heart.

You perceived, you understood the language of strangers,
Interpreted their soul! The hint sufficed
The longing one, and hints have long
Been the language of gods.[170]

Strangers, those not of this earth, found his heart, and it was with this heart that he heard and understood their language. Immediately, without the work of words, without their utterance and his own interpretation, but directly. Their hint had to have been given, lucid from the very beginning, yet perceptible, if only to someone like him. He wanted to show others this hint, to teach them instantaneous understanding, in the momentary flash of eyes that meet, in the momentary impulse that moves unseen, by the shortest path, from one heart to another. This is how Julie and Saint-Preux, the lovers in *The New Heloise*, understood one another in their best moments, or at least they knew how to dream of such understanding, as Julie says in her fever-dream: "[I]s there not a way in which two souls so tightly united could have an immediate communication between them, independent of the body and the senses?"[171] A few decades later, Zygmunt Krasiński, *dans l'amour*, will have similar dreams, spinning Delfina Potocka phantoms of wordless understanding within a wilderness of words. Both Julie and Zygmunt knew, however, that, after the fashion of "heavenly messengers," they would be able to speak such a language only in the embrace of God, past death's door, which does not admit words, veils, or masks. Here, on earth, one must speak a language of many words, one needs not just one hint, but many, a great many.

If that's how it is, then that's tough, but at least we can keep things to a minimum. As few hints as possible. That's how it used to be; in his deliberations, Rousseau would return to the undefined, primitive stages of the human condition, when there were no words at all, and later there still aren't many, not many at all. Each new word would distance us further from that directly given possibility of full expression and full understanding—a gesture, a look, one isolated utterance. And writing completed the split, uncoupled intention from expression, expression from reception, once and for all. When millions of signs appeared to replace one or two, immediacy, that primal transparency, was irretrievably lost. No, maybe not lost, but buried, obscured so much that day after day one would have to set about the painstaking and increasingly difficult work of extracting it. Does "the hint," just one hint, still "suffice"? One sign, a single word, one pure look, of which there were not enough to convince Mlle Lambercier? Rousseau fills page after page, Jean-Jacques makes his best attempts among people, every time starting from scratch, every time hopefully, nearly every time unsuccessfully. Finally, he stops. When he is writing *The Reveries of a Solitary Walker*, when he composes that first sentence, "I am alone on earth," with the feeling that no one would ever read these reveries and that he was now writing only for himself, for Jean-Jacques, he finally regains, despite his resignation, some certainty: yes, someone will hear him out, will understand in a single instant, in one flash of the word still gleaming on the paper, and he himself will be that person, he himself and he alone. Yes, the words will finally glitter like a transparent film. After so many years, he will be relieved of the fear that the black of his ink will weigh too heavily on the letters' lights and will not allow his intentions to come to the fore. Now that he is directing them only to himself, they stop, for perhaps the first time, to whither under the burden of their transmission, the imperative to get somewhere, to break through to their recipients. All that they are is instantly self-evident, is now nothing other than a sigh of loneliness, and loneliness is always transparent.

So many unsuccessful words have come before, though there were just as many abandoned glances, unnecessary words, unacknowledged smiles, misunderstood brushes of the hand. He would look, speak, smile, reach out his hand, place it on someone's shoulder, on a knee, timidly, as a sign of his good intentions. So it was good, or so it seemed, that nothing divided them, that between Jean-Jacques and others, Mlle Lambercier, David Hume, who knew to look with such exceptional warmth and kindness, and still others, Madame Dupin, Madame de Chenonceau, there was no obstruction, yet all of a sudden a raven would fly past, a ribbon would wrinkle, darkness would fall, that comb that some-one had broken, that suddenly strange, sorrowful gaze of Hume's, those hands suddenly withdrawn, heads turned away. A moment ago, these people had been completely different, but night had suddenly intruded on the brightest day. He's lost his mind, some would say, he's obsessed, others would confirm, conspiring over a theory of light. He falls into hysterics, in his imagination he spins a blemish into an entire veil, from a single shadow on the wall he whips up dusk itself, from one raven he makes an entire flock, from one spider a whole nest.

So now he walks, alone, alone on earth, more and more ex-hausted, until finally, a stranger in a strange place, he'll rest there, he'll find his grave, maybe somewhere around here, in Powązki Cemetery, next to Antoni Malczewski, martyr of such beautiful solitude, by his symbolic grave, for he has no other, or perhaps far-ther off, anywhere, at the seaside near Portbou, on an island near Saint-Malo, in Ermenonville. Alone, alone among people, among grown-ups and adults, but, as Hölderlin noted (and he was cer-tainly an adult, though also insane), "the child, trembling, clings" to his gravestone.

June, Again

We'd walked downtown to get something to eat, we didn't feel like cooking, in the air you could smell the approaching summer, which before its time had driven us out of our apartment for the last several nights; a conference at the university, the last of the year, was to start the following day, and I felt as I do before any presentation, slightly on edge and filled with gloomy doubts, and if I was hungry, it was more out of habit than the call of a belly that'd been empty since morning. We took a shortcut through Skaryszewski Park—not far from the building that had been erected in a hurry and into which we'd had to move that spring—the dogs, as always, running faster than the people and seeming as though it was only with regret that they couldn't abandon their owners, who were proudly, almost reflectively pounding their fake Reeboks, reflectors at their ankles, onto the paths. Dusk was falling, and they looked like giant fireflies zipping off on some important business. The tennis courts were already deserted, their white lines struck an increasingly sharp impression of symmetry, their whiteness lifted over the earth and hovered lightly, the idyllic sky over the Vistula was slowly shedding its deep red, the river now locked in the half-light, and quietly, yet swiftly, it decanted its waters into the distant north. We arrived at Saska Street, passed the gray mass of the church that seemed to me like a giant hangar for God-knows-what manner of vehicle, the dark Walecznych Street brought us quickly to Francuska, which was puffing here and there with little lights, some minor special effects before bed, and we were perhaps the first of the evening, or at any rate the only, and soon, though they were supposed to be closing, the last guests at Rimini, pasta, tiramisu, etc., Wednesdays two pizzas for the price of one. But we ordered the spaghetti, so as not to rip through the heaps of dough and knock our knives against our plates; we waited without saying anything, in the window I saw Olga's hands caressing her napkin, hanging gloveless over the table and disappearing from time to time in the brake lights of passing cars. A moment later the waiter, with a ceremonious gesture, as though he were presenting the freshly severed heads of our enemies, set our two carbonaras before us. Olga, now clearly hungry, quickly swallowed her first bites and then, observing my sluggish stabs, slowed down. She wound the strands skillfully around her fork and suspended them over her plate, waiting for me to take care of my own scroll; a moment later and we were just about even, a hungry, serene body on one side of the table, an unsettled soul on the other.

"Enough already," Olga said. "Relax. You'll read your paper and be done with it."

"It'll be the same as always," I mumbled. "They'll be whispering in the corners, 'What the hell is this, is it a paper or isn't it? You can never tell.'"

The waiter removed our plates; all that remained of the severed heads were the last streaks of sour cream. Olga's red dress regained its vigor, and she was once again the queen of color for the evening. I didn't feel like going back home, so we sat on the tall stools by the bar. From over the frosted glasses of our Manhattans we stared out into the now-quiet street, its squares of light spaced evenly by the streetlamps.

"Do you think it really wasn't him who broke the comb?" I asked, pushing my hat back from my brow.

"I don't know. I don't know. Maybe he did it." Olga sucked the last drops from her ice and repeated with a strange gravity, either playful or sad, "I don't know. Sometimes I think he did do it."

I said nothing and stared at the drawing on the bottom of the ashtray; it was a gondola floating straight to the Doge's Palace.

The waiter was busying himself with the espresso machine, he had several dark stains on his white blouse; I asked him for another round. "We have to believe him," I said to the air after a long pause. "It was that other one who did it, his cousin, or somebody else."

The waiter nodded and without a word placed two new glasses on the countertop. The ice shimmered against their sides like an Arctic scene in ruddy streams of rain, a landscape painting placed in a museum.

"It's possible," Olga said thoughtfully. "It's possible that that's exactly what happened. But I'm really not sure. Maybe he made the whole thing up. Maybe he thought us up, too, for that matter."

I took another, overlong gulp, which froze my throat. The first night bus drove past the window; what would be the last two dogs of the day were pissing on the grass, their owners staring into Rimini's bright window with indifferent expressions. We sipped our ruddy streams in silence, and the waiter placed a third round in front of us without asking.

"I changed the proportion of bourbon to vermouth," he announced. "To your advantage."

We laughed.

"This'll be the last," Olga said, pointing to me. "He has to be conscious tomorrow."

I pulled my hat down hard and looked haughtily at the glass, as if this were a duel; the bronze inside had become a bit tarnished, most likely from that bourbon.

We left well after midnight, and we could still hear the grating of the cream-colored, metal roller shutters being let down behind us. It was already almost a summer night, warm, and the temperate air grew thick before our eyes in this, the pleasant mineral cave of the city. We returned slowly, hugging, a little tired and full, as if we'd come to the end of a long journey. We quickly set up the pull-out bed and stretched out the sheets, and Olga fell right to sleep, letting out her usual, light sigh, after which, as if she'd crossed some threshold, she could float peacefully along in her slumber till morning.

She turned onto her other side, toward me. She took a deeper breath, opened her eyes for a second as if wanting to check that everything was alright, that the bed hadn't drifted into unfamiliar territory, or that I hadn't been frightened by something, hadn't woken up from some nightmare, after which, reassured, trusting, she climbed back onto her somnolent wave, and next to my hand I felt the minute, warm washes of air she cast to shore. I saw her face, increasingly clear in the coming dawn; the first streak of light was already gliding across her upturned cheek. My sleep went away, minute by minute what was left of my fog lifted out of me, my eyelids became light, tensed, and my eyes stretched them, pulled them back so far that it seemed to me I would never need rest again. I looked with infinite confidence at Olga's face, stirred ever so slightly by her breathing, which sort of lifted the blanket into blue and yellow dots and declared, in its own theatrical way, the hidden rhythm of her heart, yes-no, yes-no. It's you, I thought, you're my sentence, those few utterances, that tiny bundle of syllables, yes-no, yes-no, yes, it's you who settles there, whose sound this is. So long as you're here, as we are. For me, you're that sentence, there will be no other, you're my sentence that encompasses everything, you are that everything, here I am. I looked at her face, that landscape that is so familiar, with its somewhat sharp tip of the nose, which I call The Monk, with its sort of pouty lips, the bottom broader than the top, and in the increasing fullness of the light I made out her every feature, the pebbles and dips, but looking at her in this way I knew, and this knowledge was like a taste, like a morsel placed on the tongue, that the image of it in my eyes was just as real, real to the degree that this, Olga's face, might be the mirror reflection of this image, cast on the blanket from my own face, just as my face is a reflection of the image that has settled in her eyes. The first rays of sunlight stole in through the not-quite-closed curtain, promising a clear and lovely day, and they formed a delicate, barely visible square on the wall. It smoldered in the room, a little flame in the grayness, a cold light, shining, though not yet giving heat. I stared at it and felt it spreading within me, just as it was spreading in our room, and that I was illuminated by it, that it was taking on my shape. Some day, I thought, a day whose first contours were already being broadcast from the future, I would enter this square, I would become transparent, and Olga's breathing would go on forever, would rise in the emptiness of the bedroom, bump against the walls, wither like sad rain on the window, a draft in an empty attic, it would stir the body drawn up under the blanket, alone in the shoreless night, and I felt a love so tremendous, so terrible, so unutterable that it stifled this breathing, and I felt so painfully sorry for its trouble, unnecessary now, since I would disappear, and for the pointless seeking out of the hands into which it would fall, as though onto a warm dish, and after a moment I imagined, or rather understood, that however much time there was, it too would come to an end, would be absorbed into the blanket, into the floor, and, my throat clenched with pain and love, I looked at Olga's face, letting go of its features gradually, like in slow-motion, like in freeze-frame, Olga's face fading more and more, dying away like a tired wind, Olga's face shriveling in the air, radiating for a moment longer with its last detail and now invisible forever, and I saw our room, now without us, without our bodies enveloped in the blanket, empty in the gleaming dawn, enduring for no one but itself, pure, transpicuous, transparent, with a square of light on the wall.

TRANSLATOR'S NOTE

I have made every effort to avail myself of extant translations of quoted material whenever practical, or else to work directly from the original sources noted in these citations. As is common in the Polish tradition of literary nonfiction, however, the original text of *Transparency* omits scholarly attributions, and the author has on occasion quoted from memory. Where I have seen fit to translate directly from the author's appropriation of this material, I have allowed the quotation to remain untethered to its source.

—B.P.

1   James Joyce, *Dubliners*, ed. Jeri Johnson (Oxford: Oxford University Press, 2000), p. 173.

2   Ibid., pp. 175–76.

3   Charles Baudelaire, *The Flowers of Evil*, trans. Edna St. Vincent Millay (New York: Harper's, 1936), p. 157.

4   Jean-Jacques Rousseau, *The Confessions*, trans. John Michael Cohen (New York: Penguin, 1953), p. 29.

5   Ibid., p. 30.

6   Ibid., p. 29.

7   Ibid., p. 31.

8   Ibid., p. 388.

9   Ibid., p. 87.

10   Ibid., p. 415.

11   Jean-Jacques Rousseau, *Rousseau, Judge of Jean-Jacques: Dialogues*, eds. Roger D. Masters and Christopher Kelly, trans. Judith R. Bush, Christopher Kelly, and Roger D. Masters, *Collected Writings of Rousseau*, vol. 1 (Hanover, NH: University Press of New England, 1990), p. 155.

12   Quoted in *The Critical Review* 5, no. 1 (May 1805), p. 15.

13   Robert Burton, *Anatomy of Melancholy* (New York: Tudor, 1920), p. 328.

14   Rene Descartes, *Meditations and Other Metaphysical Writings*, trans. Desmond M. Clarke (New York: Penguin Books, 1999), p. 19.

15   Jean Starobinski, *Jean-Jacques Rousseau: Transparency and Obstruction*, trans. Arthur Goldhammer (Chicago: University of Chicago Press, 1988).

16   Jean-Paul Sartre, *Nausea*, trans. Lloyd Alexander (New York: New Directions, 2007), p. 52.

17   Aristotle, *De Anima: On the Soul*, trans. Hugh Lawson-Tancred (New York: Penguin, 1986), p. 174.

18   Ibid., p. 175.

19   Anca Vasiliu, *Du diaphane: image, milieu, lumière dans le pensée antique et médiévale* (Paris: Librairie Philosophique J. VRIN, 1997), p. 261.

20   Jean-Jacques Rousseau, *The Confessions*, trans. Angela Scholar (Oxford: Oxford University Press, 2000), p. 647.

21   Jean-Jacques Rousseau, *Rousseau, Judge of Jean-Jacques: Dialogues*, p. 157.

22   Jean-Jacques Rousseau, *Julie, or the New Heloise: Letters of Two Lovers Who Live in a Small Town at the Foot of the Alps*, trans. Philip Stewart and Jean Vaché (Hanover: Dartmouth College Press, 1997), pp. 455–56.

23   Jean Paul Richter, "Apologue of Jean Paul Richter," in *Supplement to the Musical Library* (March–December 1835): p. 105.

24   Joseph Joubert, *The Notebooks of Joseph Joubert*, trans. Paul Auster (New York: NYRB, 2005), p. 147. [I have modified the second of the two sentences from what appears in Auster's translation. —*Trans.*]

25   Quoted in Maurice Blanchot, *The Book to Come*, trans. Charlotte Mandell (Stanford: Stanford University Press, 2003), p. 58.

26   Stendhal, *Love*, trans. Gilbert Sale and Suzanne Sale (New York: Penguin Books, 1975), p. 284.

27   Quoted in Philippe Hamon, *Expositions: Literature and Architecture in Nineteenth-Century France*, trans. Katia Sainson-Frank and Lisa Maguire (Berkeley: University of California Press, 1992), p. 76.

28   Czesław Miłosz, *Visions from San Francisco Bay*, trans. Richard Lourie (New York: Farrar, Straus and Giroux, 1982), p. 3.

29   Gail Levin, *Edward Hopper: An Intimate Biography* (Berkeley: University of California Press, 1995), p. 139.

30   Yves Bonnefoy, *The Lure and the Truth of Painting: Selected Essays on Art*, ed. Richard Stamelman (Chicago: University of Chicago Press, 1995).

31   Jean-Jacques Rousseau, *Confessions*, p. 573.

32   Ibid., p. 437.

33 E.M. Cioran, *Écartèlement* (Paris: Gallimard, 1979), p. 31.

34 Milan Kundera, *The Art of the Novel*, trans. Linda Asher (New York: Harper, 2000), p. 139. [Kundera is quoting from his own novel, *Life is Elsewhere. —Trans.*]

35 Peter Sloterdijk, *Critique de la raison cynique*, trans. Michael Eldred (Minneapolis: University of Minnesota Press, 1987), p. 57.

36 Ibid., pp. 47-53.

37 [The American edition of *The Art of the Novel* uses sixty-three, rather than the original sixty-five, headings. —*Trans.*]

38 Milan Kundera, *The Art of the Novel*, pp. 152-53.

39 Pierre Lévy-Soussan, *Eloge de secret* (Paris: Hachette Littératures, 2006).

40 Witold Gombrowicz, *Ferdydurke*, trans. Danuta Borchardt (New Haven: Yale University Press, 2000), p. 134.

41 Serge Raffy, *La guerre des trois* (Paris: Fayard, 2006).

42 André Boyer, *L'Impossible éthique des enterprises* (Paris: Editions d'Organisations, 2002).

43 Thierry Libaert, *La transparence en trompe-l'oeil* (Paris: Descartes et Cie, 2003).

44 Florence Aubenas and Miguel Benasayag, *La fabrication de l'information: les journalistes et l'idéologie de la communication* (Paris: La Découverte, 1999), p. 73.

45 Jadwiga Staniszkis, "Niespełnione marzenie," *Rzeczpospolita* (February 26-27, 2005), n.p.

46 Leopold Tyrmand, *The Man with the White Eyes*, trans. David Welsh (New York: Knopf, 1959), p. 426. [The italicized portion of the quotation is omitted from the English translation. —*Trans.*]

47 Maurice Maeterlinck, *Hothouses: Poems, 1889*, trans. Richard Howard (Princeton: Princeton University Press, 2003), p. vii.

48   Zygmunt Krasiński, *Listy do Delfiny Potockiej*, vol. 3, ed. Zbigniew Sudowski (Warsaw: Państwowy Instytut Wydawniczy, 1975), p. 219.

49   Alfred de Musset, *Fantasio*, in Alfred de Musset, *Fantasio and Other Plays*, trans. Richard Howard (New York: Theatre Communications Group, 1993), p. 12.

50   Alfred de Musset, *The Complete Writings of Alfred de Musset*, vol. 4, trans. Edmund Burke Thompson (New York: Hill, 1905), p. 100.

51   Charles Baudelaire, *Paris Spleen and La Fanfarlo*, trans. Raymond N. MacKenzie (Indianapolis: Hackett, 2008), p. 130.

52   Emile Zola, *The Kill*, trans. Brian Nelson (Oxford: Oxford University Press, 2008), p. 17.

53   Juliusz Słowacki, *Kordian*, Act 3, scene 6.

54   Stéphane Mallarmé, *Mallarmé on Fashion: A Translation of the Fashion Magazine* La Dernière Mode *with Commentary*, trans. P.N. Furbank and A.M. Cain (Oxford: Berg, 2004), p. 174.

55   Ibid., p. 175.

56   Ibid.

57   Jules Verne, *Twenty Thousand Leagues under the Sea*, trans. William Butcher (Oxford: Oxford University Press, 2009), p. 78.

58   Ibid., p. 93.

59   Ibid., p. 50.

60   Philippe Hamon, *Expositions: Literature and Architecture in Nineteenth-Century France*, p. 9.

61   Marcel Proust, *Remembrance of Things Past*, vol. 2, *The Guermantes Way and Cities of the Plain*, trans. C.K. Scott Moncrieff and Terry Kilmartin (New York: Vintage, 1982), p. 594.

62   Roland Barthes, *Mythologies*, trans. Anette Lavers (New York: Hill and Wang, 1972), p. 65.

63   Emile Zola, *The Kill*, pp. 168–69.

64   Bertold Brecht, *Poems 1913-1956*, eds. John Willett and Ralph Manheim (London: Methuen, 1987), p. 131.

65   Walter Benjamin, *Fragments*, ed. Rolf Tiedemann (Paris: PUV, 2001), pp. 256–57.

66   Paul Valéry, "The Lost Wine," trans. Barbara Howes, in *The Anchor Anthology of French Poetry: From Nerval to Valery in English Translation*, ed. Angel Flores (New York: Anchor Books, 2000), p. 281.

67   Walter Benjamin, *Selected Writings*, vol. 2, part 2, eds. Michael W. Jennings, Howard Eiland, and Gary Smith (Cambridge, MA: Harvard University Press, 1999), p. 734.

68   Ibid.

69   Ibid., p. 735.

70   Ibid., p. 732.

71   Paul Scheerbart, *Glass Architecture*, trans. James Palmes, in *Glass Architecture, by Paul Scheerbart, and Alpine Architecture, by Bruno Taut*, ed. Dennis Sharp (New York: Praeger, 1972), p. 41.

72   Ibid.

73   Ibid., p. 46.

74   Ibid., p. 58.

75   Daniel Payot, "La sobriété « barbare » de Paul Scheerbart," in: Paul Scheerbart, *L'architecture de verre* (Strasbourg: Circé, 1995).

76   Paul Scheerbart, *Glass Architecture*, p. 61.

77   Roland Barthes, *Critical Essays*, trans. Richard Howard (Evanston, IL: Northwestern University Press, 1974), p. 3.

78   Jean-Louis Schefer, *La Lumière et la table: Dispositif de la peinture hollandaise* (Paris: Maeght Editeur, 1995), pp. 25–26.

79 Ibid.

80 Paul Scheerbart, *Glass Architecture*, p. 54.

81 Quoted in Brian Bruce Taylor, *Le Corbusier: The City of Refuge, Paris 1929/33* (Chicago: University of Chicago Press, 1987), p. 80.

82 Walter Benjamin, *Selected Writings*, vol. 2, part 1, eds. Michael W. Jennings, Howard Eiland, and Gary Smith (Cambridge, Mass.: Harvard University Press, 1999), p. 209.

83 Walter Benjamin, *Selected Writings*, vol. 2, part 2, p. 731.

84 Ibid., p. 734.

85 Ibid.

86 Ibid.

87 Ibid., p. 735.

88 Daniel Payot, "La sobriété « barbare » de Paul Scheerbart," p. 23.

89 Jean Baudrillard, *The System of Objects*, trans. James Benedict (London: Verso, 2005), p. 42.

90 Charles Baudelaire, *Les Fleurs du Mal*, trans. Richard Howard (Jaffrey, NH: David R. Godine, 1982), pp. 90–91.

91 Stéphane Mallarmé, *Selected Poetry and Prose*, ed. Mary Ann Caws (New York: New Directions, 1982), p. 17.

92 Piotr Matywiecki, *Ta chmura powraca* (Krakow: Wydawnictwo Literackie, 2005), p. 68.

93 Quoted in Marshall Berman, *All That Is Solid Melts into Air: The Experience of Modernity* (New York: Penguin, 1982), p. 239.

94 Ibid., pp. 239–240.

95 Ibid., p. 237.

96 Ibid., p. 239.

97   Johann Wolfgang von Goethe, *Selected Poetry of Johann Wolfgang von Goethe*, ed. and trans. David Luke (New York: Penguin, 1999), p. 5.

98   Nikolai Chernyshevsky, *What Is To Be Done?*, trans. Michael R. Katz (Ithaca, NY: Cornell University Press, 1989), p. 360.

99   Ibid., p. 369.

100   Ibid., pp. 370, 376.

101   Ibid., pp. 370, 372.

102   Quoted in Herman Hertzberger, *Lessons for Students in Architecture* (Rotterdam: 010 Publishers, 1991), p. 218. [The sentence beginning "The male and female workers…" is not included in Hertzberger's book. —*Trans.*]

103   Fyodor Dostoevsky, *Notes from Underground*, trans. Richard Pevear and Larissa Volokhonsky (New York: Vintage, 1993), p. 35.

104   Ibid., pp. 24–25.

105   Marshall Berman, *All That Is Solid Melts into Air*, p. 245.

106   Michel Foucault, *Discipline and Punish: The Birth of the Prison*, trans. Alan Sheridan (New York: Vintage, 1977), p. 204.

107   Ibid., p. 203.

108   Vladimir Nabokov, *Invitation to a Beheading*, trans. Dmitri Nabokov (New York: Vintage, 1989), pp. 72, 24.

109   Ibid., p. 24.

110   Ibid., p. 52.

111   Ibid., p. 223.

112   Pierre Vago, "Un hôtel particulier à Paris," in *Pierre Chareau: La maison de verre 1928-1933*, ed. Olivier Cinqualbre (Paris: Jean-Michel Place, 2001), p. 24.

113 Ivor Montagu, *With Eisenstein in Hollywood: A Chapter of Autobiography* (New York: International Publishers, 1969), p. 102.

114 Quoted in Claude Gandelman, "Représenter la verre," *Traverses* 46 (1989), p. 12.

115 Marshall Berman, *All That Is Solid Melts Into Air*, p. 245.

116 Ibid., p. 242.

117 Quoted in Joseph Frank, *Dostoevsky: The Years of Ordeal, 1850-1859* (Princeton: Princeton University Press, 1990), pp. 45–46.

118 Peter Sloterdijk, "The Crystal Palace," trans. Michael Darroch, *Public* 37 (2008), pp. 4, 12.

119 Ibid., p. 12.

120 Ibid., p. 15.

121 Fyodor Dostoevsky, *Winter Notes on Summer Impressions*, trans. David Patterson (Evanston, IL: Northwestern University Press, 1988), p. 37.

122 Peter Sloterdijk, "The Crystal Palace," pp. 13, 15.

123 Quoted in Jules Henrivaux, "A House of Glass," *The Chautauquan* 28:4 (January 1899), p. 392.

124 Emile Zola, *Au Bonheur des Dames*, trans. Robin Buss (New York: Penguin, 2001), pp. 231, 245.

125 Peter Sloterdijk, "Czy Polacy odnajdą szczęście w Kryształowym Pałacu: Rozmowa z Maciejem Nowickim," *Europa* 1 (2006). http://wiadomosci.dziennik.pl/wydarzenia/artykuly/174295,czy-polacy-odnajda-szczescie-w-krysztalowym-palacu.html.

126 Maurice Maeterlinck, *Hothouses: Poems, 1889*, p. 3.

127 Walter Gropius, "Programme of the Staatliches Bauhaus in Weimar," in *Programs and Manifestoes on 20th-Century Architecture*, ed., Ulrich Conrads (Cambridge, MA: MIT Press, 1970), p. 49.

128   Pierre Chareau, "La maison de verre," in *Pierre Chareau: La maison de verre 1928–1933,* p. 37.

129   David Whitney and Jeffrey Kipnis, *Philip Johnson: The Glass House* (New York: Pantheon, 1993), p. 160.

130   Ibid., p. 99.

131   Ibid., pp. 81, 27-28.

132   Richard Sennett, *The Conscience of the Eye: The Design and Social Life of Cities* (New York: W.W. Norton, 1990), p. 113.

133   Richard Sennett, in *Raritan Reading,* ed. Richard Poirier (New Brunswick: Rutgers University Press, 1990).

134   André Breton, *Manifestoes of Surrealism,* trans. Richard Seaver and Helen R. Lane (Ann Arbor, MI: University of Michigan Press, 1969), p. 28.

135   André Breton, *Nadja,* trans. Richard Howard (New York: Grove Press, 1960), p. 18.

136   "The Technical Manifesto of Futurist Painting," qtd. in Christine Poggi, *Inventing Futurism: The Art and Politics of Artificial Optimism* (Princeton: Princeton University Press, 2009), p. 102.

137   André Breton, *Earthlight,* trans. Bill Zavatsky and Zack Rogow (Los Angeles: Sun & Moon Press, 1993), p. 72.

138   Vladimir Nabokov, *Novels 1969–1974,* ed. Brian Boyd (New York: Library of America, 1996), p. 518.

139   Ibid., p. 489.

140   Ibid.

141   Ibid.

142   Italo Calvino, *Six Memos for the Next Millennium* (Cambridge, MA: Harvard University Press, 1988), p. 45.

143 Ibid., p. 92.

144 Ibid.

145 Francois-Rene Chateaubriand, *Memoirs of Chateaubriand, from His Birth in 1768, till His Return to France in 1800, Written by Himself* (London: Henry Colburn, 1849), p. 249.

146 Maurice Blanchot, *The Book to Come*, p. 161.

147 Ibid., p. 200.

148 Roland Barthes, *Writing Degree Zero*, trans. Annette Lavers and Colin Smith (New York: Farrar, Straus and Giroux, 1977), p. 77.

149 Ibid., pp. 77, 5.

150 Octavio Paz, *The Monkey Grammarian*, trans. Helen Lane (New York: Arcade, 1990), p. 157.

151 Ibid., pp. 159, 110.

152 Ibid., p. 159.

153 Ibid., p. 113.

154 Ibid., p. 110.

155 Ibid., p. 156.

156 Ibid., p. 41.

157 Giuseppe Tucci, *The Theory and Practice of Mandala*, trans. Alan Houghton Brodrick (London: Rider, 1969), p. 39.

158 Stephan Mallarmé, *Selected Poetry and Prose*, p. 97.

159 Ibid.

160 Francis Ponge, *Selected Poems*, ed. Margaret Guiton, trans. C.K. Williams *et al.* (Winston-Salem: Wake Forest University Press, 1994), p. 75.

161 Stephan Mallarmé, *Selected Poetry and Prose*, p. 101.

162 Roland Barthes, *Writing Degree Zero*, p. 75.

163 Ibid., p. 76.

164   Czeslaw Milosz, *New and Collected Poems (1931–2001)* (New York: Ecco, 2001), p. 195.

165   Jean-Jacques Rousseau, *The Reveries of the Solitary Walker,* trans. Charles E. Butterworth (Indianapolis: Hackett, 1992), p. 1.

166   Ibid., p. 5.

167   Friedrich Hölderlin, *Odes and Elegies,* trans. Nick Huff (Wesleyan: Wesleyan University Press, 2008), p. 89.

168   Friedrich Hölderlin, *Hymns and Fragments,* trans. Richard Sieburth (Princeton: Princeton University Press, 1984), p. 77.

169   Ibid.

170   Friedrich Hölderlin, *Odes and Elegies,* pp. 89–91.

171   Jean-Jacques Rousseau, *Julie, or the New Heloise,* pp. 270–271.

MAREK BIEŃCZYK was born in 1956. One of the most esteemed contemporary Polish writers, he is the author of the novels *Tworki* and *Terminal*, in addition to an essay collection on the subject of melancholy. Bieńczyk has translated works by Milan Kundera and Roland Barthes into Polish, and is also one of Poland's foremost wine critics.

BENJAMIN PALOFF is the author of *The Politics*, a collection of poems, and is an editor for the *Boston Review*. He teaches at the University of Michigan and has received fellowships from Poland's Book Institute and the National Endowment for the Arts.

PETROS ABATZOGLOU, *What Does Mrs.*
Freeman Want?
MICHAL AJVAZ, *The Golden Age.*
The Other City.
PIERRE ALBERT-BIROT, *Grabinoulor.*
YUZ ALESHKOVSKY, *Kangaroo.*
FELIPE ALFAU, *Chromos.*
Locos.
JOÃO ALMINO, *The Book of Emotions.*
IVAN ÂNGELO, *The Celebration.*
The Tower of Glass.
DAVID ANTIN, *Talking.*
ANTÓNIO LOBO ANTUNES, *Knowledge of Hell.*
The Splendor of Portugal.
ALAIN ARIAS-MISSON, *Theatre of Incest.*
IFTIKHAR ARIF AND WAQAS KHWAJA, EDS.,
Modern Poetry of Pakistan.
JOHN ASHBERY AND JAMES SCHUYLER,
A Nest of Ninnies.
ROBERT ASHLEY, *Perfect Lives.*
GABRIELA AVIGUR-ROTEM, *Heatwave*
and Crazy Birds.
HEIMRAD BÄCKER, *transcript.*
DJUNA BARNES, *Ladies Almanack.*
Ryder.
JOHN BARTH, *LETTERS.*
Sabbatical.
DONALD BARTHELME, *The King.*
Paradise.
SVETISLAV BASARA, *Chinese Letter.*
MIQUEL BAUÇÀ, *The Siege in the Room.*
RENÉ BELLETTO, *Dying.*
MAREK BIEŃCZYK, *Transparency.*
MARK BINELLI, *Sacco and Vanzetti*
Must Die!
ANDREI BITOV, *Pushkin House.*
ANDREJ BLATNIK, *You Do Understand.*
LOUIS PAUL BOON, *Chapel Road.*
My Little War.
Summer in Termuren.
ROGER BOYLAN, *Killoyle.*
IGNÁCIO DE LOYOLA BRANDÃO,
Anonymous Celebrity.
The Good-Bye Angel.
Teeth under the Sun.
Zero.
BONNIE BREMSER, *Troia: Mexican Memoirs.*
CHRISTINE BROOKE-ROSE, *Amalgamemnon.*
BRIGID BROPHY, *In Transit.*
MEREDITH BROSNAN, *Mr. Dynamite.*
GERALD L. BRUNS, *Modern Poetry and*
the Idea of Language.
EVGENY BUNIMOVICH AND J. KATES, EDS.,
Contemporary Russian Poetry:
An Anthology.
GABRIELLE BURTON, *Heartbreak Hotel.*
MICHEL BUTOR, *Degrees.*
Mobile.
Portrait of the Artist as a Young Ape.
G. CABRERA INFANTE, *Infante's Inferno.*
Three Trapped Tigers.
JULIETA CAMPOS,
The Fear of Losing Eurydice.
ANNE CARSON, *Eros the Bittersweet.*
ORLY CASTEL-BLOOM, *Dolly City.*
CAMILO JOSÉ CELA, *Christ versus Arizona.*
The Family of Pascual Duarte.
The Hive.
LOUIS-FERDINAND CÉLINE, *Castle to Castle.*
Conversations with Professor Y.
London Bridge.

Normance.
North.
Rigadoon.
MARIE CHAIX, *The Laurels of Lake Constance.*
HUGO CHARTERIS, *The Tide Is Right.*
JEROME CHARYN, *The Tar Baby.*
ERIC CHEVILLARD, *Demolishing Nisard.*
LUIS CHITARRONI, *The No Variations.*
MARC CHOLODENKO, *Mordechai Schamz.*
JOSHUA COHEN, *Witz.*
EMILY HOLMES COLEMAN, *The Shutter*
of Snow.
ROBERT COOVER, *A Night at the Movies.*
STANLEY CRAWFORD, *Log of the S.S. The*
Mrs Unguentine.
Some Instructions to My Wife.
ROBERT CREELEY, *Collected Prose.*
RENÉ CREVEL, *Putting My Foot in It.*
RALPH CUSACK, *Cadenza.*
SUSAN DAITCH, *L.C.*
Storytown.
NICHOLAS DELBANCO, *The Count of Concord.*
Sherbrookes.
NIGEL DENNIS, *Cards of Identity.*
PETER DIMOCK, *A Short Rhetoric for*
Leaving the Family.
ARIEL DORFMAN, *Konfidenz.*
COLEMAN DOWELL,
The Houses of Children.
Island People.
Too Much Flesh and Jabez.
ARKADII DRAGOMOSHCHENKO, *Dust.*
RIKKI DUCORNET, *The Complete*
Butcher's Tales.
The Fountains of Neptune.
The Jade Cabinet.
The One Marvelous Thing.
Phosphor in Dreamland.
The Stain.
The Word "Desire."
WILLIAM EASTLAKE, *The Bamboo Bed.*
Castle Keep.
Lyric of the Circle Heart.
JEAN ECHENOZ, *Chopin's Move.*
STANLEY ELKIN, *A Bad Man.*
Boswell: A Modern Comedy.
Criers and Kibitzers, Kibitzers
and Criers.
The Dick Gibson Show.
The Franchiser.
George Mills.
The Living End.
The MacGuffin.
The Magic Kingdom.
Mrs. Ted Bliss.
The Rabbi of Lud.
Van Gogh's Room at Arles.
FRANÇOIS EMMANUEL, *Invitation to a*
Voyage.
ANNIE ERNAUX, *Cleaned Out.*
SALVADOR ESPRIU, *Ariadne in the*
Grotesque Labyrinth.
LAUREN FAIRBANKS, *Muzzle Thyself.*
Sister Carrie.
LESLIE A. FIEDLER, *Love and Death in*
the American Novel.
JUAN FILLOY, *Faction.*
Op Oloop.
ANDY FITCH, *Pop Poetics.*
GUSTAVE FLAUBERT, *Bouvard and Pécuchet.*
KASS FLEISHER, *Talking out of School.*

SELECTED DALKEY ARCHIVE TITLES

FORD MADOX FORD,
The March of Literature.
JON FOSSE, *Aliss at the Fire.*
Melancholy.
MAX FRISCH, *I'm Not Stiller.*
Man in the Holocene.
CARLOS FUENTES, *Christopher Unborn.*
Distant Relations.
Terra Nostra.
Vlad.
Where the Air Is Clear.
TAKEHIKO FUKUNAGA, *Flowers of Grass.*
WILLIAM GADDIS, *J R.*
The Recognitions.
JANICE GALLOWAY, *Foreign Parts.*
The Trick Is to Keep Breathing.
WILLIAM H. GASS, *Cartesian Sonata
and Other Novellas.*
Finding a Form.
A Temple of Texts.
The Tunnel.
Willie Masters' Lonesome Wife.
GÉRARD GAVARRY, *Hoppla! 1 2 3.*
Making a Novel.
ETIENNE GILSON,
The Arts of the Beautiful.
Forms and Substances in the Arts.
C. S. GISCOMBE, *Giscome Road.*
Here.
Prairie Style.
DOUGLAS GLOVER, *Bad News of the Heart.*
The Enamoured Knight.
WITOLD GOMBROWICZ,
A Kind of Testament.
PAULO EMÍLIO SALES GOMES, *P's Three
Women.*
KAREN ELIZABETH GORDON, *The Red Shoes.*
GEORGI GOSPODINOV, *Natural Novel.*
JUAN GOYTISOLO, *Count Julian.*
Exiled from Almost Everywhere.
Juan the Landless.
Makbara.
Marks of Identity.
PATRICK GRAINVILLE, *The Cave of Heaven.*
HENRY GREEN, *Back.*
Blindness.
Concluding.
Doting.
Nothing.
JACK GREEN, *Fire the Bastards!*
JIŘÍ GRUŠA, *The Questionnaire.*
GABRIEL GUDDING,
Rhode Island Notebook.
MELA HARTWIG, *Am I a Redundant
Human Being?*
JOHN HAWKES, *The Passion Artist.*
Whistlejacket.
ELIZABETH HEIGHWAY, ED., *Best of
Contemporary Fiction from Georgia.*
ALEKSANDAR HEMON, ED.,
Best European Fiction.
AIDAN HIGGINS, *Balcony of Europe.*
A Bestiary.
Blind Man's Bluff
Bornholm Night-Ferry.
Darkling Plain: Texts for the Air.
Flotsam and Jetsam.
Langrishe, Go Down.
Scenes from a Receding Past.
Windy Arbours.
KEIZO HINO, *Isle of Dreams.*
KAZUSHI HOSAKA, *Plainsong.*

ALDOUS HUXLEY, *Antic Hay.*
Crome Yellow.
Point Counter Point.
Those Barren Leaves.
Time Must Have a Stop.
NAOYUKI II, *The Shadow of a Blue Cat.*
MIKHAIL IOSSEL AND JEFF PARKER, EDS.,
*Amerika: Russian Writers View the
United States.*
DRAGO JANČAR, *The Galley Slave.*
GERT JONKE, *The Distant Sound.*
Geometric Regional Novel.
Homage to Czerny.
The System of Vienna.
JACQUES JOUET, *Mountain R.*
Savage.
Upstaged.
CHARLES JULIET, *Conversations with
Samuel Beckett and Bram van
Velde.*
MIEKO KANAI, *The Word Book.*
YORAM KANIUK, *Life on Sandpaper.*
HUGH KENNER, *The Counterfeiters.*
*Flaubert, Joyce and Beckett:
The Stoic Comedians.*
Joyce's Voices.
DANILO KIŠ, *The Attic.*
Garden, Ashes.
The Lute and the Scars
Psalm 44.
A Tomb for Boris Davidovich.
ANITA KONKKA, *A Fool's Paradise.*
GEORGE KONRÁD, *The City Builder.*
TADEUSZ KONWICKI, *A Minor Apocalypse.*
The Polish Complex.
MENIS KOUMANDAREAS, *Koula.*
ELAINE KRAF, *The Princess of 72nd Street.*
JIM KRUSOE, *Iceland.*
AYŞE KULIN, *Farewell: A Mansion in
Occupied Istanbul.*
EWA KURYLUK, *Century 21.*
EMILIO LASCANO TEGUI, *On Elegance
While Sleeping.*
ERIC LAURRENT, *Do Not Touch.*
HERVÉ LE TELLIER, *The Sextine Chapel.*
*A Thousand Pearls (for a Thousand
Pennies)*
VIOLETTE LEDUC, *La Bâtarde.*
EDOUARD LEVÉ, *Autoportrait.*
Suicide.
MARIO LEVI, *Istanbul Was a Fairy Tale.*
SUZANNE JILL LEVINE, *The Subversive
Scribe: Translating Latin
American Fiction.*
DEBORAH LEVY, *Billy and Girl.*
*Pillow Talk in Europe and Other
Places.*
JOSÉ LEZAMA LIMA, *Paradiso.*
ROSA LIKSOM, *Dark Paradise.*
OSMAN LINS, *Avalovara.*
The Queen of the Prisons of Greece.
ALF MAC LOCHLAINN,
The Corpus in the Library.
Out of Focus.
RON LOEWINSOHN, *Magnetic Field(s).*
MINA LOY, *Stories and Essays of Mina Loy.*
BRIAN LYNCH, *The Winner of Sorrow.*
D. KEITH MANO, *Take Five.*
MICHELINE AHARONIAN MARCOM,
The Mirror in the Well.
BEN MARCUS,
The Age of Wire and String.

WALLACE MARKFIELD,
Teitlebaum's Window.
To an Early Grave.
DAVID MARKSON, *Reader's Block.*
Springer's Progress.
Wittgenstein's Mistress.
CAROLE MASO, *AVA.*
LADISLAV MATEJKA AND KRYSTYNA
POMORSKA, EDS.,
Readings in Russian Poetics:
Formalist and Structuralist Views.
HARRY MATHEWS,
The Case of the Persevering Maltese:
Collected Essays.
Cigarettes.
The Conversions.
The Human Country: New and
Collected Stories.
The Journalist.
My Life in CIA.
Singular Pleasures.
The Sinking of the Odradek
Stadium.
Tlooth.
20 Lines a Day.
JOSEPH MCELROY,
Night Soul and Other Stories.
THOMAS MCGONIGLE,
Going to Patchogue.
ROBERT L. MCLAUGHLIN, ED., *Innovations:*
An Anthology of Modern &
Contemporary Fiction.
ABDELWAHAB MEDDEB, *Talismano.*
GERHARD MEIER, *Isle of the Dead.*
HERMAN MELVILLE, *The Confidence-Man.*
AMANDA MICHALOPOULOU, *I'd Like.*
STEVEN MILLHAUSER, *The Barnum Museum.*
In the Penny Arcade.
RALPH J. MILLS, JR., *Essays on Poetry.*
MOMUS, *The Book of Jokes.*
CHRISTINE MONTALBETTI, *The Origin of Man.*
Western.
OLIVE MOORE, *Spleen.*
NICHOLAS MOSLEY, *Accident.*
Assassins.
Catastrophe Practice.
Children of Darkness and Light.
Experience and Religion.
A Garden of Trees.
God's Hazard.
The Hesperides Tree.
Hopeful Monsters.
Imago Bird.
Impossible Object.
Inventing God.
Judith.
Look at the Dark.
Natalie Natalia.
Paradoxes of Peace.
Serpent.
Time at War.
The Uses of Slime Mould:
Essays of Four Decades.
WARREN MOTTE,
Fables of the Novel: French Fiction
since 1990.
Fiction Now: The French Novel in
the 21st Century.
Oulipo: A Primer of Potential
Literature.
GERALD MURNANE, *Barley Patch.*
Inland.

YVES NAVARRE, *Our Share of Time.*
Sweet Tooth.
DOROTHY NELSON, *In Night's City.*
Tar and Feathers.
ESHKOL NEVO, *Homesick.*
WILFRIDO D. NOLLEDO, *But for the Lovers.*
FLANN O'BRIEN, *At Swim-Two-Birds.*
At War.
The Best of Myles.
The Dalkey Archive.
Further Cuttings.
The Hard Life.
The Poor Mouth.
The Third Policeman.
CLAUDE OLLIER, *The Mise-en-Scène.*
Wert and the Life Without End.
GIOVANNI ORELLI, *Walaschek's Dream.*
PATRIK OUŘEDNÍK, *Europeana.*
The Opportune Moment, 1855.
BORIS PAHOR, *Necropolis.*
FERNANDO DEL PASO, *News from the Empire.*
Palinuro of Mexico.
ROBERT PINGET, *The Inquisitory.*
Mahu or The Material.
Trio.
A. G. PORTA, *The No World Concerto.*
MANUEL PUIG, *Betrayed by Rita Hayworth.*
The Buenos Aires Affair.
Heartbreak Tango.
RAYMOND QUENEAU, *The Last Days.*
Odile.
Pierrot Mon Ami.
Saint Glinglin.
ANN QUIN, *Berg.*
Passages.
Three.
Tripticks.
ISHMAEL REED, *The Free-Lance Pallbearers.*
The Last Days of Louisiana Red.
Ishmael Reed: The Plays.
Juice!
Reckless Eyeballing.
The Terrible Threes.
The Terrible Twos.
Yellow Back Radio Broke-Down.
JASIA REICHARDT, *15 Journeys from Warsaw*
to London.
NOËLLE REVAZ, *With the Animals.*
JOÃO UBALDO RIBEIRO, *House of the*
Fortunate Buddhas.
JEAN RICARDOU, *Place Names.*
RAINER MARIA RILKE, *The Notebooks of*
Malte Laurids Brigge.
JULIÁN RÍOS, *The House of Ulysses.*
Larva: A Midsummer Night's Babel.
Poundemonium.
Procession of Shadows.
AUGUSTO ROA BASTOS, *I the Supreme.*
DANIËL ROBBERECHTS, *Arriving in Avignon.*
JEAN ROLIN, *The Explosion of the*
Radiator Hose.
OLIVIER ROLIN, *Hotel Crystal.*
ALIX CLEO ROUBAUD, *Alix's Journal.*
JACQUES ROUBAUD, *The Form of a*
City Changes Faster, Alas, Than
the Human Heart.
The Great Fire of London.
Hortense in Exile.
Hortense Is Abducted.
The Loop.
Mathematics:
The Plurality of Worlds of Lewis.

SELECTED DALKEY ARCHIVE TITLES

The Princess Hoppy.
Some Thing Black.
LEON S. ROUDIEZ, *French Fiction Revisited.*
RAYMOND ROUSSEL, *Impressions of Africa.*
VEDRANA RUDAN, *Night.*
STIG SÆTERBAKKEN, *Siamese.*
LYDIE SALVAYRE, *The Company of Ghosts.*
Everyday Life.
The Lecture.
Portrait of the Writer as a
Domesticated Animal.
The Power of Flies.
LUIS RAFAEL SÁNCHEZ,
Macho Camacho's Beat.
SEVERO SARDUY, *Cobra & Maitreya.*
NATHALIE SARRAUTE,
Do You Hear Them?
Martereau.
The Planetarium.
ARNO SCHMIDT, *Collected Novellas.*
Collected Stories.
Nobodaddy's Children.
Two Novels.
ASAF SCHURR, *Motti.*
CHRISTINE SCHUTT, *Nightwork.*
GAIL SCOTT, *My Paris.*
DAMION SEARLS, *What We Were Doing*
and Where We Were Going.
JUNE AKERS SEESE,
Is This What Other Women Feel Too?
What Waiting Really Means.
BERNARD SHARE, *Inish.*
Transit.
AURELIE SHEEHAN, *Jack Kerouac Is Pregnant.*
VIKTOR SHKLOVSKY, *Bowstring.*
Knight's Move.
A Sentimental Journey:
Memoirs 1917–1922.
Energy of Delusion: A Book on Plot.
Literature and Cinematography.
Theory of Prose.
Third Factory.
Zoo, or Letters Not about Love.
CLAUDE SIMON, *The Invitation.*
PIERRE SINIAC, *The Collaborators.*
KJERSTI A. SKOMSVOLD, *The Faster I Walk,*
the Smaller I Am.
JOSEF ŠKVORECKÝ, *The Engineer of*
Human Souls.
GILBERT SORRENTINO,
Aberration of Starlight.
Blue Pastoral.
Crystal Vision.
Imaginative Qualities of Actual
Things.
Mulligan Stew.
Pack of Lies.
Red the Fiend.
The Sky Changes.
Something Said.
Splendide-Hôtel.
Steelwork.
Under the Shadow.
W. M. SPACKMAN, *The Complete Fiction.*
ANDRZEJ STASIUK, *Dukla.*
Fado.
GERTRUDE STEIN, *Lucy Church Amiably.*
The Making of Americans.
A Novel of Thank You.
LARS SVENDSEN, *A Philosophy of Evil.*
PIOTR SZEWC, *Annihilation.*
GONÇALO M. TAVARES, *Jerusalem.*

Joseph Walser's Machine.
Learning to Pray in the Age of
Technique.
LUCIAN DAN TEODOROVICI,
Our Circus Presents . . .
NIKANOR TERATOLOGEN, *Assisted Living.*
STEFAN THEMERSON, *Hobson's Island.*
The Mystery of the Sardine.
Tom Harris.
TAEKO TOMIOKA, *Building Waves.*
JOHN TOOMEY, *Sleepwalker.*
JEAN-PHILIPPE TOUSSAINT, *The Bathroom.*
Camera.
Monsieur.
Reticence.
Running Away.
Self-Portrait Abroad.
Television.
The Truth about Marie.
DUMITRU TSEPENEAG, *Hotel Europa.*
The Necessary Marriage.
Pigeon Post.
Vain Art of the Fugue.
ESTHER TUSQUETS, *Stranded.*
DUBRAVKA UGRESIC, *Lend Me Your Character.*
Thank You for Not Reading.
TOR ULVEN, *Replacement.*
MATI UNT, *Brecht at Night.*
Diary of a Blood Donor.
Things in the Night.
ÁLVARO URIBE AND OLIVIA SEARS, EDS.,
Best of Contemporary Mexican Fiction.
ELOY URROZ, *Friction.*
The Obstacles.
LUISA VALENZUELA, *Dark Desires and*
the Others.
He Who Searches.
MARJA-LIISA VARTIO, *The Parson's Widow.*
PAUL VERHAEGHEN, *Omega Minor.*
AGLAJA VETERANYI, *Why the Child Is*
Cooking in the Polenta.
BORIS VIAN, *Heartsnatcher.*
LLORENÇ VILLALONGA, *The Dolls' Room.*
TOOMAS VINT, *An Unending Landscape.*
ORNELA VORPSI, *The Country Where No*
One Ever Dies.
AUSTRYN WAINHOUSE, *Hedyphagetica.*
PAUL WEST, *Words for a Deaf Daughter*
& Gala.
CURTIS WHITE, *America's Magic Mountain.*
The Idea of Home.
Memories of My Father Watching TV.
Monstrous Possibility: An Invitation
to Literary Politics.
Requiem.
DIANE WILLIAMS, *Excitability:*
Selected Stories.
Romancer Erector.
DOUGLAS WOOLF, *Wall to Wall.*
Ya! & John-Juan.
JAY WRIGHT, *Polynomials and Pollen.*
The Presentable Art of Reading
Absence.
PHILIP WYLIE, *Generation of Vipers.*
MARGUERITE YOUNG, *Angel in the Forest.*
Miss MacIntosh, My Darling.
REYOUNG, *Unbabbling.*
VLADO ŽABOT, *The Succubus.*
ZORAN ŽIVKOVIĆ, *Hidden Camera.*
LOUIS ZUKOFSKY, *Collected Fiction.*
VITOMIL ZUPAN, *Minuet for Guitar.*
SCOTT ZWIREN, *God Head.*